SHATTERED WOLF

SHADOW CITY: SILVER MATE

JEN L. GREY

CHAPTER ONE

WITH EVERY MILE we moved away from the over-crowded downtown of Gatlinburg and closer to the pack neighborhood, my heart beat more erratically. Despite my protests, Mom had encouraged me to hang out with Heather, one of PawPaw's pack members, tonight, but I was sure she hadn't meant for me to stay out until after one in the morning. It worried me that she hadn't linked with me to check if I was okay.

Lately, her silence had been saying more than her words since...well, since Dad died.

Dad.

How I missed him.

The familiar swirls of anger tightened my chest, and I took a deep breath to cleanse my mind. Thankfully, the grief was nowhere as intense as it had been right after his death.

On instinct, I played Mozart's Clarinet Concerto in A Major in my head to calm the brewing storm within.

Though I was twenty and an adult, my pack, the silver wolves, had always stayed isolated from humans and other supernaturals, including other wolf shifters, to keep our existence secret. Genetically, we were descended from an angel, and our angel blood made us more powerful than other wolf shifters, especially during a full moon. We'd been hunted and killed over our heritage. For that reason, pack members worried whenever any of us stayed away longer than expected, as Heather and I had done tonight. As of *very* recently, we were no longer hiding from other supernaturals, but secrecy was ingrained in us. Change took time, and I took my mother's silence as frustration.

It'd be best if I contacted her now so she could vent before we arrived.

We're on our way back, I sent through our link.

Silence. Even the bond seemed muted, as if she were asleep, which was odd. Maybe she'd shut down our connection—but that didn't feel right, either. Normally, it would still be warm. Well, I'd soon find out what was going on.

Great.

I dreaded arriving at PawPaw and Nana's. It would come in handy if I could link with my grandparents, but I wasn't part of their pack, so we couldn't. I was a silver wolf, after all, and had planned to stay with their pack for only a short time while I grieved my father and worked through my anger surrounding his death. I didn't want those negative emotions to take over my life.

As time passed, the plan had changed. Back at home, Mom had only grown angrier. Not needing her rage to fuel mine, I'd stayed with my grandparents' pack longer and longer. Then Mom had shown up here, and we'd started working through our issues. Heading home was finally imminent.

Wherever home was.

Our silver wolf pack had been shuffled around ever

since *they* had come into the picture. My cousins. Sterlyn—our new alpha—and her twin brother, Cyrus. My father had died protecting them, and I'd left to work through my grief about that. My rage had tried to control me, but letting it do so hadn't been fair. Dad had chosen to protect them with his life, and he'd done it out of love.

I should respect that. *He* deserved that.

I hadn't meant to leave the pack before all sorts of other attacks had descended on them. By the time I'd realized more of my pack members were dying, they'd moved from our home to a new location.

"Hey!" Heather exclaimed as she snapped her fingers at me from the driver's seat of her beat-up Ford truck. Her light blonde hair swayed across her shoulders. "None of this. You were actually *fun* tonight, and I refuse to let you change just because we're heading home."

I laid my head on the headrest and tilted my face toward the window. My auburn hair hung in shining strands around my face, and my blue eyes were so bright, they seemed to glow, even though my wolf wasn't surging forward. My olive complexion helped with that illusion.

My reflection mocked me. Outwardly, I looked confident, but I struggled to be comfortable around anyone outside my pack, especially humans. "You laced my rum and Coke with wolfsbane, so yeah, I wasn't completely myself."

"Oh, don't worry, Jewel." She rolled her light brown eyes. "You weren't the life of the party. But at least you smiled from time to time, and you weren't hiding in the corner of the bar behind the holiday tree...much."

A laugh escaped, surprising me. I rolled my head toward Heather and said, "Yeah, okay. It's just that Mom—"

"Wanted you to go out and have fun!" Heather interjected, and focused on the road. The smooth ride became jerky as she turned onto the one-lane dirt road that led to my grandparents' pack neighborhood. "She asked me to take you into town and make you forget about all the crazy since she..."

"Couldn't." I would have rather had Mom take me out. She was my best friend—well, ever since Dad had passed. Mom and I had always been close, but I'd been Daddy's little girl.

Until I wasn't.

Pain stabbed my heart, and I felt wrong for having laughed just a few minutes ago.

"Hey, she can't help that her insane ex lives close enough that if she ventures too far, he'll find out she's here." She shook her head and wrinkled her nose. "That sounds horribly soap opera-ish when I say it out loud."

I hadn't heard the full story about Mom and her almost-chosen mate from a neighboring pack, but I knew it hadn't ended well. Apparently, she'd met Dad the morning before she and her ex had been meant to complete their bond. One look at Dad, and her world had tilted...or so she'd said. I didn't know *all* the details, but the ex had said that if she didn't follow through on her promise to him, she'd better never show her face around this pack again.

The neighborhood of two-story log cabins appeared, and the hairs on my arms rose. All the lights were off, which wasn't a big deal, but it was an adjustment after being in Gatlinburg with the holiday decorations lighting up downtown. Also, the two households at the beginning of the neighborhood were full of night owls. At this time of night, their lights were usually still on, even though wolf shifters didn't need light to see in the dark. We used them to help us blend in with humans.

Mom? I linked again. Something *was* off. Maybe I should have linked with her throughout the night. Our pack link had cooled marginally and was almost the same temperature as my pack bond with the silver wolves, who were too far away for me to connect with. It felt like she was out of range.

My blood turned cold.

"Can you link with anyone?" I didn't hide the concern wafting through me. My gut screamed that something was horribly wrong.

Heather rolled her eyes. "You're overthinking things, as usual." She exhaled as her eyes glowed, and then her face fell. "No one is answering me." Her brows furrowed as she turned off the truck. "It's like *everyone* is asleep."

She took a right onto the road that led straight to the pack neighborhood and passed the first three cabins before turning into my grandparents' driveway. PawPaw's pack consisted of about two hundred individuals living in a neighborhood with sixty homes. They were spread across the mountainside overlooking Gatlinburg, isolated while blending in with other developments of touristy seasonal cabins. It was hard to see every house from this position, which was why PawPaw's home was near the start of the neighborhood. If any threats came, he would be one of the first to respond.

Nothing seemed out of the ordinary. Raccoons scurried, and deer meandered by through the eastern red cedar, American beech, and yellow birch trees. With it being early December, most of the leaves had fallen. I focused on my supernatural hearing. Apart from a bear ambling a few miles away, all was quiet.

I cranked down the window so I could sniff. Before

leaving the safety of the vehicle, we needed to ensure that no one strange was lurking nearby.

"What are—" Heather began.

I placed a finger in front of my lips. If someone was here, they would've heard us pull up. Stealth wasn't an option, but I needed to listen and smell for anything that might explain what was causing this oddity. The musky scents of shifters saturated the air, as expected. I also detected the faint smell of humans—their scent lacked any defining qualities, such as the sweetness of vampires, the herbal scent of witches, or the floral fragrance of angels.

Why had *humans* been here? That was odd. Though the scent was faint, I could tell there'd been a large number of them.

I opened the passenger door, and it creaked loudly.

"And you told me to be quiet," Heather huffed. "Should we be getting out?"

Ignoring the first comment, I addressed the latter. "No one is nearby." Since the moon was slightly more than three-quarters full, my wolf was stronger than a normal shifter's. The angel who had fathered the first silver wolves had been the guardian of the moon, so our angelic powers were tied to it. The fuller the moon, the larger and stronger we were, while during a new moon, we had the same strength as any other wolf shifter.

I only took charge when I had to, and this situation surely fit the bill. If PawPaw's pack was in danger, we needed to act before things got worse. I couldn't fathom what had caused the pack to shut down communication with Heather or why humans were involved.

"Come on," I murmured, and ran toward the cabin. The bedrooms were located on the cabin's left side, on both the top and bottom floors, and the living room and kitchen were on the right side of the main floor. As I rushed up the five steps to the covered porch and past the two rocking chairs, my hands started to shake. I forced them to hold steady and removed the key from my pocket, focusing on the cool metal, needing something to ground me.

Family was everything. Dad had instilled that in me, and the thought that the only remaining blood I had could be in harm's way nearly paralyzed me.

Inhaling, I used the calming technique Dad had taught me.

I went to slip the key into the lock, and the door swung open. My pulse pounded as I stepped inside and gazed around. From its place on the left wall, the television flickered with the sound muted, but that was normal. PawPaw liked to sit on the couch and watch TV until he fell asleep. The gray blanket Nana had knit him lay crumpled on the hardwood floor, but that was the only thing that *looked* out of sorts. *Smell*, on the other hand...

I detected a few unfamiliar scents.

Humans.

Nana's yarn and crochet needles sat on the loveseat. She normally placed them on the wooden coffee table where PawPaw kept his remote.

"Jewel, what's...what's going on?" Heather's voice broke as she walked up behind me. "Where are my alpha and his mate?"

That was exactly what I was attempting to determine. "I don't know. Let's go to your house."

"Yeah, okay." Heather spun on her heel and rushed out the door. Her brown leather cowgirl boots crunched over the gravel as she ran to the right and up the hill toward her family's place next door.

I hurried after her, not wanting us to split up. Though

no one was nearby, as far as I could tell, the threat could always come back. Since she and I couldn't pack link, we had no way of communicating other than with our cell phones. Cells just weren't as convenient as linking with your mind.

Being shifters, we didn't breathe hard as we hiked up the steep hill that led us deeper into the neighborhood. Heather's door had been left wide open. We hurried into her living room, but nothing seemed out of place. Not even the television had been left on. When I looked into the kitchen on the right, I noticed her mother's teal kettle sitting on the stove and a cup with a tea bag in it on the counter. I walked past the black recliner centered in front of their flatscreen TV and into the kitchen. The tea bag was dry, and I lifted the lid of the teapot to find it full.

A lump formed in my throat.

I stuck my finger into the pot. The water was lukewarm, meaning whatever happened had gone down anywhere from thirty minutes to an hour ago. That was still a significant range, but at least it hadn't been shortly after we had left at six.

A slightly metallic scent hung in the air, but at a glance, nothing else stuck out to hint at what had happened.

"Heather, your mom's tea." Somehow, the words had made it past my lips.

"That's good," Heather said, sounding hopeful. "Maybe they had last-minute pack business to take care of and didn't want us to come looking for them. They could all be in the garden enjoying the moonlight or the training fields."

However, when she joined me in the kitchen, her usual tan complexion paled, and she raced back into the living room. "Mom! Dad! Sean!" She opened the door to her parents' bedroom, then slammed it before taking off up the stairs in the corner of the living room.

This was the first time I'd ever heard her sound like she *wanted* to find her older brother. The two of them were usually at each other's throats since he was poised to take over the pack when PawPaw passed. He was a rule follower and believed in boundaries, whereas Heather liked to skirt the line and get into trouble.

I stayed put, certain she would find nothing, and searched the room for any clues. I walked the perimeter, taking in every nook and cranny. At the corner where the kitchen met the living room, the faint stench of blood tickled my nose again. Something had to be here.

Bending down, I examined the edge of the doorframe. *There.* A spot of blood on the bottom corner where the cabinets abutted the wall. Bile churned in my stomach.

Someone had been injured.

I squatted and lowered my head, smelling the blood. I wished I could tell if the drop was shifter or human, but our blood smelled the same.

Heather pounded down the stairs, and I straightened. I wasn't necessarily trying to hide what I'd found, but Heather was reactive. If she suspected that her family had been injured, she would become even more irrational. She was already screaming for family members we both knew she wouldn't find, especially since Sean had his own cabin. Besides, her parents' scents weren't strong enough for them to be inside or even close by.

"No one's here," she squeaked from the bottom of the stairs.

I needed to get her out of there and keep her calm while I planned our next moves.

"Let's head back to PawPaw's." I wanted to have a thorough look there to see if we missed anything.

Heather rubbed her arms and glanced over her shoulder. "Yeah, okay."

We hurried back down the hill. The coldness of December usually didn't bother me, but iciness crept into my bones. Moving faster with the descent, we were back in my grandparents' home within a minute. I removed my cell phone, ready to take the final measure.

As I punched in his number, I prayed to the gods for PawPaw to answer his damn phone.

CHAPTER TWO

WITH BATED BREATH, I put the phone to my ear and made my way to the couch. Just as I reached the edge, a shrill ringtone echoed. Vomit burned my throat.

His phone was here.

Black dots blocked the corners of my vision.

Dad had told me that my biggest strength was my ability to think differently from the rest of the pack. I came up with solutions outside of the norm, and I had a sinking suspicion I needed that talent now.

Lifting the gray blanket off the hardwood floor, I uncovered PawPaw's cell phone. Something had definitely gone down, and the tipsy sensation I'd felt from the wolfsbane-laced drinks became a distant memory.

"This isn't good," Heather squeaked.

No, it wasn't. Something had happened, and I didn't know what to do. I plopped down onto the couch, trying to wrap my head around everything and confusing myself further. How the *hell* were humans involved? They didn't even know we existed.

Heather rushed past me, grabbed the remote from the end table, and unmuted the TV.

Watching television was the last thing on my mind. I opened my mouth to ask what she was doing but froze when I read the headline scrolling at the bottom of the screen.

Supernaturals are REAL.

"We have confirmation that supernaturals are *real*, and they are living among us!" the middle-aged reporter said. "Watch the footage that has sent the entire world into a spiral, taken just a few short days ago."

The image changed to a gorgeous angel with purple-tinted hair and dark wings. She flew out of the trees where she must have been attempting to hide. Though I'd known angels existed, I'd never seen one...until now.

Pale, unhealthy-looking humans faced her from across a clearing.

A group of wolves inched out of the tree line, and the bright silver fur of Darrell, my pack's acting beta, caught my eye. His blood orange eyes were unmistakable.

I inhaled sharply and blinked a few times.

Why were the silver wolves there? Mom had told me that we were integrating back into society, but I didn't think that meant revealing ourselves to the entire *world*. My eyes focused on Cyrus, who was in human form, and what had to be Sterlyn in wolf form. The twins were now alpha and beta of the silver wolf pack.

The day I met Cyrus was also the day I'd left the pack to come and visit PawPaw and Nana here. Mom had spewed so much hatred toward Cyrus over her pain, and I couldn't be around her and deal with my own grief.

Sterlyn's hair was pure silver and Cyrus's a shade darker, similar to Dad's. The silver tones were the trade-mark of the silver wolf alpha bloodline. In human form, all the other silver wolves had ordinary hair colors, but when we shifted, our coats were the same silver shade as Sterlyn's hair.

Their iridescent eyes were strained—I could see it from where I sat. Something terrible had happened, and when they glanced at the camera, their faces twisted in fear.

The wolves hadn't known the humans would be there. But how was that possible? They should've been able to sense them.

It was fine. There were ways we could cover up this error. Blame it on cosplay, hallucinations, and the list went on and on. The damage wasn't irreversible.

The shot moved to another image, and I froze. The most delectable man I'd ever seen was standing in front of a quaint brick building in what looked like a downtown area. Dark chocolate eyes stared into the camera, and a chill ran down my spine. I tensed, squirming and feeling as if my soul had been bared to him...which was silly. He couldn't actually *see* me.

He cleared his throat and held up a microphone to his full lips, his bicep bulging under his olive green long-sleeved shirt. A breeze ruffled his short cappuccino hair, and he inhaled, emphasizing his athletic build.

For a moment, all I could do was stare. The urge to walk across the room and caress the screen overwhelmed me. I'd leaned forward, ready to do just that, when he said in a deep, sensuous voice, "It's true. Supernaturals are real, but we aren't a threat to any of you."

My breath stalled in my lungs. What was he *doing*? He had to be insane, or maybe he was using this opportunity to be in the spotlight. Not that he would've had trouble attracting attention—there was no way anyone wouldn't notice him. As delicious as he looked, it made sense that he'd be narcissistic.

"Think about it." He placed a hand in his jeans pocket and leaned toward the camera. "We've been here the entire time, coexisting with humans. We're just *like* you."

The desire to reach through the screen and strangle him raced through me. He had to be an idiot. Keeping our existence secret was a core belief for every supernatural race, and this handsome butthead had destroyed that in *seconds*.

The screen flickered, and a guy in his mid-twenties appeared. He was hunched over, his eyes jerking around as if he were frantically examining the room. His chest heaved, and he grimaced. "There's no way it was an illusion. My girlfriend was ripped out of my hands by something *invisible*. Someone was laughing maniacally as she was dragged away, screaming for help."

The woman holding the camera asked, "Why didn't you go after her?"

"I...I *tried*." He shivered. "But something grabbed my arm and held me back. I...I still can't find her."

Clip after clip presented similar stories. They all originated from Shadow Ridge and Shadow Terrace, the towns that bordered and protected Shadow City—the place where silver wolves had been created and then forced by murderous angels to flee and go into hiding for hundreds of years.

The camera panned over walls that circled a city built on an island in the middle of a vast river. A city that even I, who'd never seen it in person, knew was supposed to be concealed from human eyes. A long suspension bridge that reminded me of the Golden Gate Bridge in California connected the island to the mainland.

Shadow City.

Tales of the legendary city had stood the test of time in our pack, and the descriptions hadn't done it justice. Gold buildings glittered in the light, outshining even all the paintings I'd seen of Heaven. The sparkling buildings made the city look like Mount Olympus.

"And that appeared out of *nowhere*," a man said, gesturing wildly at the city as if viewers might not understand what he meant.

The same handsome man reappeared and opened his stupid, sexy mouth. That was when I'd had enough. I snatched the remote from Heather and slammed the power button to turn off the TV.

I couldn't handle hearing anything else he had to say. He'd already done more damage than could be undone.

Silence descended, and I had to force my lungs to breathe. Dead Sexy had ruined *everything*.

"That must be what my parents were talking about earlier today." Heather shook her head as she dropped onto the loveseat, barely missing Nana's crochet needles.

My family had been tense the past day, but I'd thought it was because Mom had mentioned us heading home. My grandparents hadn't been able to visit us before because we'd always kept the location of the silver wolf settlement secret, so the only time they had gotten to see us was when we'd visited them, which had been rare because of Mom's ex. She truly thought he'd follow through on his threat even after all these years, and I wondered why she'd been willing to commit to the man in the first place.

"How long has this been on the news?" I tended to avoid television and spent most of my time running in the woods in wolf form, hiking in human form, or reading stories about strong women who found love along their journeys. In books, I'd read about creatures that I had yet to encounter, like dragons, and magical realms. I figured most fantasy stories were based on truth, like human stories of shifters, vampires, angels, and witches. During my time here, I'd even heard murmurings that dragon shifters were alive and experiencing a resurgence.

"I don't know. Mom gave me a list of errands to run with you today, so I didn't check anything." She took out her cell phone and mashed some buttons. "It's been on media outlets since...yesterday morning."

Sirens sounded in my head. Our pack's disappearance *couldn't* be a coincidence. Humans were broadcasting about the terror they'd experienced at the hands of supernaturals, and the scent of a lot of humans surrounded the pack neighborhood. That *asshole* had led them here.

But how would anyone even know about this pack and this location? And if humans had taken PawPaw and his pack, what in the world did they want them for? Every plausible answer I could come up with made my heart stutter.

No. I wouldn't allow panic to overwhelm me, not when people I loved might be in danger. I'd been trained for this. I had to remain rational and determine the best course of action based on the limited information I had.

My mind was fixed on the only fact I could cling to. If the pack had been taken, the people who'd kidnapped them could come back. If Heather and I were still here when they came, we might be taken, too, and there was no telling when someone else would discover we were missing.

I stood, the hairs on the back of my neck rising. "We've got to go."

"What?" Heather's mouth dropped. "Why? And...*where*?"

That was a loaded question, but there was a clear answer: "To my pack."

"But my parents. My brother. My *pack*." She jumped to her feet and clenched her hands. "*Your* grandparents and your mom! We can't just leave them."

"You're right." I had no intention of leaving them, but we couldn't be stupid. "Whoever convinced them to leave or *took* them managed to get *everyone* out of here, including the kids, without anyone linking with us. How are the *two* of us supposed to go up against that?"

She scoffed and crossed her arms. "You're a *silver wolf*."

"Something that no one is supposed to know," I said. The one condition of me coming to stay here had been for PawPaw to alpha-will the entire pack to keep my heritage secret. "And the moon is waning. Every day, my power will grow weaker. Beyond that, even if I were at full capacity, I'm still *one* silver wolf."

Rubbing her temples, Heather closed her eyes. "I...I just don't want to leave. It's like I'm abandoning them."

My heart thawed. I understood how she felt. "We aren't. We're getting reinforcements." If I trusted in anything, it was my pack. They'd come through for me...at least, what was left of them. With all the turmoil that had happened in Shadow City while I was gone, we'd lost so many members. But I did believe Sterlyn and Cyrus wouldn't stand in the way of helping Mom and the others; they had to be good people for Dad to have given up his life for them. "Otherwise, we'll just be offering ourselves up to whomever took them."

She blew out a breath. "You're right. It's just...how will your pack react to me coming with you? You silver wolves have always been so secretive. They won't be happy with me rolling up."

A hardened laugh escaped me. "Apparently, they aren't worried about it anymore. They were just on *television*."

"What?" Her head turned toward the dark TV. "All I saw was an angel and that sexy-ass man."

A growl almost escaped me, taking me by surprise. I'd never reacted to anything so strongly, and to feel possessive over a handsome guy who'd told the world about *us* was even more ridiculous. He'd done so much damage, and if he was the reason my grandparents were missing, I'd find him and deal with him as well.

The anger I'd worked so hard to keep at bay swirled inside me. To calm myself, I began humming Debussy's "Clair de lune." Once my breathing had slowed, I said, "Come on. Let's go." The longer we stayed here, the more on edge I got.

I placed PawPaw's phone on the ground and put the cover back over it. Then I turned the TV on and muted the volume. After placing the remote on the end table where it had been before, the two of us rushed out the front door. I paused to shut the door.

"What are you doing?" Heather murmured. "We need to get out of here."

Turning, I headed toward her truck. "I don't want anything to look different. If whoever was behind this comes back, they could notice things were moved. We don't need them to know they missed some of us."

She rubbed her arms and hurried to the driver's side. "Yeah, okay. I'll feel better once we get out of here."

I reached the passenger door and glanced back at my grandparents' cabin one last time. I didn't want to leave, but I'd just explained all the reasons we needed to. Teeth gritted, I forced myself to open the car door. The *creak* sounded even louder this time, and I quickly jumped into the vehicle. At least that had gotten me moving.

Heather started the engine, the sound deafening. She pressed on the gas and peeled out of the parking spot to head back down the curving gravel road.

"So...where do I go?" Heather asked as she navigated, not bothering to turn on the headlights.

Good question—one for which I, unfortunately, didn't have the answer. My pack had relocated, and I'd left before learning about the new location. I couldn't pack link with them because they were too far away. "They're near Chattanooga, so head in that direction. I'll text Chad to get an address." I typed out a message and sent it to him.

"Chad, huh?" She tightened her grip on the wheel. "You talk about him a lot."

I kept the phone in my hand, knowing it wouldn't take Chad long to answer me. "He's like a brother to me. We grew up together in the same home. If there were feelings between us, they would've surfaced a long time ago."

"But you've never been apart from each other like you have the past several months." She lifted a brow.

"Seriously, it's *not* like that." My phone buzzed, and I was thankful for the distraction. "Can we not talk about this right now? We have more pressing matters. And will you turn on the lights? We don't need to draw any more attention to ourselves." I hated talking about myself, especially when it came to the men I cared about.

"Sorry. I'm just trying to distract myself from..." She grimaced as she flipped on the headlights before we turned onto the paved road.

As we picked up speed, a black van drove past us, heading in the direction we'd come. As I glanced behind us to see if they'd passed the turnoff to the pack houses, they slammed on their brakes.

A drunk tourist who'd gotten lost?

My phone buzzed again. I read the text quickly, not wanting to worry Chad more than I already had.

It's about damn time you came home, J. But why in the middle of the night?

I didn't want to share with him like this, but I didn't want to lie, so I gave him a brief synopsis of everything that had happened.

He responded immediately. **We're in Shadow Ridge with the local pack. I'll send you the address. Get here, and we'll decide the next steps.**

After a second, I received the address. I plugged it into my map and started the GPS. "They're less than three hours away."

Heather sighed. "Yeah, but it still doesn't feel right leaving."

I had to admit that part of me agreed.

Bright lights shone in the rearview mirror. They were coming up fast. I spun around, and reality crashed over me. It was the same van that had passed us...and they had no plans of stopping.

CHAPTER THREE

"GO FASTER," I said through clenched teeth as my eyes remained locked on the car behind us. The lights were almost blinding, but I wanted to make out more about the vehicle. All I could confirm was that the van was black and had at least two people inside—the driver and a passenger.

The vehicle increased its speed, though the road down the mountain was steep and curvy and passed through several cabin communities that were rented out year-round.

Heather hissed. "My truck is old, and the bed is light. I can't go crazy around these curves, or we'll tip over."

"They're about to ram us." There had to be a way out of this situation. These people could be part of the group that had taken PawPaw's pack.

As if the driver had heard me, the van swerved onto the other side of the road and raced to catch up to us. That was a risky move since the driver couldn't see oncoming traffic with all the curves. However, it was after one in the morning, so the roads were likely deserted.

I lifted my phone and dialed 911. Though I doubted the cops would arrive before they ran us off the road, the threat of someone coming should at least make these people wary.

"What are you doing?" Heather growled as she glanced in the side mirror. The van was gaining on us. "Now isn't the time to make a call."

"I'm calling for help."

The line rang once before an operator picked up. She asked in a nasal voice, "What's the emergency?"

"A black van is chasing us." I tried to sound calm, but my voice shook with fear. I rattled off the approximate area and the direction we were going in.

"Can you tell me anything more about the van? A license plate?" the operator asked.

I'd opened my mouth to respond just as Heather screamed, "Hang on!"

The van slammed into the driver's side midway up the truck bed, spinning us left across the road. My right side slammed into the door, and pain exploded through my shoulder and ribs.

Tires squealing, Heather slammed on the brakes. The stench of burned rubber choked me.

When the truck went still, the silence was over-whelming.

I looked at Heather, afraid she'd frozen in fear. Her hands clutched the steering wheel, and her eyes appeared to stare forward but were actually turned slightly to the left, toward our enemy. Her right leg was tense, prepared to stomp on the gas at any time.

She had a plan, and I had no choice but to trust it.

I tried holding my breath, not wanting to inhale more of the polluted air, but my lungs screamed in protest.

When the van doors opened, Heather stomped her foot

back on the gas. The tires squealed as she peeled back onto the right side of the road.

"Get your ass in the car!" the driver said in a deep, booming voice.

I glanced over my shoulder to find the front end of their van dented and the passenger-side headlight broken. A woman in her mid-twenties lunged back into the van. We were gaining ground, but not for long. "They're coming after us."

"I'm aware." Heather's eyes stayed fixed on the road as she revved the engine harder, trying to gain more distance. "But I don't know what else to do. It would be nice if those cops got here quickly."

The police.

I glanced at the phone and realized that the operator was still on the line. I reached down and swiped the cell phone from the floorboard. "Sorry, I dropped the phone."

"The police should be there in five minutes." The operator sounded more animated than she had at the beginning of the call. "Are you okay?"

"Yes." I wanted to add *for now*, but Heather was barely hanging on. I was thankful that so far, stress hadn't broken her, and she was coming through. Wolf shifters had a natural instinct for self-preservation. "Just a little upset and clumsy with everything going on."

The problem was we couldn't wait for the police and needed to determine a different solution—one that Heather probably wouldn't like. However, while I hadn't been around lately to help my own pack, I'd be damn sure to protect Heather's.

There was a cutout on the road about fifty yards ahead of us. "Heather, pull over there."

"What?" she asked, and looked at me.

"Trust me. We can't outrun them in the truck, but we can on foot." I tapped into my wolf, knowing it would make my eyes glow brighter. "We need a head start." Especially since we didn't know what weapons they might have.

"Don't get out of the vehicle," the operator commanded. "Try to keep some distance between you and the other car."

If we did that, we'd be hit and killed or taken. "We'll be fine. Just send the cops here, and have them look for our truck. I'm hanging up, but I'll leave my phone in the truck so you can use the GPS to find our location."

"N—" the operator started, but I hung up.

We had no choice. If we had to shift, I didn't want to chance the operator hearing it and asking more questions.

"You're right." Heather nodded but didn't lift her foot off the gas.

Good. We couldn't slow down until we had to. I spun in my seat again and watched the van rushing toward us.

I hoped we had enough time to run into the woods and blend in, even if we had to change into our animal forms. Shifting wasn't ideal with the cops coming. Still, even in human form, we could run faster and climb better than any typical human. We just had to hide until the police arrived.

Seconds before we reached the dirt cutout, Heather slammed on the brakes and skidded to the side. The truck felt as if it might topple over, but she kept us upright.

"Grab the keys, and let's go," I commanded as I reached for the handle. My right side smarted, but I ignored it and swung the door open. "Get out on this side."

Heather killed the engine, removed the keys from the ignition, then slid across the bench seat and landed on her feet beside me.

The van appeared and didn't bother to pull in behind the truck. Instead, it parked right next to it on the road.

Heather and I took off into the trees about ten feet away. We had to be careful where we went since the leaves were gone. Our best option for cover was either thick brush or a bunch of red cedars. Of course, the American beech and yellow birches were closest to us.

Doors opened. We pushed our legs hard as we moved deeper into the woods. I could hear metal clicking, and my heart sank.

They had guns, confirming my suspicion. They were human.

The image of the sexy guy on TV flashed through my mind. After I found Mom and the others, I would hunt him down and make him pay for the damage he'd caused my family.

Anger washed through me, and I was at its mercy. Dad had always told me that some anger was healthy, but too much rage could consume me. The rage Mom harbored had caused a terrible rift in the silver wolf pack I'd left behind and between us as well. She'd been repairing her relationships, but the pain still lingered.

I didn't want to be that kind of person. I wanted to be like Dad—calm, loyal, and strong.

Even though I could run faster than Heather, I refused to leave her behind. We might not be family, but we were friends, and she was pack to my grandparents. Besides, silver wolves were meant to be protectors. I'd already missed battling beside my pack, and it was time to become what Dad had trained me to be.

A gunshot rang out, and I almost froze at the sound of a bullet whizzing toward us. Dad had been against us training with firearms. Our new alpha had changed that policy a few months ago, but I hadn't been around to learn. I didn't know anything about guns.

Something brushed my arm, and a sharp, stabbing pain followed. I glanced down to see a deep scratch and blood trickling down my skin.

I'd been hit.

Bastards.

"What the *hell*, Ajax," the woman chastised. "We aren't supposed to shoot them."

"It's better than having supernaturals running loose," he countered. "You're the one with the tranq gun—use it!"

Their little dispute worked in our favor. My wolf surged forward, granting me speed. We ran deeper into the woods where the trees grew closer together. It would be harder for them to hit us. The darkness would make it harder for them to see us, too, and even if they had night-vision goggles, it was nothing compared to what we could see. With our wolfish eyes, we could see at night as if it were day.

My breath puffed in front of me as Heather and I continued at a steady pace, making some turns to throw off our pursuers. After putting a quarter mile between us, I lifted my hand, telling Heather to pause. I could clearly hear the two humans arguing over the best way to find us. They didn't know which direction we'd run, so they probably weren't hunters.

Who the hell were these people?

The faint wail of sirens had tears burning my eyes. Maybe we'd get out of this after all. I turned to Heather, who was hiding behind the trunk of a thick red cedar across from me. Her body relaxed slightly, informing me she'd heard them, too.

The humans couldn't hear the sirens...at least, not yet. They were still stumbling through the woods. We wouldn't be safe until the cops got here and checked everything out.

The two humans continued to walk toward us, heading

a little west of where we'd stopped, probably thinking we were running down the mountain.

Though they were aware of us, they clearly didn't understand us. If they'd known anything about wolf shifters, they'd know we could hear for miles. Though they were whispering, they might as well have been speaking in a normal voice.

The sirens grew louder. At some point, the humans would hear them, too.

The bullet wound still stung, but not as badly. The blood was clotting, meaning my quick healing had already kicked in. The pain in my right side was almost completely gone.

"Shit! Do you hear that?" Ajax rasped. "It sounds like sirens heading this way. I need to move the van. You keep—"

"You aren't leaving me out here by myself," the woman replied. "I'm going with you. Besides, none of the others know about these two, and they don't know where their pack is. I say we forget about them and go."

Again, they confirmed how little they knew about us. Though they'd taken the pack, Heather could find them, and I could find my mom via our pack link. The farther out of range the shifters were, the longer it'd take. But we *would* find them eventually.

"You're right. Let's go." Ajax grunted. "The sirens are getting louder. We've got to move."

Heather smiled at me. She murmured quietly to avoid the humans overhearing us, "Your plan worked. I had my doubts. You never offer suggestions or give your opinion."

I shrugged. "I prefer listening to others instead of talking about myself." I felt rather awkward whenever I said anything at all, especially when someone put me on the spot. I preferred to daydream and read, keeping myself company, though one day, I hoped to learn how to play the clarinet. "We can head back and make sure they're gone."

She nodded, and the smile fell from her face.

About halfway back to the truck, we heard doors shut and an engine start.

We picked up our pace and were nearly back at the truck when the sirens stopped. Red and blue lights strobed through the trees. The cops had arrived. Good. The people in the van wouldn't return while they were nearby.

We hurried out of the woods and found two older men walking around the cutout, dressed in their black cop uniforms, searching the ground with flashlights...likely looking for us.

When the older one with gray hair hit me with his light, he let out a huge sigh. "These must be the girls."

"Thank God." The younger one, who was probably in his forties, sighed. "I was worried you two might be hurt."

I rushed over to them. "Thank you so much for coming to help us."

"Did the car chasing you damage your truck?" The older one flashed his light on the huge dent on the driver's side then back around. "I don't see another vehicle, but they could still be out here."

"Actually, I think I was being paranoid." Thankfully, these cops were human, so they couldn't smell my lie. "There was a car behind us, but it kept going after we pulled over."

"The operator said she heard something." The younger officer grabbed the front of his dark blue police hat and repositioned it on his head. "That they could've rammed into you."

Heather cut her eyes to me but didn't say a word. Her

nose wrinkled. Though they couldn't smell the sulfuric stench of my lies, she and I both could.

"Heather lost control and ran off the road into a huge tree a ways back." I waved a hand, trying to downplay it. "We were freaked out and pulled over because the truck doesn't handle curves well. Though they drove by, we thought they were going to stop and hurt us, so we ran away in a panic. They called out for a couple of minutes and left when we didn't answer."

"Then why were you still hiding in the woods?" the older cop asked, and crossed his arms, watching my every move.

I spoke up quickly before Heather could jump in. "Because we *thought* the van was chasing us, but after they drove by, I had to pee." I shrugged and glanced at the ground, my cheeks burning. I didn't even have to pretend to be embarrassed. "You guys got here right when I... uh...finished."

The younger cop opened the passenger door of his vehicle and pulled out a form. "Well, let's write a report for your insurance."

"It's fine," Heather said hurriedly. She examined the road as if she thought the men would reappear. "I only have liability on this big ol' clunker. Insurance won't cover it. I can fix it."

"You can fix it?" the younger cop asked as he rubbed his forehead like he was trying to smooth out the lines. "I can't even do that."

She shrugged. "I like working on vehicles. I can get the dents out."

That was one of her jobs around the neighborhood. She worked on equipment, vehicles, and anything mechanical.

"We appreciate your help, but we need to go home." We

needed to leave so we could reach the silver wolf pack. "I'm sorry we wasted your time. We were just scared."

"Are you sure you don't want to file a report?" the older cop asked.

"No," Heather cut in. "We just want to go somewhere s—"

"Home." She'd been about to ruin the cover I'd carefully constructed. "We need to go home. It's past curfew."

"Look—" the younger officer started again.

"Just let them go." The older man tilted his head. "They're young and out late. Let's let them off the hook. If they say they're fine, we have no reason not to believe them."

I grabbed Heather's hand and pulled her toward the truck. "Thanks again. Seriously. And I'm sorry we alarmed you all for no reason."

The older man smiled kindly. "If you ever feel like you're in danger, never hesitate to call 911. The operator knew you were scared, and you did the right thing."

"Thanks," Heather squeaked as we climbed into the truck.

She started the engine and headed back down the road, then glanced at me and chuckled. "Look at you, being all devious. You've been holding out on me."

I fidgeted. I'd never lied like that before, but it had been to protect us. All of us.

Mother's link cooled in my chest, becoming the same temperature as the rest of my pack links, meaning she was out of communication range. Heather's face fell. She must have felt the same thing from PawPaw's pack members. Rubbing her chest, she pushed the gas harder, racing toward Shadow Ridge.

A LITTLE BEFORE five in the morning, we were driving down a two-lane road in the middle of nowhere. The GPS instructed us to turn left, and soon, we were approaching a town. A quarter of a mile later, a large sign declared we had reached Shadow Ridge.

Finally. Some of my unease ebbed now that I was close to my pack again. Though Mom's link wasn't nearly as strong, the rest of the pack's bonds were back to the lively warmth I hadn't realized I'd missed so much.

In front of us, the quaint downtown I'd seen on the newscast came into view. Of course they had broadcast from here. The place was so picturesque. I just prayed I didn't run into *him* during my time here. Surely Sterlyn and Cyrus would want nothing to do with the person who'd revealed our presence to the world.

The downtown area was composed mainly of brick and featured shops and bars and restaurants that connected for a couple of miles. Though no one was around, it was clear it was prosperous—or had been before the whole supernatural world was outed.

We're in Shadow Ridge, I linked to Chad.

Thank gods, Chad answered. *I'm with Killian, Sterlyn, Griffin, and Cyrus. We'll be on Killian's porch, so you'll know where to stop—that's the address I gave you. Darrell and Theo are running the perimeter, but they're aware of what's going on. You'll be safe here. Killian's the alpha of the Shadow Ridge pack.*

Of that list, I was familiar only with Cyrus and Sterlyn. Mom had mentioned Griffin, Sterlyn's mate, and it made sense that he'd be there. This was the first I'd heard about

Killian, but apparently, I'd meet him soon. We were in his territory, after all.

My connections with Darrell and Theo were warm, but they didn't link to me. Chad must have informed them that we'd arrived.

The GPS told us to take a right onto a road that led away from downtown. "They're waiting for us outside the house. We're almost there."

Heather had been quiet for much of the drive, which wasn't that odd for the two of us. Other than last night, we didn't hang out much. She was pretty popular in her pack, whereas I was the strange loner who was tolerated due to PawPaw being their alpha. She'd taken me out last night only because Mom had asked her.

Darrell finally linked with me. *It's good to have you home.*

Yeah, we've missed you, J, Theo added.

Some of the coldness seeped out of my bones. *Sorry I stayed away too long.*

You're home now, and we'll find Mila, your grandparents, and their pack. Don't you worry, Darrell assured me.

The two of them went silent, leaving me to my thoughts...just like I preferred.

The road wound through thick groves of trees. Only the cypresses stayed green year-round. We took another turn, and houses broke through the mostly bare trees. They were all built in the warm, cozy Craftsman style, and the entire neighborhood felt welcoming. Each house captured the same inviting feeling, and they were painted in varying shades of white, blue, green, and yellow.

Two large figures captured my attention. Chad stood in front of a house, his brow furrowed. When he caught sight of the truck, warmth surged through our bond. He was happy that I was back, and his smoky topaz eyes glowed faintly in the light.

Cyrus stood next to him. He had five inches on Chad, coming in just under six and a half feet, and though he was leaner than Chad, he seemed more muscular.

We pulled into the driveway of the hunter green house. Around the back, I glimpsed an in-ground pool with a diving board and a water slide. As soon as the truck stopped, I jumped out of the car, eager to hug Chad.

Before I could reach him, the front door of the house opened. Something jolted inside me and *yank*ed my attention away from my friend.

I blinked, not believing my eyes.

No. This had to be a sick joke.

CHAPTER FOUR

MY FEET STOPPED. Hard as I tried, I couldn't take my eyes off *him*—the man from TV who'd confirmed the existence of supernaturals to the world. He'd been handsome on the screen, but in person... Drool pooled in the corners of my mouth. As it dribbled down one side of my chin, reality came crashing over me, and I tried to wipe it away discreetly.

Blood boiling, I focused on my rage instead of the attraction. Even though he was handsome, he could be the reason my entire family had been kidnapped. I clenched my teeth as my breathing turned ragged.

The door opened, and a woman who had to be Sterlyn and another ridiculously handsome male walked outside. The guy beside her had a foot on her and had a similar stature as Cyrus. His navy blue shirt hugged his chest and arms, leaving little to the imagination, and his honey-brown hair, cut longer on top, flopped into his eyes.

But he didn't hold a candle to Dead Sexy. My attention snapped back to him.

I could *not* find *him* attractive.

"Hey, you okay?" Chad asked, his concern bringing my gaze back to him.

Wiping the corners of my mouth again, I focused on the question. I exhaled, and my voice hardened. "I will be once we get Mom, my grandparents, and their pack back." I glared at Dead Sexy, wanting him to feel my wrath.

My glare didn't quite work because Chad pulled me into his arms for a bear hug. I breathed in his familiar musky honeysuckle scent.

Dead Sexy growled from the porch, and my wolf surged forward, restless. That didn't make sense. I'd been shifting and running regularly. Maybe tonight's attack, on top of losing Mom and my grandparents, had made her antsy.

My mom and grandparents were all I had left of my family.

"Uh...you *know* him?" Heather asked in disbelief as she gestured at Killian. "You left that part out."

Before I could answer, Cyrus's musky hydrangea and pine scent assaulted me, as well as something heavenly. The scent was so exquisite, it had to be from the nearby trees.

Who's the girl with you? Cyrus asked, linking to Chad and me.

"This is Heather," I answered out loud. "She's from my grandfather's pack. She and I were out together when something happened to them, which, strangely enough, wasn't long after *he* told everyone about our presence." I didn't tamp down my anger. I needed to focus on something other than his mouthwatering looks.

Cyrus sighed. "It wasn't like that."

I stepped back, removing myself from Chad's brotherly embrace. My traitorous gaze darted to Dead Sexy, whose shoulders seemed to relax marginally—but I had to be seeing things.

We shouldn't even have been here with him after what he'd pulled.

"Why did you bring someone outside our pack here?" Cyrus asked gruffly, his silver eyes glowing. "We have enough going on without bringing in more outsiders."

That was what he was focused on? Not the fact that this man here might be the reason my family and their pack had disappeared?

Heather laughed humorlessly. "Why am I not surprised that the secretive silver wolves aren't happy that I'm here?"

"What should she have done? Left her friend and grandparents' pack member behind?" Dead Sexy marched off the porch toward us.

With each step he drew closer, I felt something inside me *yank* toward him more. My wolf stirred in excitement, and my head screamed in frustration. How could I feel anything remotely positive for him?

Down, girl, I chastised her. I was inexperienced around men outside my pack, and if I were to gain experience, it would *not* be with him. I took a step back, more to put my wolf in place than anything else. *We are not interested in him.*

I'd hardly been around anyone outside the silver wolf pack until I'd left to stay with my grandparents. Even so, PawPaw's pack was more like family, and I'd been focused on mourning Dad and determining a healthy way to move on without feeling guilty.

Cyrus turned to Dead Sexy and rasped, "She's part of my pack—"

I rarely caused problems since Dad was a big proponent of working together, but I couldn't just sit here and let *him*—the man who'd shattered my world—stand up for me.

"And mine," Sterlyn interjected. "And Killian is right." She gestured to Dead Sexy.

This was Killian, their friend and ally, and the local alpha? Great. Now I had a name for his annoying, sexy face. I would've thought knowing his actual name would have made him more ordinary, but *his* name made him more alluring. Clearly, I'd never been around someone I found attractive before because these feelings were insane. No one should feel such intensity toward someone they'd just met, especially not someone who'd put *every supernatural race* at risk.

"Jewel did the right thing by bringing Heather here," Sterlyn continued, and made her way to her twin brother. She placed a hand on Cyrus's shoulder.

He exhaled and ran a hand down his face. "You're right." He glanced at me and pressed his lips into a firm line. "Of course you should've brought her. She's part of your grandfather's pack, which makes her extended family."

When Mom had shown up at my grandparents', she'd expressed a lot of remorse. She'd caused problems for Cyrus and, indirectly, Sterlyn as the new pack leaders. She'd blamed them for Dad's death and had spewed so much negativity that she and Chad and a few other silver wolves had chosen to break off from the pack at a time when staying united had been crucial. I didn't know the half of what had happened, but apparently, many wolves had been in danger, including Cyrus's fated mate, Annie, who was another unique kind of shifter, a demon wolf. Mom had later apologized, even to me, and made amends. At first, I'd doubted her sincerity, but then she'd started talking about Sterlyn and Annie. She'd spoken so highly of them, and she'd even spoken more warmly about Cyrus.

I could have understood her about-face if they hadn't been friends with *him*.

"You'll have to forgive us," Sterlyn said as she walked over and placed her hands on my shoulders in a friendly gesture. "It's been stressful the past few..." She trailed off as if she wasn't sure how to finish that statement.

"Weeks?" the tall man who'd come out with her offered. "No, months." He came to stand next to her and focused on me. "With all the turmoil going on, I've lost track of time. Although one good thing happened. I found the love of my life." He kissed Sterlyn's cheek.

I noticed their scents—her musky freesia and his musky leather—were blended. They were fated mates.

A lump formed in my drying throat. Their connection reminded me of Dad and Mom. The ghost of Dad again hovered in my presence.

"You'd better get used to this." Chad rolled his eyes, trying to lighten the mood. "A bunch of them act just like Sterlyn and Griffin, if not worse. Cyrus has been more lovesick since Annie birthed their twins."

"Dude, don't even suggest that Cyrus is more smitten than me," Griffin growled, wrapping his arms around Sterlyn. "I'll beat your ass, silver wolf or not."

I rubbed my arms, and a shiver ran through me. I always felt at home with Chad, but his friendly dynamic with the non-silver wolves made me feel like an outsider.

Taking a step away from him, I rubbed my chest where my links pulsed. At this hour, most of the silver wolves were asleep. Soon, they'd wake up, and once they realized I'd returned, they'd bombard me with questions. My stomach clenched, and unease coursed through me. Chad had filled me in on some things when we'd gotten close enough to link. All these shifters had just finished fighting—and winning—a catastrophic war against demons. And here I was, bringing in another problem when they hadn't had a chance to rest from the last one.

Heather cleared her throat, reminding us that she was here.

Using her interruption, I recentered the conversation. "I appreciate you waking up to greet us, but we need to focus on the threat."

Sterlyn turned to Dead Sexy. "Kill, can we talk in your house?"

He nodded. "Of course." He gestured toward the door but remained standing in front of the porch, mere feet from me, staring.

I shook my head. There was no *way* I was going in there. "Let's stay out here." It was bad enough being this close to Killian; I wasn't entering his house. "We can figure out what to do about my grandparents' pack disappearing."

"It would be best to go inside. Since Shadow City was revealed, things around here have been tense, not only between us and humans but among some of the supernaturals as well." Sterlyn bit her bottom lip. "I don't want to worry anyone about a new problem if we don't need to."

"Then maybe *he* shouldn't have told the world about us." I still didn't understand why he was here.

Griffin stepped next to Sterlyn and growled, "I understand that you're upset, but Killian is part of our alliance. Plus, he's the best friend I've ever had. If you have an issue with what he did, then you have a problem with every single one of us."

"Maybe it was a mistake to come here." I turned, ready to get back into the truck.

A strong hand grasped my upper arm. The calloused fingertips dug into my skin, but I knew who it was—Chad.

Look, I don't agree with what Killian did, either, but he's helped us the entire time, both with support from his pack and personally, Chad linked. *If you want to find your mom and your grandparents, you'll need our help. You came all this way because you know that. Do you really want your anger to get in the way of saving the people you love?*

He always knew how to get through to me. He was right —I wasn't thinking clearly. *Fine.* I switched to speaking out loud. "I'll go inside and *talk*, since Mom, my grandparents, and the lives of their pack members are more important than my concerns with *you*." I glared at Dead Sexy. *Killian.*

Sterlyn's shoulders relaxed. "Okay, great. Rosemary and Levi got home a few hours ago, and since they're sleeping it off at our place, I didn't want to wake them yet." She gestured toward the house next door. "Let's go to Killian's and discuss what we know." She strode to his front door with Griffin right behind her.

Playing Beethoven's Symphony No. 9 in my mind, I tried to squash some of my irritation. I wanted to stay far from Killian, but Chad was right. I needed their help. If I let my pride alienate everyone, I'd be doing the same thing as Mom had when she'd let her anger control her. A few days before she left our pack, she'd called to tell me she was considering breaking away. I'd tried to dissuade her, but when she became like that, she was impossible to reason with. So when she did split, I'd felt the loss but hadn't been surprised. She tended to think only about herself when upset.

Instead, I focused on what Sterlyn had said and linked to Chad, *Rosemary is your angel ally, but who is Levi?* Mom had told me about Rosemary, a female angel who'd been indispensable to our pack.

Levi is her preordained mate, which is what angels and

demons call their fated mates. He's a demon. No one's had one for hundreds of years 'til them. He didn't hesitate to follow Sterlyn, Griffin, and Cyrus into the house.

My gaze flicked to Killian, hoping he'd move next. Though part of me wanted to brush past him, the sane part told me to stay far away. His dreamy eyes locked on me, and my internal war increased tenfold. Goosebumps broke out across my body, and my pulse thudded against my skin.

"Let's move inside before another car chase or something worse happens," Heather said, and stepped up beside me.

Killian moved a few inches closer. "Car chase?"

I'd failed to tell Chad about the chase. He'd been worried enough about the disappearance of Mom and PawPaw's pack, and then he'd filled me in about the war. I'd planned on telling everyone about it when we arrived. Killian, however, didn't need to pretend to care. "Yeah, *humans* chased us since they know all about us now."

He flinched, and his irises darkened.

"Not only did they take my pack, but they damaged my truck, too." Heather gestured at the dent in the side of her truck. "Believe me, I wouldn't have hurt Betsy like that. It took me two years to get her up and running."

I forced my attention to the front door, not wanting to look at him more than I had to, but I could feel his gaze on me even without a link to him. He was supposed to go inside. Was he worried I'd change my mind and drive away?

Damn irritating man.

My hands were shaking, so I tucked a piece of hair behind my ear and rushed to follow the others. I'd rather be around them inside *his* home than out here under his scrutiny. As I scurried past him, his scent surrounded me—musk and sandalwood, the amazing scent I'd noted and thought was from the nearby woods. Unable to stop myself, I inhaled deeply. He smelled delicious.

How appealing could one man be? I had to be hyper-sensitive tonight because I also couldn't stand him. That was what happened to the women in the books I read, but unlike those stories, he and I wouldn't wind up together.

"Hey," Killian murmured, and touched my arm where the bullet had grazed me.

A jolt sizzled through me, heading straight for my core. I jerked my arm away and glared at him. "Do *not* touch me."

He lifted his hands, eyes wide, and stepped back, but he focused on the spot he'd touched.

I didn't know what I was expecting—a burn, the wound to reopen—but my arm looked fine. The faint scab was still there, and the sensation had been pleasurable, not painful. The echo of its effect still coursed through my arm to my soul.

Lungs not working, I stood tall and glared at him. I wouldn't allow him to affect me.

"Is everything okay?" Heather asked, breaking whatever was happening between him and me. "Did he hurt you?"

If I'd been more comfortable showing affection, I would've hugged her. I didn't know what strange thing was going on, but I didn't have time for a distraction, especially of the opposite-sex variety. "No, he just touched me without permission."

The front door opened, and a girl with sandy blonde hair stuck her head out. I started.

Killian's attention was still locked on the scab on my arm as, irises glowing, he growled, "What happened?"

"Oh, my gods," the new girl gasped, cutting him off as her gray eyes turned to slits. "We're waiting to discuss that here, together. You're going to scare these poor ladies away.

What have I *told* you about being grumpy and overbearing?"

Those two words didn't describe the man I'd seen on TV or the one here. The word I'd choose was *intense*.

"Please forgive him." The new girl sashayed over and looped her arm through mine. "He doesn't get out much, so the constant frown on his face is the norm. For women, it's called 'resting bitch face.' I'm not sure what the male version is, so we'll just go with 'resting Killian face.'"

Tugging me toward the door, she gave me little choice but to follow, not that I would've put up a fight. I needed to get away from him. Strangely, I wasn't uncomfortable with her. I always felt awkward around supernaturals outside my own pack.

"Sierra, you're butting—" Killian started, but Sierra kept on babbling.

"He's a good guy, so we forgive him. But he's very protective." She pulled me through the small foyer toward a large, open living room with gorgeous blue-gray walls.

Somehow, I swallowed my laughter. I wouldn't consider him a good guy. He'd made things extraordinarily worse for the supernatural world. Continuing to point it out would only derail the conversation more, however, so I forced my mouth to stay closed.

A sizable brown leather couch was against the far-left wall with a television hanging above a tiled chimney across from it. A matching loveseat sat perpendicular to the couch, facing five windows. The room opened into a gigantic kitchen with dark oak cabinets and a circular glass-topped table. The door leading to the backyard was positioned between the kitchen and living room. In one corner of the living room, near the couch, sat a fishing pole and a tackle box.

My attention landed on a huge portrait hanging over the couch. It showed a younger version of Killian, a girl about his age who looked so much like him that they had to be siblings, and two older people standing behind them.

He was a family man. So where was his family now?

Chad stood next to the fireplace, his attention on me. *You're acting stranger than usual.*

I couldn't deny that one. I was usually calm and collected, but Killian had thrown me off-kilter.

Griffin, Sterlyn, and Cyrus were sitting on the couch, and Sierra led me to the loveseat. "We'll sit here." She winked as she plopped down. When I didn't immediately join her, she patted the open spot.

Trust me, Chad linked to me. *Just sit down. It'll be easier that way.*

I could already tell she wasn't one to take no for an answer. I'd have preferred to stand after sitting for so long in the truck, but then I might wind up next to Killian. At that thought, I obliged her eagerly.

Killian stood on the other side of the TV, and Heather squished onto the loveseat beside me.

Sterlyn leaned forward, her elbows on her knees. "Tell us everything that happened."

My body loosened, ready to determine what we could do to save my family.

Heather launched into the tale, informing them of how we'd come home and what we'd found. She left out that we'd been having a girls' night at a bar when our family and pack were taken.

The entire time, I could feel Killian's attention on me. Even avoiding his gaze didn't lessen the tingles and aggravation I experienced under his gaze.

"And here we are, in need of your help to find my pack and Jewel's family," Heather concluded.

"That's not all." Killian pushed off the wall, walking straight toward me. "She got hurt during the altercation, and I...*we* need to know when and how."

My blood turned cold. Of course he'd push the matter. Clearly, he had a habit of sharing information that wasn't his to share. I hadn't even told Heather I'd been hit because I was fine.

Pivoting toward me, Heather gasped, her face twisted. "You got hurt? When? Was it the crash or the bullet?"

All seven pairs of eyes focused on me. The last thing we needed to discuss was my almost-healed injury. "It doesn't matter. Let's just—"

Apparently, that had been the wrong thing to say, because Killian's nostrils flared. "Like hell it doesn't." I could hear him move toward me, and I glanced up as Chad stepped in front of me.

Chad clenched his hands as he said, "Back off and give her a chance to explain."

CHAPTER FIVE

I HATED one thing more than drama, and that was being in the center of it. I always felt as if I needed to help Dad in his alpha role, so I strove to make peace and blend into the background.

Killian's neck corded. For whatever reason, he was determined to know what had caused my injury, despite it now being a mere scab. I wasn't sure why he was so upset—he'd only just met me—yet he and Chad were already in a testosterone-fueled battle. The prick needed to learn that it wasn't his place to worry about me.

I stood and placed my hands on Chad's shoulders. His muscles were so tight that they could have passed as rubber bands.

A low growl emanated from Killian's throat. It had to be because Chad was interfering. Though Chad wasn't alpha-strong by silver wolf standards, he was stronger than most shifters. I'd almost bet that Killian could give him an equal battle as long as they weren't in wolf form when the moon was in our favor.

"Guys, we aren't enemies," Sterlyn interjected, straightening as if she might stand.

"I'm not so sure," Chad said through gritted teeth. "If he keeps talking to J like that, we might end up that way."

"Are you threatening me?" Killian snarled.

Chad's back spasmed, informing me that he was becoming upset, too. I'd only seen that happen once when he and Dad had gotten into it about Chad wanting to attend a local high school. All silver wolves were homeschooled, but Chad had been desperate to get away from the pack for a short while.

"Slow your roll, Kill." Sierra leaned back and crossed her arms. "You've been distancing yourself and stressed since all the craziness happened, and now you're imploding. That isn't good for anyone. Maybe you should get laid. I mean, the last woman you were interested in found her fated mate before you could confess your feelings. I understand that everything sucks right now, but getting your world rocked might do you good. I'd even be willing to find that scatterbrain Deissy for you."

Pain shot through my heart, and I held in a whimper. He had feelings for someone else.

Likely someone who had boundaries he kept disrespecting, like the need to keep earth-shattering secrets and mind his own business.

Chad stepped backward into me, brushing against my chest. "That's what I'm thinking, and I won't allow him to take it out on J. It's not her fault that her grandparents' pack disappeared. She knows how to hide and blend in. Bart taught us *all* that."

Hearing my father's name brought me strength. I didn't need a protector; I was more than capable of handling things on my own. "I didn't inform anyone about the supernatural races or my grandfather's pack, or what species of wolf I am."

Head jerking back as if he'd been smacked, Killian clenched his hands.

"We all need to *calm down*." Cyrus rubbed his temples. "Hell, I'm not sure how we got to this point, but I'm sleep-deprived. Between two newborns and waking up an hour ago with Chad filling me in on everything, I'm lucky to get two hours of sleep at a time."

"Dude, you're not alone, and I don't have the newborn excuse." Griffin snorted. "I'm just as confused as you are. And now Killian's taken your place as the angry and irrational one."

Diarrhea mouth would've been a better description. He'd shared things that were not his to share.

Killian waved a hand at my arm. "She got injured tonight, and I want to know how. I've seen the speed at which you silver wolves heal, so that injury was recent."

One thing was clear—if I didn't speak, things would escalate, and the focus wouldn't return to Mom and the pack. Even though Killian wasn't a silver wolf, alpha power wafted off him, and he was determined to get an answer.

Begrudgingly, I couldn't blame him. He didn't know me, and after months away, I come back with a stranger and ask for their help to find Mom and my grandparents' pack. That was a hefty request, especially if I wasn't willing to answer his questions.

"She doesn't deserve to be talked to that—" Chad started, but I shut it down.

"A bullet grazed my arm when Heather and I were running in the woods. They didn't shoot me with a tranq gun, so I'm fine." My wolf stirred inside me, wanting to release Chad and touch Killian, so I dug my fingers deeper into Chad's shoulder.

"And you didn't think *I* should know that?" Heather slid off the couch and onto her feet. "I was with you when it happened!"

This was why I hadn't told her. I'd seen her overreact before. "We couldn't pack link, and we were running for our lives. Yeah, they were human, but we needed to be quiet and blend in. Between that and the police showing up, by the time we got back in the truck, I'd forgotten about it." I pointed at the scratch. "It's almost completely healed. I've had worse injuries while training."

You should have told me, Chad linked, and my stomach sank from the hurt permeating through our pack link. *We had an agreement.*

I dropped my arms from his shoulders, and Killian exhaled. He must have been content with my answers... which made me want to take them back. I didn't want to appease him. I just wanted him to let this go.

I agreed to tell you if I got hurt during training. I hated almost any kind of attention, especially pity. *This wasn't training.*

Though my dad had never been meant to be the true silver wolf alpha, he'd had alpha blood running through his veins. When I was born without silver hair, he'd known that my uncle, Arion, whom I had never met, would have children of his own. Fate had a funny way of revealing her plan.

I didn't have alpha power, which I was at peace with. I was fine with not being in the spotlight. But I still wanted to be just as strong of a fighter, despite being a rare female silver wolf—which, funnily enough, wasn't so rare right now, with my best friend, Emmy, Sterlyn, and me in the same pack. As the firstborn, I'd always been determined to keep up with the men, so while training, I wound up getting hurt every so often.

Something uncomfortably warm, akin to rage, added to his hurt as Chad replied, *Not making things better. I said let me know when you are* hurt. *I didn't specifically say during training.*

Clearly, it was a misunderstanding. He'd asked for that promise after I'd suffered a minor injury during training, blowing it out of proportion. He was like an older, protective brother even when I didn't need one —like now.

Heather shook her head. "I can't believe they had tranquilizers."

"That doesn't surprise me." Killian rolled his shoulders. "The people who tried to capture Sterlyn used tranqs too, although they were supernaturals."

Breath catching, I replayed his words in my head to see if I understood what he'd said.

Heather laughed. "Says the official face of the supernatural world."

"Don't start." Sierra rolled her eyes and rubbed her hands down her thighs. "There wasn't a lot of time to decide what to do."

Killian snorted. "Don't make it sound as if I didn't decide to inform the world."

My chest constricted as I focused every ounce of self-control on not stomping across the room and punching him. Thankfully, the familiar tug of my best friend linking with me pulled at my core.

Emmy linked, *Jewel? You're home!*

Her excitement relieved some of my tension, but that would only last until she learned what happened to PawPaw's pack.

Just as expected, her joy lessened. *Wait. I can't feel your mom. Did you leave her in Gatlinburg?*

Mouth drying, I had to remind myself she'd asked because she cared. I didn't want to keep repeating the story. *Hey, Emmy. I missed you, too. Cyrus or Chad can fill you in.*

When she didn't respond, I knew what she was doing.

Martha's link warmed as if she'd awakened, and I guessed that Emmy and Martha—Emmy's mom and Darrell's mate—would be here soon.

"What's wrong?" Heather asked, bringing me back to the present.

Shaking my head, I focused on the room again while linking to Chad, *Emmy is heading over.* Though I loved and appreciated her, she could be overwhelming. I'd almost broken down with Chad; I wouldn't be able to hold it together if Emmy came here, too. I hadn't seen her since she'd left my grandparents' pack a few weeks ago to head back here. Sitting around was beginning to wear on me. "Some of the silver wolves are waking, and I've been away for a while. With Mom and my grandparents at risk, it's a lot." I rubbed my hands down my arms to shake off the chill that had penetrated deep within. "I want to focus what energy I have on finding them."

The tension dissipated as Chad stepped to the side. "I'll head them off and buy you some time." His eyes glowed as he linked with Darrell, Theo, Cyrus, Sterlyn, and me. *I'll stop Emmy from coming in and fill in the rest of the silver wolves while J stays here to finish. I heard the entire story.*

I sighed with relief as my heart warmed. That would help tremendously.

"It'll be hard to find them. Everyone was out of pack-link range before we got off the mountain." And now we were south of Chattanooga and likely even farther away.

We could still find them, but it would take much longer. We'd have to follow the pull of our links. It sounded easy in theory, but it rarely offered a straight line to the source. We'd wind up taking detours, adding to our time.

"We have a solution for that," Sterlyn said. "Our witch friends could help us."

"Witch?" I parroted. I hated when people repeated the exact thing someone had just said, but I must have heard her wrong. Mom had told me that a coven had begrudgingly helped the shifters take down the demon wolf pack that had threatened Annie, and they'd lost one of their own in the process, so to hear that they would help again surprised me.

A sharp pain pulsed in my chest. While mourning, I hadn't been there to help with the battles the silver wolves had endured. Guilt weighed heavily on me. I should've been here to fight alongside them. Dad would've never left them in time of trouble. Granted, I hadn't realized there would be any threats of this magnitude. Then several members of our pack died, and Mom and the others had wanted Emmy and me to stay away. They'd even moved without telling us where the pack had resettled. I could have looked for them myself, but they'd have felt me, and I'd have distracted them, potentially causing more injuries or deaths. Forcing my way down here would've been selfish.

I was still working on forgiving Mom for leaving the pack and taking Chad, Theo, and Rudie with her, so her failure to inform me that the silver wolves had faced dire battles, again and again, had only further strained our relationship. That was the whole reason she'd come to PawPaw's pack despite the risks—to mourn Dad's death and make peace with me.

I shook my head, trying to get over my reproach. All I

could do going forward was make Dad proud by standing with my pack.

"Mom said the witches didn't like helping the wolves." The words rubbed my throat raw. If I'd stayed, I wouldn't need an explanation.

Sierra tossed her hair over her shoulder and smiled. "Girl, please. Once people meet me, they can't stay away. The bonds I form *are* magic. You'll soon see for yourself."

Biting my bottom lip, I examined her. I was certain she believed every word she said, yet she didn't seem narcissistic. It was a quandary.

"She's joking." Killian sighed and gestured at Sierra. "Kind of."

The urge to comfort him surged through me, and I clenched my jaw. I should have wanted her to annoy him... to death.

"What she *really* means is that the witches realized they couldn't keep hiding." Sterlyn sat on the edge of the couch. "Kind of like what Cyrus and I decided with the silver wolves. Trying to hide gives others more power. I know Dad and Bart—" She paused, and her eyes glistened. "They believed we needed to hide to protect our packs, but we were born to protect supernaturals *and* humanity. We can't do that from the shadows. The witches are meant to protect the balance of good and evil, and they have to be immersed in the world to fulfill their obligations, too."

No one had ever explained it to me that way. Her view held merit. The fact that I hadn't contemplated it bothered me. I tried to see every angle of a situation, and my obliviousness reinforced that growing up with fundamental beliefs made it hard to challenge them. Regardless, the truth had come out, and there was no turning back—not that I could see.

"And they willingly *help* you?" Heather's brows furrowed. "My pack wasn't in hiding, but we only interacted with other wolf shifters, and mostly with our own pack, despite other packs attending the same local schools."

Griffin smiled adoringly at Sterlyn and wrapped his arm around her waist. "My mate has an uncanny way of bringing supernatural races together."

She reached up and patted his cheek lovingly. "It's not just me. We have a group of outstanding friends and family who came together to make a difference."

Their interaction reminded me so much of Dad and Mom that sorrow nearly drowned me. Cyrus's irises darkened to a gunmetal gray as he watched me as if he understood. But that was impossible. His mate was nearby with their children.

My gaze flicked to Killian again, and I froze when I caught him staring at me. A similar frisson to the jolt I'd felt when he'd brushed my arm sizzled through the air between us.

I scowled. *That* was crazy, and I refused to find the man who'd informed the world of our existence alluring. Though Sterlyn's belief about not hiding had merit, supernaturals hadn't hidden for our own protection, but rather to protect humans from their irrational fear of *us*.

Fresh air. That was what I needed. "Point me in the direction of the witches, and I'll head over there."

"They aren't here." Cyrus stood and shoved his hands into his jeans pockets. "Annie and I can take you to them. Aurora has been harassing us to see the twins."

"I'll go with you guys, too," Killian said. "If my decision to inform the world is the reason your mom and your grandparents' pack are in danger, I need to help, and there's no telling what sort of mess you're getting into. Whatever is happening to Jewel's family's pack will make its way down here to mine. Besides, Billy has acted as alpha for years, so I'll tell him to make sure the towns are covered." Killian scratched the back of his neck and glanced at Sterlyn and Griffin. "Unless you guys need me to stay here."

He seemed remorseful, but intent never mattered. His actions had consequences, and this was one of them.

"You didn't kidnap her grandparents' pack. But I understand why you want to go." Griffin stretched his arms. "I'll call Ronnie and Alex and coordinate who's going to keep an eye on things while the rest of us are busy."

Sterlyn smiled at her mate. "That's a good plan. I'll pack us a bag and wake Rosemary and Levi. We need to move. If humans organized the disappearance, I'm afraid it's just the beginning."

Though that was the last thing I wanted to hear, she was right. "If that *is* what happened, we need to act fast. Who knows what else the humans have planned?" I turned to head out the door, eager to make my way to the witches.

Sterlyn linked with me, *Can Cyrus and I talk to you alone for a second? Annie is getting the twins ready and will pick you up in a minute. Some things are better said out loud.*

She seemed to be giving me the choice, and though I wondered if that was an illusion, only concern and warmth wafted from her to me.

One thing was certain: The two people my dad had died to protect wanted to talk to me alone. There was only one answer I could give. *Yes.*

As soon as I answered, my stomach fluttered. What was so important that they wanted to say it out loud?

CHAPTER SIX

WITH A SMALL SMILE, Sterlyn headed to the back door. "While Annie gets the twins ready, Cyrus, Jewel, and I are going out back to talk."

A jolt rushed through my body, warning me that Killian was looking at me again. I glared at him and caught his gaze darting away.

My cheeks burned. I was hyper-aware of him, and I would wager he was only paying close attention to me because of my abrupt arrival. He was probably watching Heather just as much, trying to learn all our secrets so he could tell the world.

The thought of him paying her extra attention strangled me. I wanted *all* of his attention, though I already knew he was interested in someone else. A pang of jealousy shot through my chest, and I rubbed it, hoping to alleviate the discomfort.

It didn't help. The sensation was emotional, despite it manifesting as if it were physical.

I was losing my mind. The stress was taking its toll. That was the only explanation.

I needed fresh air. Between that and gaining space from Killian, I'd be able to level out these strange emotions.

"Maybe I should come, too." Heather bounced on her feet.

She didn't want to be left alone with strangers, and I'd rather not hear what these two had to say by myself. Though Sterlyn seemed kind and strong, I suspected she wanted to address why I'd stayed away for so long. Although that could be my guilt rearing its head.

They wanted to speak out loud instead of using the pack link, so it had to be something serious. They wouldn't want Heather there.

I patted her shoulder and said, "I think they want to talk to me alone." Avoiding the conversation was pointless.

The corners of Heather's mouth tilted downward as she laughed, the sound a little too high-pitched. "Of course. Silver wolf business."

Even though Heather and I weren't super close, I'd seen her act like this often enough back at PawPaw's pack home to realize her feelings were hurt. His pack was full of outstanding men, but their attitude was still outdated, like most of the supernatural world, where women were discounted because they tended to be weaker physically. When I'd first told PawPaw that a female was the rightful alpha of the silver wolves, he'd thought I was joking.

Cyrus bobbed his head from side to side. "Something like that."

I squeezed her arm comfortingly before dropping my hand. If she saw a hint of hesitation, she'd cling to it and push to come with me.

Sierra snorted and scurried past me, looping her arm through Heather's. She leaned her head on Heather's shoulder and murmured, "You get used to it...kind of. I allow it to happen occasionally 'cause Sterlyn's my girl. Stay with me, and tell me about your pack."

Shoulders relaxing, Heather seemed relieved; she wasn't the only one being left out.

Killian tilted his head down and ran his hands through his short, thick hair. He dropped his hands, leaving his hair messy. I wanted to lick—no, I wanted to *smack* him.

My wolf inched forward, showing her approval of my first instinct. My wolf needed to settle, but she had a mind of her own.

"Let me know if you need me." Killian homed in on Sterlyn. "I'll link with Billy and inform him of our plans. He'll step into the alpha role while I'm gone."

Cyrus opened the back door and waved the two of us outside. The cool breeze of an early morning in December blew across my hot skin as I stepped onto the covered concrete back porch. My wolf calmed, either from the temperature or the distance from Killian. I didn't care which, so long as she did.

I scanned the backyard. A black iron handrail stood on one side of four brick steps that descended to the grass. About twenty feet away was the pool with a black cover on top. There was no fence, which I found odd. Humans always had fences around their pools. But this was a supernatural community, where even kids had no problem swimming. The tree line started seventy-five feet past that, and I guessed the woods went all the way to the Tennessee River a couple of miles away.

The patter of paws deeper in the woods revealed that wolves were running the perimeter. I estimated five. They were in various parts of the forest, circling the neighborhood.

After jumping gracefully to the ground, Sterlyn headed

to the edge of the covered pool and faced us. She clearly wanted to put some distance between us and the house so we wouldn't be overheard. Following his sister's lead, Cyrus jumped onto the grass, whereas I walked slowly down the stairs, using those few extra seconds to level out my emotions.

As I approached, Cyrus glanced at his sister and tugged at the collar of his light gray cotton shirt.

My curiosity was piqued. He was uncomfortable. They wanted to talk to me, so why would he feel uncomfortable? Alphas didn't usually have a problem addressing their pack members.

Placing his hands behind his back, he looked at me expectantly. Did he expect me to talk first?

I remained silent as I reached them, keeping a few feet between us. We were close enough to murmur so the others wouldn't hear, but we weren't in each other's bubbles. I inhaled, filling my lungs with fresh air, and smelled the fescue grass under my feet.

"Sorry to pull you away from everyone inside, but it might be a while before we can talk with you alone." Sterlyn twirled a piece of hair around a finger.

She was nervous, too...and it clicked. This was about one or both of my parents. Not trusting my voice, I nodded.

"I know things with Mila were tense for a while," she started, lifting her head high. "And I understand why. I can't imagine what it would be like to live in a world without Griffin, and if he died..." She closed her eyes. "If he died protecting people he barely knew, that would be hard to overcome."

Eyes burning, I swallowed, trying to keep my tears at bay. "Don't worry. I won't cause problems like Mom did. That was one reason I went away."

"That's not what I meant." She opened her eyes again. "What I wanted to say is...I'm sorry. Because Bart was protecting me, you lost your father, and I know how hard it is to lose a parent."

"He wasn't only protecting Sterlyn." Cyrus tugged at his ear. "He was protecting all of us. He helped me get in touch with my wolf and work through the anger I'd allowed to control me all my life. He made me feel like part of the pack. Like I *could* be part of it."

I already knew all of this. Though Dad had stayed here to help Sterlyn and Cyrus, he'd called Mom and me daily. He'd told us that Cyrus had been kidnapped as an infant and raised by people who'd never cared for him. They'd used him to train armies, and because he'd been taken from the silver wolves, he hadn't been able to shift and had grown up completely out of sync with his wolf. Dad had felt responsible for my cousins, not only because they were silver wolves but because they were his niece and nephew. He'd loved them.

"If I could take it back..." Sterlyn pressed her lips together. "If I could somehow bring him back—"

They were being kind and, more importantly, sincere. They were both struggling with emotions like I was—not only could I see it, but I felt it through our pack connection. They loved Dad. Everyone did. He'd embodied goodness, strength, and empathy. Without him, the world had been stripped of one of its few bright lights.

My throat thickened further, making it more of a challenge to swallow. "Please don't apologize." I had a feeling that was where Sterlyn was heading, and although I appreciated the sentiment, I wouldn't be able to keep my emotions together. I didn't like feeling vulnerable in front of anyone. "You have nothing to be sorry about. Dad *chose* to protect you because you are pack and family. You didn't ask him to because with Dad, you never had to. He was self-less and courageous—everything a silver wolf is meant to be. I left because I wanted to respect his sacrifice, and I needed the time and space away to be able to do that without spewing anger or falling apart. I *failed* you and every one of my pack members by not being here to help you fight. So if anyone has anything to apologize for, it's me."

Sterlyn placed her hands on my shoulders and leaned down so we were at eye level. She had an inch on me, and I came in at around five feet seven. She rasped, "You also have nothing to apologize for. If you needed time to mourn your father's death, you had every right to take it, and frankly, I admire that. Not many people take the time for self-care."

I hadn't thought of it as self-care, but that description worked. It had been a struggle not to succumb to the pain while at PawPaw and Nana's, and I could only imagine how catastrophic staying here would have been, dealing with the fallout of my emotions on top of everything else. I didn't want my emotions to rule me and turn me into a person I didn't like.

"We're—" I stopped, steadying myself to say the word. Dad had loved them. I'd heard it in his voice when he'd spoken about them, and I'd been so eager to finally meet them when the time came. Here it was, and I had to remember what he'd wanted. "We're *family*. He was so excited for the day I got to meet you both and the future we would all have together. So...that's what I want—to fulfill his vision and be what he hoped we could be. It may take time, but I'm willing if you two are."

Exhaling, Cyrus chuckled. "I should've realized that

Bart's daughter would be like him—honest, loyal, and self-aware."

Those words did describe Dad, but he'd been so much more than that. He'd been patient, kind, and dependable. He'd been more than my dad and best friend; he'd been my mentor.

"You do remind me of him." Sterlyn lowered her hands to her side and smiled. "And I'd love for us to be family." Her happiness swirled through our connection, which was stronger than mine was with the other silver wolves because she was my alpha.

"Me, too." Cyrus winked. "Especially now that we have twin newborns. I could use all the family we have to help out with them."

Babies. I hadn't been around a newborn since I was a young child myself. Silver wolves had only one or two kids their entire lives. Our reproduction cycles were long, due to our angel heritage, and the newer mated couples like Theo and Rudie hadn't birthed any children yet. "I'd *love* to help."

My heart both ached from the loss of my father and warmed from finally connecting with family from Dad's side. The crippling fear that plagued me due to the Gatlinburg pack and Mom vanishing was never far away, heightening the other emotions. The sensations pulled at me equally, along with an irrational urge to run back inside to see Killian, adding to my frustration. If anything, I should have been running *away from* him.

A ticking bomb best described everything roiling inside, and I despised feeling that way. If I wanted to save everyone, I had to keep a level head.

Cyrus beamed, bringing back my joy. "Then it's settled." His irises glowed faintly. Someone was linking with him. "I'm going to help Annie. Arian is giving her a hard time."

"That's fine. We'll make a plan and fill you in," Sterlyn said as she waved her brother on.

Without hesitation, he took off, rushing past the white house next door and farther down the neighborhood.

She walked by me, gesturing toward the white house. "Griffin and I live here. Why don't you come over while I pack a bag and grab some coffee before we head out?"

Tears still threatening to spill, I spoke slowly, trying to keep my voice level. "I should find Heather." I didn't want to leave her on her own any longer than I had to. "But thanks."

"If you change your mind, just link me. We won't be here much longer."

She turned and walked toward her home, and I realized there was one more thing I was desperate to know. "Sterlyn?" When she looked back at me, rather than speak aloud and risk someone overhearing, I linked, *Why aren't you upset with Killian for telling the world about us?*

She regarded me steadily. *The truth had already come out, thanks to human videos, and we wanted someone we could all trust to talk about us to the world,* she answered simply. *Killian suggested it was the best way to control the narrative.*

That was the problem—a narrative wasn't needed, let alone required—but I kept my mouth shut.

When I didn't respond, Sterlyn smiled and slipped inside the house as she linked, *I'll be back soon.*

A chill racked my body, and I felt truly alone. I wished I had someone to confide in.

I wish Dad were here.

Tears spilled down my cheeks as the ache of missing

him, Mom, and my grandparents submerged me. I hadn't cried in a few weeks after finding a balance between mourning Dad's death and cherishing my memories of him. It had taken me months to find my way to that place, but being back here with the pack, meeting Sterlyn and Cyrus, and with the threat of losing Mom and my grandparents hovering over me...it felt like my world was falling apart again.

To find my strength, I had to allow this moment of weakness. Bottling up emotions wasn't healthy and would only fuel my rage. I'd seen it happen with Mom, and that hadn't ended well.

I turned away from the house in case anyone was watching me. Though I didn't like to cry in front of others, I didn't consider tears a weakness. Rather, they were a vulnerability I was willing to share with only those I trusted completely. I believed Sterlyn and Cyrus would become that, but we weren't there yet. We might be related, but a close bond hadn't formed.

A sob built inside me, but I refused to let it out. Someone might hear me. Instead, I focused on silent tears that would keep my broken secret.

I sniffled just as the back door opened. Loud footsteps hit the concrete, and the tantalizing scent of sandalwood swirled around me. A jolt shot through my body and increased in intensity with every step he took nearer to me.

Even with my back facing the door, I knew who it was.

Killian. The traitor.

And there was nowhere to run.

CHAPTER SEVEN

I WIPED the tears from my face, hoping he hadn't heard the sniffle. The last thing I needed was for him to know I was upset. He'd jump at the opportunity to shout that information at the top of his lungs for anyone to hear.

"Why are you crying?" he rasped, and his voice had the same calming effect over me that Beethoven had. A perfect, soothing combination would have been Killian humming "Ode to Joy."

I snorted softly to myself. That would *never* happen. He probably had a horrible singing voice that would crack every glass in the neighborhood. I closed my eyes, imagining his rough, jangling singing voice. It helped ease the effect he had on me, at least while my back was to him.

My first instinct was to lie, but that would accomplish nothing but add a horrible odor to an already tense situation. Maybe if I answered him quickly, he'd leave me the hell alone and head back inside.

"It's a combination of everything." Whoever had come up with *the truth will set you free* must have been drunk. I'd rather be vague than pour my heart out to *him*. If I didn't give him a little bit of information, though, he wouldn't be satisfied.

"We'll find your mom—" he started.

"Don't." Heart pounding, I spun and faced him. "Do *not* give me false hope or guarantees that are beyond your control. For all I know, they're in this situation because of *you.*"

His expression fell, and he closed his eyes.

I'd hurt him. *Good.* He needed to realize the impact of his decision to expose us to the *entire* world.

My wolf whimpered, and I clenched my hands. With his eyes closed, I could see how long his lashes were. And when he licked his lips, I wondered if they tasted better than he smelled. Not that I would ever find out. But no matter how hard I tried to ignore my attraction, my senses kept betraying me. Hurting him bothered me.

"I'm sorry." Killian opened his eyes, and they darkened. "The last thing I'd ever want to do is cause you pain."

My heart lurched into my throat, and my palms grew sweaty. *Keep a level head, Jewel*, I warned myself. "You don't even know me." Saying that to a complete stranger wasn't normal. He *didn't* know me from Jack, and his audacity to pretend he did should have infuriated me.

No. It *did* infuriate me.

"Don't try to manipulate me into not being upset with you." My feet stepped toward him without my permission, and I shoved my finger into his chest. The jolt sparked, but anger took over. I relished the distraction—anything to prevent me from feeling this strange attraction to him.

He groaned in frustration. "I'm not manipulating you. I knew there would be backlash, but I thought they might attack *here*." He lifted his hands out to the side.

I laughed. I couldn't help it. His logic was completely

flawed. "You thought that humans would come to a place they know is infested with supernaturals instead of picking off individual groups outside this cursed city?" That was the problem with most supernaturals, even my cherished silver wolves. We thought people would come after *us*. We couldn't fathom a group going after another pack, a different supernatural race, whatever, instead. We were part angel and part wolf. We had ties to the moon.

Obviously, Killian employed similar logic. Humans had witnessed the huge battle that had occurred in his territory, and he'd thought humans would come after them. "They're going to pick off the isolated packs and groups that don't have allies close by," I said.

Massaging his temples, he sighed, and I dug my finger deeper into his chest.

My strange attraction to him sparked as my anger ebbed. *I'm still touching him.* I dropped my hand and took a step back.

"Why would they hunt down others when they know so many supernaturals are here?" He winced, then answered his own question. "Because they don't know we're not on great terms."

There, he was finally getting it. "Exactly. The news showed wolves, angels, and super-pale humans working together. They must think there's an alliance among all supernaturals, and even if there isn't, that you would all rally together against a common enemy."

"*We*," he rasped.

Brows furrowing, I blinked. "What are you talking about?"

"You're a silver wolf. Bart and Mila's daughter. You're part of this neighborhood and Shadow Ridge," he murmured.

He was missing the point, and worse, I liked how the word *we* sounded on his full, delectable lips. I had to focus on the problem, not on how hot he was. "I realize that you didn't foresee this, but you still told a secret that wasn't only yours to tell. I was raised in isolation, and not only am I trying to adjust to the supernatural world knowing that silver wolves exist but to humans knowing now, too. Everything my dad stood for, you essentially demolished in five seconds."

Dad hadn't shied away from helping others, but he had tried to protect his pack by doing what he thought was right. He hadn't forced us into anything without listening to the pack's opinions. Killian should have consulted with most of the supernaturals before appearing on that broadcast, and probably not even half of the world's supernatural population lived in this area. "While I do believe you didn't mean to cause harm, that's irrelevant. Every choice has consequences, and your decision may have led to my family being tortured, killed, or used as test subjects."

"I will make this right," Killian vowed, and took a step toward me.

The insane part was that he actually thought he could achieve that. "The damage is done. There's no making it right. We can only try to mitigate the consequences. Lives will be lost, and I pray to the gods it isn't my family's lives. I can't lose anyone else close to me. I might turn into someone I don't want to be." My capacity for anger scared me, and if I didn't have Mom or my grandparents, I was afraid fury would consume my soul.

Tears spilled from my eyes without permission, and Killian's forehead lined with either regret or worry. I wasn't sure which, but all I knew was that I was crying in front of him. I lifted my head, refusing to look ashamed.

He clenched and unclenched his hands, then rubbed his palms on his jeans as he chewed on his bottom lip.

Part of me wanted him to say something...anything. But there was nothing he could say. Admitting he was wrong wouldn't fix the problem, and promising again to find my family was something he might not be able to follow through on.

We had nothing left to say.

Wiping the tears from under my eyes, I prepared to go inside. If I stayed out here with him any longer, I'd unravel. My anger and attraction toward him were ripping my heart out more than if I'd settled on one emotion. It was like watching one of Chad and Theo's ping-pong matches in the basement of my house growing up. Instead of a ball, the thing in play was a mess of jumbled sensations.

When I stepped past Killian, he caught my wrist. The shock that charged between us damn near stole my breath.

"I..." He trailed off, but his hand remained firm on me. He looked down at where we were touching, eyes wide.

I already knew what he had almost said and rasped, "Let me go. I don't want to be around you, and all you want is to not feel as burdened by your decision."

He huffed but released his hold.

Something sharp panged my heart. I forced my legs to move. I didn't have time for some psychotic episode—my entire focus needed to be on locating my mom and grandparents. I couldn't let a self-absorbed man with a god complex distract me.

Tapping into my wolf, I listened to see if he was following me, but I heard nothing other than his ragged breathing by the pool. Good. Maybe he'd gotten the hint that I wanted nothing to do with him.

I swung the door open and stepped inside the house.

The living room was empty, so I had a moment to myself. Unable to sit, I paced in front of the windows. My attention flicked outside the living room windows that faced the back-yard just as the gorgeous angel I'd seen on TV walked out of Sterlyn's back door toward the pool.

Killian smiled at her, and something *squeezed* my heart. His face lit up, and the darkness emanating from him vanished. He didn't look like the same person.

Gigantic black wings exploded from her back, making her burnt orange long-sleeved shirt resemble a sunrise. The TV hadn't captured her true beauty. If I hadn't known better, I'd have assumed she was a goddess.

A door closed down the hallway, and Sierra said, "See. I told you we'd find you and Jewel some clothes. Olive had style, so you're in good hands."

The two of them entered the living room, Heather with a sizable pale pink duffel bag slung over her arm. She asked, "Are you sure Killian won't mind?"

"I don't think he plans on wearing the clothes." Sierra shrugged. "But I've been known to be wrong on occasion."

"We appreciate it, but we're good." I didn't want to take anything from him. "Besides, shouldn't we ask Olive, not Killian?"

Sierra smiled sadly. "That would be hard to do since she passed away several years ago."

"Oh." The sinking sensation in my stomach threatened to bring more tears. *Damn it.* Killian had lost someone, too. My focus went to the family picture on the wall. "Is that Olive?"

"Yeah. She was my best friend." Sierra walked to the picture and brushed her fingers along the frame beneath the young woman. "And one of the best people I've ever known."

I wanted to ask about Killian's parents, but the back door opened, and Killian, Rosemary, and another man who towered over them entered the house. The man had a dangerous edge along with short espresso-colored hair and mocha-brown eyes. He was an inch or so taller than Griffin and half a foot taller than Rosemary. A sweet peony scent, mixed with a hint of rose, wafted from him. His and Rosemary's scents were combined, indicating they were fated mates.

He had to be Levi.

Her dark purple irises contained sparkles that reminded me of stars, and when they focused on me, I could feel the pure essence radiating from her soul. She seemed familiar, even though we'd never met. Levi, however, didn't have any essence I could identify. Odd. I'd never met anyone from whom I couldn't get a slight read.

"You must be Jewel," Rosemary stated.

Heather placed a hand on her hip. "How do you know I'm not Jewel?"

"I can sense the angel in her." Rosemary nodded, and her long, purple-tinted mahogany hair brushed her arms. "We're family, after all."

I'd forgotten that Rosemary was a distant relative. Her uncle, Ophaniel, had fathered the silver wolf line. That had to be why she felt familiar.

"This is my preordained mate, Levi," Rosemary said as she waved her hand at the ruggedly handsome man. "He's a demon, but not evil."

Sierra snorted. "Leave it to Rosemary to throw facts out there. It's like Levi's demon blood defines him."

"But it does." Rosemary arched a brow. "Just like being an angel defines me."

"What my Rosey is trying to say is that I'm the love of

her life." Levi chuckled as he took her hand. "It's a pleasure to meet yet another silver wolf."

Instead of countering, Rosemary shook her head, reminding me of all the times I never understood the subtext of a conversation.

Annie and I are pulling out of our driveway now, Cyrus linked with Sterlyn, Chad, and me. *We'll be there in a minute.*

Energy surged through me. Good, we were finally moving. I wasn't sure how witch magic worked, but if they could locate Mom and the others, I'd owe them big time.

Sterlyn replied, *Griffin and I are ready to head out, too. We can take five more people if anyone wants to come with us.*

Count Heather and me in. Anything to ensure I wasn't stuck riding with Killian. I faced Heather and said, "Sterlyn and Griffin are about to pull out, so we need to catch a ride with them."

"Sounds good." Sierra clapped. "Come on, Killian. Let's roll."

Shoulders tense, I jerked my attention to him. "You're going with them, too?" That sounded rude, but I didn't care. Killian needed to ride with Cyrus and Annie or take his own damn car.

"I can take my truck—" he started.

Rosemary cut him off. "Absolutely not. We all know the Nightshadow Sisters could be watching us, and we would be none the wiser since the other witches aren't here to tell us if they're using a spell. We don't need a string of vehicles leaving to draw attention to us, especially this early in the morning."

Heather pursed her lips. "Convoys are not ideal."

"No, they're not. I've learned that carrying more than

two people at one time really wears me out." Rosemary huffed in disappointment. "Something I need to work on. A true warrior should be able to carry however many people is necessary to get the job done."

"Dear, convoy as in a group of vehicles traveling together, not you carrying someone to Eliza and the witches." Levi brushed his fingers down her arm, staring at her adoringly.

Sierra marched to the front door, not bothering to address my concerns. "You have to excuse Rosemary. She was locked up in Shadow City her entire life, so modern speech isn't her strong suit."

I didn't even care what they were talking about. I didn't want to ride with Killian, but arguing would only cause further delay and possibly put us on the radar of these Nightshadow Sisters. I just wanted to find Mom and the others and get them back.

Eager to get moving, I hurried over to the vehicle.

A Honda Pilot had pulled up to the curb in front of Griffin and Sterlyn's house. Cyrus sat in the driver's seat with a stunning dark-haired girl beside him. Chad stood at the driver's-side window, talking to Cyrus.

When Rosemary and Levi walked out, the angel called to us, "We'll meet you there." As she took flight, Levi dissolved into something I'd never seen before, a dark form that was more like a blob with only his eyes visible.

Heather stopped in her tracks. "Where the *hell* did he go?"

Waving a hand, Sierra didn't miss a beat as the garage next door opened and a brand-new Navigator backed out.

"I call back seat with J in the middle," Chad exclaimed as he hurried toward the Navigator ahead of Sierra.

That was something Theo and Chad had always done

growing up. Whenever we'd gone somewhere with Dad in his beloved Honda Accord, the boys had always made me sit in the middle. It was a running joke now that we were older.

Killian growled, low and threatening. A shiver ran down my spine.

I spun around, searching for the threat.

CHAPTER EIGHT

THE HAIR on the back of my neck rose since I couldn't find any sort of danger. The houses across the road were quiet. I had no clue what had rattled Killian.

Wanting to check on my pack, I linked with Emmy, *Are you all okay?*

That's a horrible question. Your mom, grandparents, and pack are missing, she answered, and my heart constricted as her concern mixed with mine. *And I can't find Chad.*

"The three women should sit in the back, or Jewel, me, and Sierra," Killian nearly bellowed.

Ears pounding, I forced myself not to react. Did he think Sierra needed to be in the back seat to keep an eye on us, or that we needed to be in the middle row so he could watch us himself? I tried to think of other reasons he would be so adamant, and I came back with nothing, which pissed me off even more.

I shifted my focus to answering Emmy instead of dealing with him. *He's with us. We're visiting the witches to see if they can locate Mom and the pack.*

Oh, good! They'll be helpful. Do you want me to come with you?

The truth was, I did. She was my best friend, and I trusted her explicitly. But that would mean waiting to move out. I sighed. *No, I'm good, but I'll keep you updated.*

You'd better, bish! she replied as a fluttery sensation swirled inside my chest.

She meant business.

"If I want to sit back there with J, there's not a damn thing you can do to stop me." Chad's shoulders tightened until he resembled a statue.

Focusing back on making our way to the witches, I faced the dirty-blond bombshell. In just the first few minutes, I'd gotten a good read on Sierra. She was snarky, bubbly, loyal, and blunt, and I knew how to resolve this testosterone-fueled issue. "Wanna be the cream in the center of the Oreo?"

Sierra's eyes bulged as she placed a hand on her chest. "Uh...*hell*, yeah. A question I've *always* wanted to be asked."

The question distracted Chad, his face twisting into confusion. "I'm sure there are Oreos inside, but don't you think we should go see the witches first?"

"Here I thought you'd come so far," Sierra said as she rolled her eyes and looped her arms through mine and Heather's. She dragged us toward the back door. "She was asking if I wanted to sit in the back row between her and Heather."

Even though my back was to Killian, I could feel him relax—which was impossible. I was imagining it. Whatever, it didn't matter. Killian and Chad could sit in the middle row and glare at each other the entire way as long as we got moving.

I walked by Chad and climbed in first. I slid past the two captain's seats in the middle row and sat in the back on the passenger side. Heather followed me, sitting on the driver's side, then Sierra bounded in and sat between us. She wiggled her bottom and got comfortable, reminding me of a dog.

Ugh, I hated when wolf shifters reminded me of dogs. We got enough dog jokes without our own kind adding to them.

When Chad got in and sat in front of me, I exhaled. I'd been worried that Killian would sit there and I would have to smell his scent for the entire drive.

Once we were all settled, Griffin grumbled, "Finally," and pulled out of the driveway.

As soon as the air began to circulate, Killian's scent assaulted my nose. It was as if my senses were attuned to him.

Something was *definitely* broken inside me.

The first man who'd ever intrigued me to this degree had incited everything. I bit my tongue, and the faint taste of blood exploded in my mouth. How could I feel any attraction toward him?

Heather rubbed her hands on her jeans and yawned. Dark circles had formed under her eyes, and I was sure I looked the same. We'd been up for about twenty-four hours, and I didn't foresee sleep anytime soon. Eventually, the lack of rest would catch up to us, but I hoped the adrenaline of losing Mom and the pack would drive me long enough to save them. Once that was done, I'd sleep for as long as my body needed to recover.

Maybe sleep deprivation was causing the insanity I felt toward Killian. I could hope.

As the houses disappeared behind us, the sky began to

lighten. It was approaching seven in the morning. I grimaced, realizing the pack had been missing for close to eight hours, and that was just a rough estimate based on the temperature of Heather's mother's tea.

I stared out the window. If I didn't, there was no telling where my attention would go. Actually, that wasn't true. I knew *exactly* who would occupy my attention, and it was best that I did everything possible to mitigate the decision.

It's going to be okay, Chad linked.

He was the second person to tell me that in the last half hour. Temples throbbing, I rubbed my forehead as my body heated. Sweat beaded above my lip, and I licked it, tasting the salt. That all-too-familiar anger threatened to consume me. *I wish people would stop lying to me. There's no way you can know that.*

Remembering all the times I'd offered that phrase to someone going through a hard time made me wish I could take those words back. They weren't comforting. Even though Chad believed it—the stench of a lie was missing—that didn't mean it was true. He only hoped it was, and that was what he should have said: *I hope it'll be okay.*

A heaviness floated over my body as Chad replied, *I'm not lying. It's just...I feel your worry.*

My stomach knotted, and regret wafted through me. He wasn't trying to be insensitive. Quite the opposite. I was just having a hard time coming to grips with the last of my family being in danger. So much had changed in less than two days, and I was struggling with processing it, especially after losing my father not even a year ago. *I'm sorry. I'm being a jerk. The only reason I'm holding it together is because I can feel my mom's link.*

The truth of my words settled over me. If I lost that warmth, I wasn't sure what would happen. Though I knew

I would continue to live, the loss of my entire family would wreck me.

I'll always be here for you, he vowed, and pushed the warmth of his devotion toward me.

Though Emmy was my best friend, Chad was like my brother. I sometimes forgot that. *And I for you.*

We'd turned onto the two-lane road that led in the direction from which Heather and I had come. We drove for several miles down the road, and I realized the turn onto the interstate was close.

Just as I opened my mouth to ask where we were going, Griffin took a sharp left onto a dirt road. The vehicle kicked up a dust cloud behind us, which wouldn't have been a big deal if Cyrus hadn't been driving into it. I noticed that Cyrus had slowed, having expected it.

The dirt vanished. Griffin slowed onto a trail that cut through the woods. The car jerked and jarred over dead roots and uneven ground. The deeper we went, the more we were jostled. My head hit the window, forcing me to look straight ahead. Out of the corner of my eye, I found Killian watching me, his body turned to me, ready to climb into the back seat.

His guilt about potentially being responsible for the pack's disappearance must have been getting to him.

It wasn't fair for only Heather, her pack, and my family to feel the dire effects.

"Uh...are we supposed to be off-roading?" Heather asked as she placed her hands on the back of Killian's dark leather seat.

"The location is hidden and off the beaten trail." Sterlyn glanced over her shoulder as she clutched the armrests on her sides. "It'll be over soon. Just hang on."

I wondered if this was the backup location my father

had intended for the silver wolves originally. Some of the pack had been there, but I'd never gotten a chance to see it. He'd died before our pack's intended relocation.

Just as I thought there was no way we wouldn't tumble over, the ground leveled out and turned back into a packed dirt road. Between two tall, barren oak trees, a neighborhood peeked through. There were around fifty houses, similar in structure to the homes in our original pack settlement. The ones closest to us were completed with solar panels on the roofs, while the ones farther away were in various stages of construction. The makeshift dirt road ran down the center of the subdivision. There were eight rows of six houses each, putting three houses on each side. The tightly clustered trees hid the residences from aerial view.

As we approached the first row of houses, I noted Rosemary, Levi, and two women standing in front of the house on the left, closest to the road.

Griffin parked the car on the left edge of the dirt while Cyrus pulled up beside us on the right.

The older lady was frowning, but when her sea green eyes focused on Cyrus's car, she smiled. A few tendrils of light caramel hair fell from her bun, and she tugged at the sleeves of her forest-brown dress. The faint glow of light from the rising sun highlighted her figure in a picturesque silhouette. Even if I hadn't known we were meeting with witches, that was the exact supernatural that would have sprung to mind.

As we climbed out of the Navigator, the older woman hurried to the back seat behind Annie, and the younger woman rushed to the seat behind Cyrus to reach the babies. The younger woman was in her early forties, with midnight hair that hit mid-back and rich brown eyes. Her warm beige skin seemed ageless; only the faint crow's feet around her eyes hinted at her years. Her sage-like scent didn't surprise me since all witches smelled of some sort of herb, likely from the spells they cast.

"I informed Eliza and Circe of what happened while we waited on you guys," Rosemary said as she appeared in front of Cyrus's car, watching the two ladies remove the infants from their car seats.

The twins were gorgeous. One had silver hair and honey-brown eyes that matched her mother's, and the other had Annie's brown hair and Cyrus's silver eyes.

Annie got out of the car and hugged the older lady while saying to the angel, "Rosemary, you're home."

Our group moved to stand in front of the vehicles as the two witches held the infants.

Rosemary smiled sadly. "When we saw Killian on the news, Levi and I knew we had to get back."

I laughed, though it was devoid of humor. "I think most people couldn't believe what they saw and heard."

Killian flinched. A pang of regret shot through me, but I pushed it aside.

"It would've been nice if you could've held off for another few hours." Levi scowled at Killian. "Rosemary and I only had a few days together as it was."

Apparently, Killian hadn't annoyed just me, although Levi had more problems with the timing than the actual message.

Annie came over and pulled me into a hug. "Though I wish it were under better circumstances, I'm glad to finally meet you and that you've come home."

The warmth coming off her had tears pricking my eyes. My emotions were so thick that all I could do was nod.

Heather turned to the two witches as she wrung her hands. "Can you help find my pack?"

When the younger woman glanced at the older one, the older one said, "Go ahead, Circe. You're the priestess."

There was a story there, but at least now I knew who they were.

"Do you have any personal belongings of theirs?" Circe asked as she rocked the baby.

"No." I hadn't even considered packing a bag for myself, let alone finding personal items from Mom and my grandparents. "I don't. Can you use my blood?"

"Though they're your family, your blood is full of your own magic and not theirs." Circe pursed her lips. "It can be anything of theirs. Hair. Watch. Even toenail clippings."

Ew. I gagged a little at that last one.

Sierra lifted a hand. "If either one of them has someone else's toenail clippings on hand, they're crazy, and I'm not willing to help them."

Griffin arched a brow. "But you're okay with them carrying around their own toenails?"

Sierra crossed her arms. "More so than them carrying around a family member's."

Rosemary scratched her head. "You find the oddest things romantic. Like someone cutting live flowers so they can die and giving them to a mate. 'Here, take these withering plants as a symbol of my love.'"

When she put it that way, maybe flowers didn't make the best gift.

Levi blew out a breath. "Good thing I've never done anything like that for you." He glanced around as if a hideous bouquet might magically appear.

"They're worse than the infants," Cyrus groaned. "What about you, Heather? Do you have anything?"

She shook her head. "We ran out of the neighborhood in

such a hurry that we didn't even pack any clothes. We'll just have to rely on the pack link to find them."

There had to be another solution. "What if we went back to the pack neighborhood and got some things?" I hated to lose another five to six hours, but that would still be faster than following a cold link.

"I can do better than that," Eliza said as she handed Annie the baby. "I'll go with you so you don't have to back-track. A small group shouldn't alert anyone. We can be cautious."

I wanted to be honest because if I found out my family was farther away, I wouldn't waste time bringing Eliza back home first. "If they aren't near Chattanooga..." I started.

"Child, I won't allow you and your friend here to go up alone against whatever made an entire pack vanish. That would be silly, and I won't stand by and watch people run into danger anymore." Eliza rocked on the heels of her feet. "I plan on helping you get them back, wherever they are."

"Me, too," Killian said gruffly.

Sterlyn chewed her bottom lip. "Eliza's right. We shouldn't include too many people until we know where the pack is. Cyrus and Annie, you can stay here to keep an eye on things with the humans. Griffin, Killian, Rosemary, Levi, Heather, Jewel, Eliza, and I will travel up there. While Eliza, Jewel, and Heather look for belongings for the spell, the rest of us can keep an eye out for danger. Once we know what we're up against, we'll call here for reinforcements."

"I'm going, too," Chad interjected. "Mila is like a mother to me."

"Fine, but no one else until we do some recon," Sterlyn agreed.

Though I hated the idea of waiting for backup, Sterlyn's

plan had merit. We didn't need to rush into danger, or we'd wind up being captured, too.

Heather's phone dinged, and she hurriedly took it out. When she glanced at the message, her face paled, and she jerked a hand toward the car door. "We've got to go!"

CHAPTER NINE

THE WORLD TILTED, and I sidestepped as I lost my balance.

A gigantic, warm hand wrapped around my forearm and jolted me.

I swallowed my gasp and nearly choked on the delicious breeze around me. Panic and desire coursed through my veins, warming me in conflicting ways.

My traitorous head turned toward Killian. I wanted to tell him to take his hands off me, but that would have been ungrateful. If he hadn't caught me, I would've toppled over.

I straightened and removed my arm from his grasp, though it was the last thing in the world I wanted to do. "What's wrong?" My voice came out steady despite the nerves and terror swirling inside.

"Sean installed smart fire alarms in our house a few months ago in case something happened while the pack was away, since we aren't connected to the fire department. I thought he was insane, but—" Heather turned her phone around so I could see the notification.

Dangerous CO2 Levels Detected

That couldn't be possible. "Why would they set the place on fire?"

"To send a message," Levi interjected. "The princes of Hell used to do that to anyone who defied them, often before they beat them to death. It was a warning to the residents that bad things were coming."

My knees almost buckled. "We need to hurry and see if we can stop the fire before it destroys everything. We need something to help Eliza perform that spell."

Rosemary fluffed her feathers. "It's unlikely that we'll get there in time."

The trees closed in around me as I struggled to breathe. "No, but we can't just say, 'Oh well.'"

"Let's call the fire department." Heather bounced on her feet.

Under normal circumstances, that would have been ideal, but the situation was too unpredictable to involve more humans.

"The firefighters could be hurt in the crossfire," Sterlyn interjected. "Can you give Rosemary and Levi the address so they can head there? They'll get there faster than the rest of us can. For now, Eliza, Chad, Kill, Heather, and Jewel, let's go."

"What about me?" Sierra pouted.

Killian growled, "Ride back with Cyrus and Annie. You can join us later with the others. We need to get moving."

I rattled off the address, and Rosemary tapped it into her phone. As soon as she had put the device in her jeans, she took to the air as Levi flickered into his shadow form again.

Killian, Chad, and Heather climbed into the back of the Navigator. My wolf surged forward, not happy with the seating arrangements, until we noted that Chad was in the middle. Chad tensed and glared at Killian, daring him to say something, but Killian stayed quiet. The two men looked awkward as they leaned away from each other—not that it did any good with their bulky forms. I slid over to sit in front of Heather so Eliza could climb in on Griffin's side. Once everyone was inside, Griffin took off.

Silence filled the vehicle, which seemed fitting. Hopefully, it would stay that way until we got to the cabins.

Leaning my head back, I closed my eyes and played Mozart's Piano Sonata No. 16 in C Major in my head to calm myself down. After a few seconds, my eyes grew heavier, and I drifted off to sleep.

I DIDN'T GET much rest. Every time Killian moved, my wolf surged, stirring me awake. I was way too keenly attuned to him, and the urge to climb into his arms had me digging my nails into my palms.

Chad and Killian kept fidgeting, not comfortable sitting next to each other. When one of them grunted in annoyance, the corners of my mouth tilted up. It served Chad right for acting like an overbearing brother, and anything that caused Killian discomfort made me happy.

Heather snored in the back seat, and Griffin muttered, "Please tell me I'm not that loud."

Though Sterlyn didn't verbally respond, I was certain she had through their mate link, because Griffin grimaced.

The only person who hardly made any noise was Eliza. She sat perfectly still beside me, deep in thought.

I wondered if she was practicing a calming technique similar to my meditation with classical music, something I'd started as a child. For whatever mood I was in, there was a piece that spoke to me. As young as ten, I'd gotten through emotional circumstances using the technique, which helped keep people's attention off me. I hated feeling out of control. I'd seen Mom react so rashly at times, albeit not as extremely as she had when Dad had passed.

When Sterlyn's phone dinged, I lifted my head, not bothering to attempt to doze off again. She glanced at her phone and said nothing, and I wanted to scream. That had to be Rosemary.

When I was about to ask, she turned toward the back and said, "Every cabin is in flames. The fire is contained, though, and not spreading to the forests. Rosemary and Levi flew around the perimeter and didn't see anyone. They're landing to look for a way to put out the flames and salvage some of the property."

"Do you think it's a setup?" I had to consider it, though I couldn't guess as to anyone's motives since the two humans chasing after us clearly thought Heather and I couldn't survive in the woods.

"I want to say no." Sterlyn chewed on her bottom lip. "Rosemary checked the area, but whoever set the fires could always come back. We'll have to be careful and as quick as possible."

"I know it made sense not to call the fire department, but...I don't understand how the firefighters aren't there anyway. The smoke should be visible for miles."

"That's a question we're all wondering," Griffin gritted out. "Every plausible explanation only makes the situation more dire."

Looking out the window, I realized we were already in Pigeon Forge. We'd be in Gatlinburg soon, since the traffic was light for nine in the morning, and back at the pack neighborhood within fifteen minutes. "What took them so long? I figured they'd be there quicker than that."

"They were checking the area first and trying to douse the flames before they called." Sterlyn ran a hand down her face. "It doesn't look promising, so they were wondering how far away we are. They need Eliza's help, and Rosemary asked for a location to come pick her up."

The lines at the corners of Eliza's eyes deepened. "I'm only one witch, but I'll see what I can do. We'll need to focus on the houses we can salvage."

"We're almost there. There's no point in Rosemary coming to get you. It would take just as long since we'd have to pull over somewhere remote for her to land."

Time was ticking, and something akin to a caffeine rush surged through me. All the tiredness I'd felt moments ago vanished as I anticipated arriving at the pack homes and extinguishing the fire. The pack needed their homes to come back to.

Maybe Rosemary shouldn't bother to land somewhere remote—though if humans saw her, that could garner more unwanted attention and add to the chaos. While *Killian* had informed them about us, not hiding at all might make this situation worse.

I wondered if that was the message whoever was behind this was trying to convey: *We'll destroy you and all traces of your existence.*

We breezed past one of dozens of Flapjack's Pancake Cabins, and I remembered the back road shortcut to the pack neighborhood. "Take the next left!"

The route would take us past Dollywood, but there were fewer traffic lights that way.

We were in the far-right lane, but Griffin turned the

steering wheel hard, swerving into the left lane. The car behind us slammed on its brakes and honked manically.

"A little warning would've been nice," he snarled as he gripped the steering wheel, his knuckles white.

A large SUV in the oncoming lane barreled toward us, but that didn't stop Griffin. Besides, we should have time to pass.

He redlined the Navigator, causing the engine to rev. Instinctively, my hands clutched the armrests like the time I'd been on a flight long ago, when Dad had taken Mom and me to California. If I hadn't been in the car and had only heard the noise, I would've thought it was a plane taking off.

Eliza's eyes widened as she clutched her chest. I worried she might be having a heart attack.

The oncoming SUV blared its horn as its tires squealed. Heather started awake with a shriek, adding to the tension.

Throwing her arm past me, Eliza held her palm toward the window and the oncoming car, and said, "*Desine currus.*"

The stench of burning rubber penetrated inside the Navigator as the vehicle stopped twenty feet away. Eliza kept her palm facing the car until we'd coasted onto the road leading up to the mountain.

When she dropped her hand, she murmured, "Oh, dear goddess."

At the same time, Killian rasped, "What the hell, man! You could've killed h—" He stopped and cleared his throat. "Us!"

He'd almost said something else, and the sad part was that intrigued me. I wanted to know what he was thinking.

I scowled. I shouldn't give a damn.

"Oh, please." Griffin's hands loosened on the wheel. "I had plenty of time. He was human and overreacted, unable to gauge the distance. Regardless, Eliza stopped the vehicle."

Sterlyn chuckled. "He's right. Though normally I would agree not to make a scene, we're running on precious time to stop the fires from consuming all the houses."

"Well, I made sure we didn't get run over." Eliza fidgeted. "That was too close for comfort for an old lady."

Chad had been oddly quiet the entire ride, maybe because he knew me well enough to realize I needed time to unwind. Now he linked, *Things are never boring with these guys.*

I hadn't been around this group for long, but even if Mom hadn't filled me in on all the chaos that had ensued during the six and half months I'd been away, I would've gathered as much. Trouble had a way of finding them, and I was adding more to their plate. *Mom didn't exaggerate.*

Not like usual, he replied with warmth surging into me.

Mom had a flair for the dramatic, something Dad, Chad, and I had always teased her about mercilessly. She was well aware of that attribute, but it was part of her endearing charm...at times. Dad had always grounded her anger and theatrics, and with him gone, that responsibility fell on me.

How could I help when I feared the same darkness swirled inside me?

"Well, I'm awake now," Heather grumbled. "And I have a headache. I hit my head on the glass."

"Hey, you chose the window over my shoulder." Chad snorted. "At first, I was offended, but then I noticed how much you were drooling."

She gasped. "I did *not*."

"Uh...ya did." Chad laughed. "Look at the glass."

The scent of sandalwood thickened. Stomach fluttering, I held my breath. Killian must have shifted or something.

His shoulder brushed my arm, creating a slight jolt. He was leaning between Eliza's and my captain-style seats, meaning he was touching her as well. He asked, "Is everyone okay?"

I kept my eyes forward. He was checking on us, and that was problematic. I didn't need him to pretend to be a good guy. That's what it had to be—an act. And if I risked glancing at him and he appeared concerned, I didn't want to fathom how much more conflicted I'd be about him.

A deep, threatening growl left Chad. "She doesn't want to talk to you, and you're practically in my lap."

Why in the world would Chad be upset over Killian's concern? And he'd said *she doesn't* instead of *we don't*. He must have been talking about Eliza. They were...friends? I wasn't sure what the right word was. She was a lot older. Ally? Acquaintance?

Not on purpose, I glanced at the back seat. Killian's dark, mesmerizing eyes were locked on me, and I froze.

For a moment, I forgot about the fires, my family's capture, and even my dad's death. Killian was the center of my world.

Chad gripped his arm and shoved him back into his seat. My cheeks burned from the guilt that assaulted me. How could I let *him*, of all people, affect me this way?

Killian's irises glowed as his wolf inched forward, taking control. He bared his teeth. "Keep your hands off me."

"You'd best handle this." Eliza pointed at me. "Especially if you want to get there in time."

"Have the two of you always been at each other's throats?" Heather asked, brow furrowed. "We don't have time for whatever alpha match is going on."

I wasn't sure I had any control over the situation, but I was willing to try. My annoyance bled into my words as I said, "Everyone in the SUV is fine. We didn't get hit. Can you two please knock it off so we can focus on the actual threat? I *have* to find Mom and the pack."

Chad, please, I linked. *Cool it until we find them.* I rarely asked him for anything, so I prayed this plea found its mark.

Chad lowered his hand. "Fine."

That was enough for Killian's irises to dim back to their normal color.

I focused forward and continued giving directions. When the familiar two-lane highway appeared, pinpricks nipped all over me as if my entire body had fallen asleep and circulation had been restored. The faint stench of smoke filled the air. The blazes were probably worse than I'd feared.

When the familiar red cedars that marked the one-lane gravel drive leading to my grandparents' home came into view, my wolf became anxious. She was ready to break free and run to help in whatever way she could, but handling fires would best be done in human form.

"Here!" Heather shouted from the back, sounding breathless. She had to be struggling with the same urge as me, and hers was probably worse. Her home was likely on fire.

Griffin expertly turned onto the gravel road without slowing much. Dark, billowing clouds of smoke became visible through the leafless trees, and the crackle of fire surrounded us.

The first home was engulfed in flames, and Griffin stopped about fifty yards from the nearest cabin, not wanting to park too close to the burning homes. The autumn foliage had already fallen, so the trees weren't thick with damp leaves. The wind wasn't blowing, and the smoke rose straight upward.

Eliza threw her door open and lifted her hands as she stumbled from the vehicle. The clatter of logs falling and the roar of fire drowned out her words.

I jumped out of the vehicle, and a wave of heat slammed into me.

Rosemary and Levi appeared through the smog. Dark smudges covered their faces, and their eyes were bloodshot.

Wherever Eliza pointed, the flames shrank. I wanted her to go to my grandparents' home, but the smoke was so thick, it would be hard to find even with my senses. We needed to find something, *anything*, from a house to locate the pack.

The others ran toward the first house, looking for a place the fire hadn't consumed to find a way inside.

I searched for something to use against the flames. My eyes burned from the ash, but I ignored the discomfort and glanced toward the vegetable gardens the pack grew about a quarter mile away. Though the gardens were currently barren, there was a shed full of shovels and other tools that could help. We needed to salvage one house enough to locate at least one item.

Spinning on my heel, I ran toward the gardens. No one noticed me leave, but that was okay. I could let Chad know if I found something useful.

The air got less dark with every step I took away from the burning homes, easing some of my worry. The arsonists hadn't gone far enough to destroy the garden.

Something flashed at the edge of my vision, and I paused, turning in that direction.

No, it couldn't be. Rosemary and Levi had checked the

area. But no matter how many times I blinked, I still saw a human hiding under shrubs, holding a weapon.

The person hadn't noticed me yet.

I squared my shoulders, debating the best way to protect us. I'd do whatever it took.

CHAPTER TEN

THE HUMAN'S attention was focused on the road, not the burning houses. Rosemary and Levi must have missed them due to all the smoke and their position in the bushes.

A knot formed in my belly. The person had probably seen us drive by. Would they launch an attack? Or, more likely, they'd called for backup and were waiting for rein-forcements.

Where the hell are you, Jewel? Chad linked with me, his annoyance almost suffocating. *Killian just realized you vanished, and the smoke is covering your trail. He's going apeshit, and I can't even communicate with him.*

Killian was likely feeling more guilt from seeing the consequences of his decision. I linked with Sterlyn and Chad, *There's someone hiding in the woods.* I hurried behind the trunk of a large red cedar to duck out of sight in case the person looked over.

Where? Sterlyn asked. After a brief pause, her panic slammed into me. *I don't see anything.*

In the brush south of the cabin. I was heading toward the community garden to look for supplies to fight the fire. The person has twigs and stuff covering them. I only noticed them because they moved their gun, and the motion caught my eye.

I'm on my way, Chad replied.

My initial reaction was to tell him not to come, but if we'd missed one human, there could be more. *The thing is, they aren't moving. They're watching the road.*

Confirming my fears, Sterlyn answered, *They must be waiting for backup or a sign to attack.*

We needed to get out of here, but we needed something from the pack, or our trip here would've been in vain. *Maybe you should stay with them in case more people come,* I linked with Chad. *The person didn't see me.*

Oh, hell, no. I'm not leaving you out there with someone who has a gun.

A choking sensation coursed through the link, intensifying my rage. I wanted to tell him where he could shove it, but I inhaled to calm myself. He was only trying to protect me. I'd do the same for him.

Instead, I began to cough from the thick smoke that had enveloped me. I covered my mouth, but the irritation was deep in my lungs, making the sound loud even over the crackle of the fire.

I pressed my back to the large trunk, hoping the person in the bushes hadn't heard anything. If they had, and if they couldn't see me, maybe they wouldn't risk exposing their position.

Closing my stinging eyes, I focused on my hearing.

After a minute, I peeked around the trunk. The person was standing, examining the area. At this angle, I noted long hair with twigs stuck in it and a short, slender figure.

A woman.

I quickly hid behind the tree. If she was alarmed, she

might notify anyone nearby. That might give us an idea of what we were up against.

I sniffed, this time more carefully, not wanting to set off another coughing fit. The fire had dampened some of my senses, putting us on even ground with the humans. Had they planned it that way, or was it an unintended benefit? Either way, the result was the same.

We're almost there, Chad linked.

Those words were strange. I hadn't expected Sterlyn to head this way with him since the human cavalry could arrive at any second. *We?*

Killian demanded to come, and I didn't want to waste time arguing. We might need to use him as a distraction.

Chad was all talk when it came to threatening people he was even upset with. Sterlyn considered Killian a friend, and Chad wouldn't do anything to Killian that could lead to problems. He was just protective of me and always had been. It was his way of showing his thanks to my parents.

Be careful as you approach. If the woman decided she'd imagined my cough, it would be better not to alert her to Chad and Killian's presence. We could scout the area, keeping in mind the enemy was using tactics of war.

War.

A lump formed in my throat, making it hard to swallow.

Chad's displeasure seeped into my bones as he replied, *I'm a silver wolf, for gods' sake, J. I know how to be quiet. Even Killian knows.*

That's not what I'm getting at. He could be a tad reactive, which was one reason he and Mom got along. *She heard me cough. She's no longer hiding. If you come barreling through in the open, you could set off an attack.*

Fine, he said. *We'll be careful. I'll let him know.*

I leaned forward slightly and glanced in the direction

they'd be coming from. The two of them soon came into view, though I could barely make out their frames through the smoke and tree trunks.

I see you, I connected. *You're getting close.* Some of the weight lifted from my shoulders. This was the second time ever that I'd been in a threatening situation. Though I'd trained for it my entire life, I'd never been in true danger until early this morning. *I'm ahead on your right. The same goes for the woman.*

My eyes blurred from tears, and I closed them. Goggles would've come in handy right now.

I glanced down at my white shirt, noting it wasn't white anymore. At least it helped me blend in with the dark surroundings now that the smoke blocked out the sky.

Again, I wondered why the hell firefighters weren't here. This was more than just a brush fire.

At a loss, I rubbed my eyes and winced as tears threatened. My eyelids felt like sandpaper taking a layer off my cornea. Everything hurt worse.

White-hot rage pounded through my veins. I couldn't use my breathing technique to help calm the storm because I'd wind up choking again, so music was the only tool I had. The urge to play one of my favorite classical tunes was overwhelming, the instinct natural after employing that talent for so long. But I needed to keep my ears open and focused.

This situation was shit.

Not only had these assholes probably taken Mom and the others, but they had also destroyed our homes and were waiting in the trees to attack anyone who came back. This wasn't a respectful fight but one of domination and fear.

It had to be humans.

My attention darted back to Chad and Killian. Now that they were closer, I could make out who was who, mainly due to Killian's darker hair. If the humans had taken *anyone*, it should have been *him*.

My heart ached at even considering it. The truth was, I didn't want anyone else to be taken.

They darted left, going deeper into the woods, away from the woman. That was a smart plan, as long as they didn't come across someone else.

Be careful and look in the brush. She's camouflaged, and it's harder to see because of the smoke, I told Chad. *More people could be out here.*

As if Fate agreed with me, a twig snapped close by.

The woman was moving.

I'd hoped she would give up when she didn't find anything, but she must have known that what she'd heard hadn't been a coincidence. Though I hated to say it, she was right.

Pulse pounding, I couldn't hear much of anything else.

J, the woman is almost on you, Chad linked, his alarm causing my ears to ring even louder.

I bit the inside of my cheek, watching how I responded. Though I wasn't speaking out loud, it still served as a reminder: communication was communication, orally or telepathically.

Is she alone? From where I stood, I heard only her footsteps, but I didn't trust my senses.

So far, he answered. *We're moving closer now that we see where you are. Stay still. We'll be right there.*

She was so close, I could hear her ragged breathing. She hadn't made the mistake of stepping on any other fallen branches, but each step was louder. She was almost right on this tree.

There was no way they'd reach me before she found me.

I inched toward her, still behind the tree trunk. I didn't have a weapon, but I was faster and stronger than her. That had to count for something. And if my hearing and sight were impaired, hers were, too. This was still a somewhat even playing field...except she had a gun.

She took a quick breath. Chad and Killian darted between two trees and caught her attention. She muttered, "Fuck." Then I heard her shuffling. "How far out is backup? I see two people running—it could be the two women from this morning."

All was quiet for a second. Then a man's voice filled the air. "Five minutes. Take out the targets if you have a shot."

That was a whole lot of awful information handed to me all at once, but it gave us warning. Though Sterlyn and I had suspected more people would come, hearing it confirmed was alarming, and we had no clue about the numbers.

I linked with Sterlyn and Chad, giving them a quick update.

My heart constricted as Sterlyn replied, *We're going into a house to search for something. You three go back to the car so we can leave before more people arrive.*

The girl reached my tree trunk, her gaze locked on Chad and Killian.

She sees you, I warned as my throat closed. The smoke had already burned my airways, but this was the pain of apprehension.

They split up. Killian darted behind a red cedar and Chad behind a yellow birch. There was no way they'd get out of the situation that easily, meaning that rescue had to fall on me.

If she glanced right, she'd see me. I had to move.

She lifted her gun toward the guys. Her hands were

shaking, but her attention was focused steadily between the two trees they were using as cover.

I'm attacking her. Be ready, I linked, then stepped out from around the tree. Her Caribbean blue eyes widened upon seeing me. I had four inches on her, which wasn't unusual. Shifters tended to be taller than humans.

She swung her gun at me, and I let instinct take over. I stepped left and grabbed her wrist with my left hand so the gun wasn't aimed at me. I shoved my right hand into the hand that held the gun, snapping it to the side, then head-butted her cheek and pried the weapon free. I swung the butt of the gun at her face, but the woman ducked, countering my move.

My arm hit air, leaving my right side open. She kicked me, and pain exploded through my kidney.

I tumbled to the ground on my right side and rolled onto my back. I still had the gun in my hand, which felt foreign. Luckily, I hadn't accidentally shot it during the attack.

Killian raced toward me as the woman lifted her leg to stomp on me. I kicked her leg, and she fell backward. She landed on her ass, and a cloud of dirt kicked up around her. I jumped to my feet and aimed the gun at her head as Chad barreled my way, too.

Stay back! I linked with Chad. These guys had an overblown hero complex.

Though I had no intention of pulling the trigger, the girl didn't know that. I added Sterlyn to the conversation. *I have the woman who was hiding. What should I do with her?* I'd never killed anyone, and I didn't want to start now.

Bring her with you as a hostage. Maybe she can give us some answers, Sterlyn replied. *There's no way we can find anything salvageable in this house. Rosemary and Levi flew around again and tried to access the last house that caught fire, but they couldn't. The flames were all-consuming. They're checking other houses, but it's not looking good.*

Killian reached my side and rasped, "Here, give me the gun."

My instinct was to tell him *no*, only because he was ordering me around. Truthfully, I didn't like the feel of the metal in my hand. It wasn't natural, and if I kept the gun, I'd have to be willing to use it. Instead of letting my dislike for him control me, I handed the weapon over.

"Thanks," he said, sounding surprised. "Now you— walk." He pointed the woman in the direction of the cabins. "We know you called for backup. Is anyone else here?"

"Yes," she said confidently, but even through the smoke, a rancid smell circled us. She was lying and didn't know we had a way to tell.

He leveled the gun at her. "How many?"

"I...I don't know." Her voice trembled, the first hint of fear. "All I know is more are coming."

If she was speaking, then I had a question for her. "How come the fire department isn't here?" I was worried that a group of humans were about to become involved and get themselves hurt.

"You have no idea what you're up against." She straight- ened her shoulders. "The fire department won't come because this is a controlled fire, and we were given clear- ance to handle it."

"Even better." Killian beamed like she'd told him the best news ever. "Now move! Unlike her, I won't hesitate to use this."

The urge to smack him took over again. At least I couldn't smell him right now, or I'd be more conflicted. As long as I held my breath and didn't touch him, maybe my sanity would stay firmly in tow.

The one thing I could hold on to was that innocent humans wouldn't get involved. But who the hell was after us, and how did they have so much power?

With all the dirt on her face, I couldn't gauge this woman's age, but she was young enough to move without much issue. She lifted her hands as she turned and headed toward the cabins. Killian stepped behind her, watching her closely the entire way.

When I went to follow, Chad snagged my forearm, holding me back. His irises glowed as he sneered and asked, *What the hell was that?*

Me surviving. I wouldn't apologize for what I'd done. *She would've noticed me at any second. Don't pretend you could've reached me in time to help.* He was fooling himself if he thought that.

His expression softened. *You could've gotten hurt.*

Some of the bite of my anger faded. *I was less likely to get hurt if I took her on while she was distracted.*

He pursed his lips but didn't say anything. Instead, the two of us followed Killian and the girl.

Before the roar of the fire could overwhelm my hearing again, the woman's walkie-talkie sputtered to life. A man said, "They're pulling down the road. They'll be there in less than a minute."

Chad stiffened as my heart sank. I linked to Sterlyn, *We're out of time.*

CHAPTER ELEVEN

STERLYN'S UNEASE mixed with mine, and my throat burned worse than from the fire. I hadn't thought it was possible, but boy, was I wrong. Acid churned in my stomach, but at least we'd gotten one thing out of this inferno: the woman who had been hiding.

How many are there? Sterlyn asked.

That would be helpful to know. *She said she wasn't sure, but I overheard them on the walkie-talkie, and they said they'd be here in less than—*

A black Suburban charged down the gravel road toward us.

There's one vehicle, Chad linked, and then another one came into view, blowing through the first one's dust cloud. *No, there are two.* But then a third appeared.

Why don't you wait a second before continuing? I said as I picked up my pace. We couldn't just stand here like dummies, especially since the others would be attacked within seconds.

Despite my wolf nudging me to stay close to Killian, I

rushed past him. My legs slowed of their own accord, but I forced them forward.

His attention darted back and forth between the Suburbans and the girl. As I jogged past, he scowled. Part of me rejoiced in aggravating him, which was childish, but I didn't care. I enjoyed my effect on him since he had too much influence over me.

Sterlyn, can you tell Killian to hurry up? We need to get out of here before it's too late, Chad connected as he rushed to catch up to me.

He hadn't thought the situation through, which was one of the things Dad had been working on with him. Chad was strong, almost as strong as Dad, but he didn't have the kind of critical thinking skills that an alpha or beta needed. *Chad, there's one road in and out.*

His tension washed over me, adding to mine. That was one detriment of a pack link—the ability to feel the emotions of the other members. I could feel Sterlyn's emotions more than Chad's, but his turmoil still affected me.

We're heading to you guys, Sterlyn informed us. *We don't want to make finding us easy. There's no telling what weapons they have on hand.*

I stopped about a hundred yards from the cabin we'd parked by and watched as Sterlyn, Griffin, and Heather ran toward us. The vehicles were almost on us, but with the thick smoke and the trees, their human drivers would struggle to detect us.

The idea that it was now late morning blew my mind because the smoke had darkened the world around us. Though the sun filtered in the farther we got from the pack houses, the surroundings appeared more like twilight than afternoon.

I hid behind a yellow birch tree. The trunk was on the small side, but I wasn't worried. The Suburbans drove past the Navigator and pulled over in front of it, staying close.

That was both a blessing and a problem. At least we were behind them, but they knew we were here.

Where's Eliza? Chad linked, appearing beside me.

Rosemary flew off with her since she can't run fast, Sterlyn answered. *We're supposed to meet them a quarter mile south at the garden.*

Sweat dripped down Griffin's and Heather's faces, streaking the ash. Noting the contrast between the wet trails and their skin made me realize we were dirtier than I'd thought. I could only imagine the damage the smoky air was doing to our lungs.

We needed to get out of here. I glanced back at the vehicles. The enemy was already jumping out. I hadn't even heard the doors open. Having my senses muffled was severely disorienting.

Sterlyn's iridescent purple irises glowed, and I expected her to link with Chad and me again. When she didn't, I assumed she was talking to Griffin, Killian, or both. Mom had informed me that although Killian was the alpha of the Shadow Ridge pack, he'd recognized Griffin and Sterlyn as stronger alphas, allowing them to link with one another without being pack. It was something most wolves would have refused to do. When she'd told me, I'd admired him for it and wondered who this unthreatened, confident alpha might be to agree to that.

That was before he'd taken liberties with our world.

Griffin shook his head, confirming my assumption. They were having a disagreement, but after a moment, he kissed her lips and motioned for Heather and Killian to follow him.

They're going ahead since Heather is struggling and the human is in our hands, Sterlyn linked, answering my unasked question. *I thought the three of us could stay here to get their numbers before we left, but you're more than welcome to go with them.*

My head jerked back. I hadn't expected her to invite me to stay with her, figuring she'd see me as a liability. *Of course I'll stay with you.* If my alpha wanted me here, I'd damn well stay.

Maybe she should go with the others, Chad inserted. *She's never fought a battle.*

My shoulders sagged as my chest tightened. Yet another reminder that I hadn't been around to help them fight. I hadn't meant to abandon my pack, and even though Chad hadn't meant it that way, there was no other way to take it. If I had stayed, I would have fighting experience, but now I was a potential liability.

I prepared myself for her to agree with him, and I got ready to walk away. I didn't want to cause an issue while our lives were hanging in the balance. That was a conversation for when we were out of harm's way, and Chad would learn that I *would* be helping save Mom and my grandparents. I didn't care if I had to wear armor.

Killian told me how she handled the human. Sterlyn kept her focus on the enemy. *Cyrus and I are aware that your pack didn't train with guns, yet her natural instinct was to disarm someone holding a firearm. If that isn't proof that she's battle-savvy, I don't know what is. We all had to learn, and she's trained for this, just as you and I have.*

My entire life, I had never believed anyone could hold a candle to Dad's leadership, but Sterlyn had me second-guessing. A lightness filtered through me, and my guilt and doubt vanished. She was *right*. Everyone had to have a first battle at some point.

Chad tensed behind me, informing me he was unhappy with her answer. Good. I was unhappy with how he'd reacted to me staying with them. I was a silver wolf, and this was my destiny.

I brushed those thoughts away. I wouldn't let him negatively impact me, and I would prove to Sterlyn that she was right to trust me. I counted the enemies from the first vehicle and linked, *The first car carried seven people, which is full capacity. Worse case, we could be up against twenty-one, unless more vehicles appear.*

Nodding, Sterlyn connected, *They were hoping you and Heather would show up, unsure where else to go, and probably thought that twenty-one would be a safe number.*

We had nine on our side, plus one hostage. The hostage was good but could complicate things when we tried to get away.

Two of the enemy headed toward the Navigator. They inspected the area, possibly searching for us. The rest of the group huddled together, and I counted, confirming the total we suspected. They each had two guns strapped to their hips—one handgun and one longer one.

Chad stepped up beside me as if he were considering blocking me and linked, *They all have tranquilizer guns.*

I swallowed hard, not even acknowledging the raw pain in my throat.

Out of the group, there were five smaller-statured individuals I assumed were women. I had to be careful about that assumption, though; it wasn't necessarily easy to tell just by body type. Dad had always said we should make our best guess but remember the most important part—without confirmation, it was still a guess. His motto had been to trust your gut because most of the time, our instincts weren't wrong. But be ready for anything.

The bulkiest person appeared to be the leader. Even through the polluted, murky air, I could see his biceps. He pointed to ten people and motioned toward the cabin we'd parked near, and with the remaining ten, he gestured toward the woods.

They were splitting up, which was good. We could pick them off one by one as long as the people we attacked didn't alert their friends.

Come on. Let's head toward the others. Sterlyn turned to follow her mate and Heather.

The bulky guy tapped something on his phone and glanced our way, his gaze landing on me. My instinct was to duck, but that wouldn't do any good if he'd seen me. But he turned his head, continuing to examine the area.

He *hadn't* seen me. His sight was worse than mine. Every few minutes, his attention went back to the vehicle. I connected with Chad and Sterlyn, *I think he knows the Navigator isn't the vehicle Heather and I were driving earlier, and he keeps glancing around like he expects the girl we captured to show up.*

Killian just linked with Griffin and me. They're calling on the walkie-talkie for the woman we captured. Sterlyn squatted and removed something from under her pants leg. When she straightened, she had a knife in her hand. *We need to incapacitate whoever gets in our way and leave. I'm telling the others we're heading their way so we can move as a unit. The leader could call for more backup, and the clock is ticking.*

We shouldn't head back, I suggested. *We should pick them off one by one. If we can knock them out, we'll buy ourselves time.*

You heard Sterlyn. Chad turned his head and glared at me. *She said we should stay together, and I want our group to stay together to protect you.*

He was older than me by a couple of years, and he'd taken on the role of my protector at a very early age. He'd never realize I was more than capable on my own unless he gave me a chance. One thing Dad had instilled in me was to never let a man make me feel as if I wasn't a competent fighter. Though most men were physically stronger, it made them fall that much harder. Women were strong and nimble, and we could use our smaller size to our advantage. In many ways, women were better fighters because of that, and it helped that most men discounted us.

She's right. Sterlyn halted. *I was split on the decision, but if they find us and alert the others, our group could become overwhelmed. Plus, they have weapons. I'll link with Griffin and Killian and let them know what's going on. Maybe Rosemary and Levi can help. The humans won't expect there to be an angel and a demon in the mix.*

Someone should confiscate the woman's walkie-talkie if they haven't already, I linked. *We can use it to keep tabs on them.*

They already have—Killian was worried she'd warn them somehow, Sterlyn responded.

The second group dispersed, all ten heading toward our side of the woods. The bulky guy must have assumed we'd be near the cabins where we'd captured our hostage.

The humans spread out, staying close enough that if there were an issue, they could reach each other, but their hearing and sight would be limited.

Chad, take the guy coming up on your left, Sterlyn instructed, and waved her hand at me. *Jewel, follow me.*

I followed her lead without question, and we ran to the

right. A man was slowly making his way toward us. She probably planned on us attacking him together, but she proved me wrong when she continued running to the right. She ran faster, tapping into her wolf, and I had to pull from my animal to keep up. We soon reached two red cedars that had grown close to each other. They were massive, with thick needle leaves that would hide us much better.

Two enemies would be crossing our paths soon on either side of us.

We faced the cabins, the flames dancing between nearly bare branches as a breeze blew softly. The place that had become my second home was burning right in front of my eyes. Every home I'd ever known had been shattered.

I'll take the guy on the right, and I want you to take the woman coming up on your left, Sterlyn linked.

She hadn't asked if I could handle it.

With my mission at hand, I turned to my left, waiting for the right moment to attack. The figure coming up on my side was shorter than the others. She waved a flashlight into the smoke as if that would significantly improve her view.

Palms sweating, I waited. I didn't want to rush the attack. If I gave my hand away too soon, she could call for help.

As I waited, my discomfort made itself known. My eyes burned worse. My throat was so dry I could barely swallow, and my lungs were raw.

Out of the corner of my eye, I saw Chad attack his target, and a moment later, I sensed Sterlyn leave my side. They were both engaged, but not me. Not yet.

When the woman came within fifteen feet, I crouched, preparing myself for battle. She held a short rifle in one hand and the flashlight in the other. I'd need to get rid of the gun first.

As she stepped a few feet away from me, I pivoted out of hiding. I tapped into my magic, borrowing speed, and raced toward her. Her dark eyes widened, but I wrapped my arms around her waist and dropped her onto her back, the fallen leaves softening the impact.

Her knees slid under my stomach as she fell, and I noted my first mistake. I'd underestimated her. She extended her legs, throwing me off her.

She rolled onto me and placed the gun to my head. I released her waist and jerked my right hand hard toward myself, hitting the wrist that held the gun. The weapon sailed somewhere over my head.

I punched her in the face. Her head flew sideways, and I twisted my hips and knocked her off balance. She crumpled as I jumped to my feet, eager to grab the gun. Then she went for her tranq gun.

No.

If I got hit, I would be out of the battle.

I pivoted and kicked her in the stomach. Then I redirected her hands toward her midsection. I'd expected her to cradle her stomach, but she grabbed my foot instead and lifted it.

Luckily, I'd trained for this. I jumped off my other leg, raising it higher than the one she was lifting, and rotated so I landed back on the same foot, facing the opposite direction. I easily removed my foot from her grasp and squatted, going for the tranq gun.

Something slammed into my back, most likely her foot, and I stumbled back a few steps and caught my balance. I spun around, not wanting my back to her any longer.

This girl was trained, and I'd been taking it easy, not wanting to hurt her fatally.

That ended now.

CHAPTER TWELVE

MY WOLF SURGED FORWARD, and I didn't stop her. I'd been restraining myself, but that had been the wrong decision.

Before I could reach the woman, she had the tranq gun aimed at me. She gritted her teeth and pulled the trigger, the release silent. Had I not seen her do it, I never would've known.

I tapped into my speed and moved three steps to the side. The dart whistled by, and the puff of air brushed me.

Too damn close.

As my gaze returned to her, she swiveled the gun's barrel a few inches to where I'd moved. She was determined to knock me out. That had to be how they'd taken the pack —tranqs and gods knew what else. I couldn't move too soon, or she'd adjust her aim.

Pretending to be oblivious was so damn hard. I took a few measured steps toward her, knowing she could pull the trigger at any time.

Her finger tightened.

Leaping in the opposite direction, I linked with Sterlyn and Chad, *The tranqs have more than one round.*

Of course they do. Chad's frustration bled through. *My guy's passing out. I'll be there in a second. Just don't fall asleep.*

I shouldn't have been surprised that he'd assumed I'd been hit with a tranq. Instead of moving several steps, I pivoted away from the tranq. She could easily fire another dart. So far, I'd gotten lucky.

She fired, and the tranq snagged on a loose section of my shirt where it hung over my shorts. I waited for the needle prick and fatigue to hit, but I felt nothing.

"Hell, yeah!" the woman crowed. She scrambled to her feet and made her way to me.

I glanced at the tranq. The dart had lodged in my shirt, but my jean shorts had protected me from the needle. I grabbed the end and pulled it out.

None of the liquid had leaked, thank gods. I tossed it to the ground as the woman watched me expectantly. She thought I'd hit the ground, unconscious. She pointed the tranq gun at me.

Though I'd always dreamed of acting in a play, I'd never gotten the opportunity, since the silver wolves were home-schooled to remain hidden. Here was my chance. One thing to cross off my bucket list.

I lowered my head as if it were too heavy and half buckled my knees. I had to time this right so I wasn't passing out too quickly or too slowly. Hopefully, she wasn't sure what to expect from wolves, so if I mistimed it, she wouldn't realize.

I kept tabs on her in case she pulled the trigger again.

As I dropped to my knees, the woman grinned. She was dressed all in black, unlike the woman who'd hidden in the bushes. Her long ebony hair was braided down her back, and her golden skin had grayed with ash.

Sagging my shoulders, I continued my charade. I needed her to lower her guard. I fluttered my eyes as if I were struggling to keep them open.

She headed over, smiling cockily, and my anger spiked.

Humans had bad seeds just like supernaturals did. Every group had extremists who corrupted others of their kind. For a long time, the silver wolves had resented angels for that very reason. They'd killed us for being half angel and half wolf, and the only reason we'd survived was that Ophaniel, the angel who'd fathered our supernatural race, had secreted the last two silver wolves away from Shadow City before the angels could kill them off, too.

She stepped toward me and reached for her walkie-talkie. I couldn't allow her to contact her team.

Her concentration split as she patted her hip for the walkie-talkie with her free hand.

This was it, the moment I'd been waiting for.

I snatched the tranq gun from her hand and straightened.

Her eyes widened as she stumbled back in fear.

The irony of the situation wasn't lost on me. She was *afraid*, yet she was the hunter. Fear made us do stupid things.

A shiver ran down my spine. I wasn't comfortable with firearms, as we'd never trained with them, but the last twenty-four hours proved that would be changing. To win against humans, I'd best get comfortable with projectile weapons.

I leveled the dart gun at her and spoke just loudly enough for her to hear, "Don't do anything stupid." I leaned over, keeping my gaze on her, and picked up the handgun she'd dropped.

Her gaze darted around like she was coming up with a plan.

Hell, I had to come up with one, too. I didn't want to hurt her, but I couldn't let her go.

What the hell are you doing? Chad asked, stepping from between a birch and a cedar tree.

Good question, because I didn't have a clue.

The woman snapped her head in his direction. He snarled, looking even more menacing as fur sprouted on his arms.

She stepped back, forgetting all about me.

I wanted to smack him. He was validating their fears.

Needing to end the standoff, I did what I should've done a few seconds before he arrived. I dropped the rifle, took the butt of the handgun, and smacked it against her head.

Her eyes rolled back, and I caught her before she could fall onto the ground. She didn't need to break something on top of the killer migraine she'd have when she awoke.

Sterlyn appeared beside me, chest heaving. Her silver hair looked dingy brown. We needed to get out of the smoke.

I eased the woman onto a leafier part of the forest floor. A knot had already formed where I'd hit her, and my heart constricted. I wished things didn't have to be this way, but I'd done what was best for everyone involved.

We need to meet the others closer to Griffin's vehicle, Sterlyn linked. *Did you two have any problems?*

I didn't, but clearly, she did, Chad connected, and gestured at me.

My heart raced from a mixture of the fight and his

anger. *I didn't want to hurt her, but she was a better-trained fighter than I'd expected.*

Chad frowned. *That's why you should've gone fast and hard.*

The three of us took off toward the others, keeping an eye out for any threats.

Acting like monsters will only confirm their fears. He again reminded me of Mom. Being reactive had benefits, but sometimes, it blinded us to better alternatives.

Chad lifted his hands. *And you think not hurting her will make her think we're less scary? You were aiming a weapon at her!*

Because she aimed it at me! I would've rather not touched it. Arguing wasn't helping matters, but I refused to let him treat me this way. I'd fought her and knocked her out without being hurt. I didn't understand what the big deal was.

Let's not lose focus on the real threat, Sterlyn linked and placed her hands on my shoulders. *I understand it's hard to hurt someone. We're born to be protectors, not only to our own kind but to all. I know how hard it is to fight someone you've disarmed. I struggle with it every time, and it's not a weakness. Compassion and empathy are what separate us from those who hurt others without remorse. Remember, do what you must to get the job done, and we're doing this for the greater good.*

Though she hadn't made me feel like it, I'd just gotten lectured. But everything she'd said was true. After disarming the woman, I'd struggled to see the bigger picture —the very thing Dad had always told me I was good at. My cheeks burned, and for the first time, I was glad he wasn't here to see me fail. A sob built in my chest, making me feel worse. I hadn't meant that I wished he was dead, but that was what it had sounded like.

Sterlyn dropped her hands and glared at Chad, lifting her chin. *As for you, stop trying to scare the humans. Yes, we need to knock them out, but they'll remember everything when they wake up. By becoming what they fear, you're making things harder on us and for Mila and the pack in their custody.*

He averted his eyes like a good pack member. *Fine. I hadn't thought about that last part.*

A person flicked into view beside Chad, and my wolf surged forward, growling. Though Chad could be over-bearing and critical, he was my family, and I'd die to protect him.

After a second, I realized who it was—Levi.

The demon smirked as he whispered, "As much as I'd love to see you try to take me down, now isn't the time."

The corner of Chad's mouth tipped upward. *At least I know you still love me, even if you're not happy with me.*

I rolled my eyes. He knew I cared about him; he just loved it when my protective side came out for him.

Wingbeats grew louder as Rosemary descended toward us with Eliza in her arms. Rosemary's feathers blended with the smoke, camouflaging her. Even her purple-mahogany hair was hidden from the soot that coated it.

As Eliza stepped out of Rosemary's embrace, Levi flickered back into his shadow form. This time, I knew he was there and could see his outline. That was something I'd have to get used to.

Levi said, "I'll head back to the others. They're nearby, but the humans are closing in. I wanted to ensure Rosemary and Eliza didn't run into trouble while locating you." His gaze landed on Rosemary as he inched toward the garden. "I'll link with you if we need you."

"Should we go with him?" Sterlyn murmured, her forehead lined with worry.

"No, they're very close." Rosemary stood behind a large red cedar and faced the bulky man still standing beside the Navigator.

It was clear he was guarding the vehicle in case we tried to get to it. Or perhaps he was waiting for our hostage.

Eliza coughed. "I can't fathom why anyone would do this to nature."

"Because they don't care." Rosemary crossed her arms. "It's not that hard to fathom. I can feel the vileness of that man's soul from here."

Her words made me realize something about the woman I'd fought. I hadn't felt evil from her—in fact, she'd radiated good. She hadn't had bad intentions.

I glanced at the woman just as she snatched the walkie-talkie from her side. She'd woken without making a noise.

I lunged for her, but she pressed the button and yelled, "They're near the cars!"

I jerked the walkie-talkie out of her hands as Chad growled, his irises glowing.

Eliza lifted her palm at the human and said, "*Fac eam somnum.*"

The woman's head rolled back, and she went to sleep.

But the damage had been done. I turned around, but the bulky guy hadn't moved, seeming unaware that she'd radioed the group. The humans farther away from the fire, though, had likely heard her.

A man's voice came through the walkie-talkie speaker. "How many?"

Eliza kept repeating the words, her hand shaking. I

didn't know much about witches, but I'd heard that while they were powerful on their own, if they weren't with their coven, they could burn out quickly.

The voice came again. "Alexis, how many are there?"

Now we knew her name, but I wasn't sure how that would help us.

A new voice came over the speaker. "Sir, I see some. They have Savannah. Everyone, circle around to me."

Killian. The thought of him in danger turned my blood ice cold.

Stupid, treacherous heart.

Rosemary turned to Eliza and held out her arms. "We need to help the others before they're swamped. We'll meet the rest of you there."

"But the spell for this woman..." Eliza gestured to Alexis.

"I'll take care of her." Chad snatched the tranq gun from the ground and shot her in the leg.

Eliza nodded, and Rosemary held her by the waist and took off.

Stomach lurching, I swallowed down bile. It burned the back of my throat. There was no telling how much of the drug they'd put in each dart. I assumed a larger dose than for a typical human, meaning it could kill her. I jerked the dart from her leg, hoping not all of the tranquilizer had gotten into her system. She snored faintly.

At least she was breathing.

Sterlyn turned to Chad and linked to us both, though she was talking to him. *Go grab the weapons from the person you took out. We need guns and tranqs to fight them.*

I still held Alexis's handgun. Though it didn't feel natural, I'd do whatever was needed to protect them, even Killian.

Sterlyn took off toward the man she'd knocked out, while Chad headed toward his assailant.

I'm heading to the gardens to catch up with the others, I linked with them, not wanting to run off like last time. I set off, following Rosemary.

Annoyance flashed through Chad, but Sterlyn interjected, *Be careful. I'll be right behind you.*

I allowed myself a grim smile. The fact that the alpha had given me her blessing meant Chad couldn't act too ornery, but I was sure I'd catch hell from him later.

Keeping close to the larger trees, I tapped into my wolf and pulled from the magic of the moon to enhance my senses. Even though dark clouds of smoke surrounded me, I could still see and hear better than the humans could.

No animals scurried by. The fires had cleared out all the wildlife, and even my wolf was desperate to leave.

But not without everyone else.

A little ways ahead, Heather's light blonde fur caught my eye. She'd shifted into wolf form. I frowned. She was probably trying to compensate for being slower than the other wolves.

Rosemary walked in back, watching their six, with Griffin in the lead. Heather trotted on the outer edge of the group, keeping an eye on the area, while Killian walked behind the human, gun still in hand. Eliza was on the other edge of the group, her body coiled tightly.

Seeing them drove my legs to move faster. My gaze landed on a man about twenty feet away, his tranq gun raised.

Sterlyn! A guy is aiming at them! Lungs failing, I jerked the handgun upward. I aimed, no hesitation this time, and as I pulled the trigger, a dart left his rifle.

Though the *crack* from my gun jerked his head around, I hadn't shot fast enough.

Killian, Griffin, and Heather heard the noise too late. They didn't have time to dodge as the tranq dart raced toward its mark.

CHAPTER THIRTEEN

HEATHER STOOD SLIGHTLY on her hind legs, trying to twist out of its path.

No.

The dart hit, and she crumbled. It stuck out of her wolf's lower chest, dangerously close to her heart—an organ that, if pierced, even a shifter couldn't survive.

My eyes burned, and this time, it wasn't just from the thick smoke. Her chest slowed, and my throat tightened, making me unable to swallow.

However, more of us might become injured if I didn't get my head on straight.

Forcing my gaze back to the man, I tried to see whether I'd hit him. If not, he could fire again.

I'm on my way! Sterlyn linked, her fear choking me. *Do what you can to help them, but don't put yourself in unnecessary danger.*

Even with her mate on the line, she was concerned about my safety. The qualities Dad had seen in her were becoming more apparent, and in this moment, she reminded me a lot of him.

Crimson spread across the left shoulder of the man's shirt. I'd hit him there instead of in the arm as I'd intended. Under the circumstances, I was thankful I'd hit him at all.

He still held the tranq rifle in his right hand, but he scurried behind a tree. He knew the general vicinity that the shot had come from.

I needed to distract him, or he'd take another shot.

J, don't do anything stupid, Chad linked.

He'd always been a worrywart, but this was even more intense than before. Maybe the loss of Dad plus Mom's disappearance was taking a toll.

Choosing not to answer him, I glanced at the others.

"Take cover!" Rosemary said, and landed next to Heather. She lifted her hands, which glowed white, contrasting with the dark air swirling around us. She pulled out the dart and covered the wound with her hands.

I had no clue what she was doing, but I needed to cover her. I couldn't let them hit *anyone* else.

We're almost there, Sterlyn linked. Some of her panic had receded, making breathing a tad easier for me.

Another man, dressed in all black, appeared a few yards down from the injured one. Soon, we'd be swarmed. Though we'd taken out three humans, there were eighteen more nearby. Maybe some were too close to the roaring fire to have heard the communication.

I lifted the gun, the weapon still alien in my hands, and concentrated on the threat I could see.

The new guy didn't see the risk and rushed past where the injured one was hiding. Aiming at his feet, I fired. The bullet hit the ground beside him, and I groaned. Shooting was not one of my strengths.

The guy paused and jumped into thick brush behind a

yellow birch. At least two of them would think twice before approaching.

Something snapped behind me, and I spun around, ready to fire my weapon. My finger itched to pull the trigger, but I inhaled, calming my nerves, then exhaled. It was Chad and Sterlyn.

Chad stopped abruptly and lifted his hands, each holding a rifle. *Watch where you're aiming.*

Unlike Chad, Sterlyn didn't pause as she hurried to her mate. She held her guns at the ready in case a threat appeared.

If I wasn't being careful, I would've shot you. I wouldn't admit that it hadn't been easy not to fire out of panic. I'd kept a level head. Before he could respond and irritate me, I linked with both of them, *There are two men hiding over to my right. I shot one in the shoulder but didn't hit the other. I'm assuming they're waiting for backup.*

Chad rushed by. *I'll take care of them.*

I wanted to smack him for recklessly running into danger, but at least I was here to provide backup. As long as I shot near them, they would hesitate to come out, and the one I'd hit would weaken the longer he bled.

Rosemary lifted her hands from Heather's body. A tear trickled down her cheek, and she used her bloody hands to wipe it away. She reached over and closed Heather's eyes. My friend's chest wasn't moving.

Gods, no.

I was supposed to protect her.

My own chest convulsed as despair swirled inside. I'd failed Heather just like I'd failed my pack.

Anger surged through me, and I didn't have the gumption to stop it. So much had been taken from me...from all of us. It wasn't fair that Heather's life had been stripped from her.

Black spots crowded my vision, but I didn't care. Darkness surrounded me both emotionally and physically.

Refusing to lose another person, I turned my sights back on the two men hiding from us. Gunmetal peeked from the shrub in which the new guy hid. Chad was close enough for the new guy to see him.

I tightened my grip on the gun as if that would make holding it more comfortable. It didn't matter. I'd do anything to protect Chad.

He's about to shoot you, I linked with him, then aimed and fired at New Guy's shrub. The bullet missed the shrub by five feet.

The guy didn't even flinch, that was how wide my shot had gone.

Damn it, I was done hiding. The threat was contained, if only marginally.

I tapped into my wolf and pivoted around the trunk that partially hid me. I had to move closer before he shot Chad.

Hide! I commanded Chad as New Guy tumbled into view. He dropped the gun as he did several forward rolls and hit a thick red cedar trunk.

What the—

A dark shadow form came soaring from the spot where New Guy had been hiding. Levi was helping us fight, and the humans couldn't see him.

The back of my neck tingled, and I spun around to see a man and a woman racing toward me. They hadn't noticed me yet.

I jumped behind a red cedar and squatted, chest heaving. My lungs burned, and I couldn't ignore the pain any longer.

We still had more enemies to watch out for. They could come from any direction. Taking the reprieve I had, I placed the gun on the ground beside me and wiped my sweaty palms on my shorts. Maybe I could take out New Guy and the other man in the bushes without the firearm.

Tapping into my wolf, I listened to the two newcomers' quick footsteps. They were a little unsteady, probably from fear, and not as silent as they had been when they'd arrived.

Dad had always told me that I should carry a weapon at all times, as Sterlyn did, and I'd brushed him off. It was one of the few things I hadn't taken seriously. But today, I *got* it. How I wished it hadn't taken me being in actual danger to understand.

The footsteps stopped as something hit the ground loudly a few feet away. The girl yelped in fear.

Had Levi made it past me again without me seeing him? I wouldn't put it past him, and I wasn't even trying to be punny.

I moved to help him. *Can demons get hurt in their shadow form?* I hated that I had to ask. If I'd been around to help them fight the huge demon war a week ago, I'd already know that answer.

Yes, Sterlyn linked. *Griffin is heading past Chad and Levi to look for the other human on that side, so he'll be passing you soon. I'm heading in the opposite direction, looking for the last one there. We need to disable them so they can't move, but try not to kill them if possible.*

When the man and woman came into view, I could have sworn I'd swallowed lead. Killian was fighting both of them.

No one else, *especially him*, would be getting hurt with me around.

The woman had dropped a few feet away as if she'd

been tossed aside, and Killian lifted the man by his neck. His fingers dug into the guy's flesh, and the human's face turned red. The enemy would pass out soon, as long as the woman didn't interfere.

As if she had the same thought, the woman sat up. A puddle of blood pooled underneath her, but the smoke was so thick, I couldn't smell it. A pained groan left her, and she held up a shaky hand, pointing her tranq gun at Killian.

My wolf howled inside my head, desperate to break free. My fear of him becoming injured damn near paralyzed me.

I was a fucking silver wolf. I would *not* freeze in the face of danger.

I snarled, and the woman and Killian diverted their attention to me.

That hadn't been my intention.

As she swung the tranq toward me, I lunged.

"Jewel!" Killian shouted, and released his captive. The man's vileness swirled around me, which made breathing even more of a struggle with the smoky air.

What the hell was Killian doing? I was protecting *him*, not the other way around.

I passed the barrel of the rifle just as she pulled the trigger. The dart missed me by maybe a millimeter as I landed on her chest. Her dark blue irises locked on my face as she opened her mouth to scream. But instead of sound coming out, she began hacking.

The pollution was affecting all of us. Maybe they should've thought that through.

The man used Killian's distraction to punch him in the back of the head. Killian stumbled, but I had to contend with the woman.

I grabbed the tranq rifle from her and spun it toward

her. I hated to inject her with the drug, but I had few other options. I yelled, "Will this amount kill you?"

Killian regained his balance and spun in time to duck the man's second punch. The man hit air, giving Killian the upper hand. But the guy still had both guns holstered.

Her bottom lip quivered. "Why do you care?"

"I don't *want* to kill you. None of us do! Even though you just murdered one of us!" This woman didn't feel evil. There had to be a reason she was trying to hurt us. "But I do need to knock you out. This would be the least unpleasant way with your injury."

Brow furrowing, she shook her head. "It's a strong dose, but it won't kill me."

I whispered, "With so many of your friends close by, I'm sure someone will find you."

She stiffened, and I pulled the trigger. Once the dart had sunk into her arm, I carefully laid her against a tree where she would be less likely to get trampled, positioning her so the branch wouldn't injure her further. She stared at me, something unreadable passing through her eyes before they dimmed and shut. The drugs had worked quickly.

Jumping to my feet, I spun to face Killian as he attempted to swipe the tranq rifle from the guy's waist. The man grunted and stumbled back, fast enough for Killian to miss by an inch. The man reached for his handgun, not the tranq, confirming how malicious he was. Unlike every other person we'd fought, he'd gone straight for the actual gun. I wasn't sure if I was relieved by the simplicity or disgusted that he didn't value our lives at all. At least the latter made him a true enemy instead of confusing me with a good soul.

"If you hurt him, I *will* kill you," I rasped, the sound like rocks grinding in my raw throat.

But the threat had been worth it because the man

glanced at me. His face was painted black, likely to blend in with the surrounding darkness. It was his almost white eyes that revealed his cruelty.

He smirked and aimed the gun at my heart.

That was what I thought he'd do. I pressed the trigger of the tranq, not wanting to kill him. I wanted him to remember that I'd outsmarted him.

As I tapped into my wolf, I used my speed to move to the side as the dart embedded in his shoulder. He reacted as expected and fired desperately to kill me before he passed out. But I'd already moved out of range, and the bullet whizzed by me.

Killian grabbed the gun from the asshole's hand and bent down to take the tranq. The enemy tried to remain standing, but he soon stumbled to the ground. He'd be asleep just like the woman across from him soon, but unlike her, I wouldn't move him to safety. He was on his own.

I'd spun to head back to the others when an all too familiar large hand clutched my upper arm. Tingles ran down to my toes. At the mercy of our connection, I wasn't thinking and allowed Killian to pull me back in his direction.

My gaze eagerly went to his face, wanting to etch it into my memory. He almost didn't look like the same guy. His irises were dark, and soot covered his face.

"What was *that*?" He waved a hand at the man. "Do you know how reckless that was?"

"You mean like when you took on two people with two guns each on your own?" I'd never gone up against an alpha, even one outside my own pack. The position had power and so much responsibility that I *never* wanted to understand. But this man had my blood boiling in all kinds of ways, and the longer I was around him, the worse it got. I wanted to punch the angry look off his face.

"I had it *under* control," he murmured, and stepped closer to me.

I laughed and ended up choking. Damn stupid air! If I hadn't been embarrassed already, I'd have flipped the smoke off, but then I'd look crazy and prove Killian's point.

He arched a brow, and I swallowed, trying to moisten the parched thing that was once my throat.

"Yes, the woman with the branch in her side could've tranqed you, but what do I know? So yeah, I *saved* your ass. You're welcome." I squared my shoulders, and my breasts brushed his chest, shooting a hot flash through me. I hadn't noticed how close we were until this very moment, but I couldn't make myself step back. "It's not—" I stopped. I had no clue what I'd been about to say, so instead, I stood there with my mouth gaping open.

I'm about to take the final one down. Griffin got the one he was after, Sterlyn linked. *Hurry back to the Navigator. We've gotta get out of here. Rosemary is flying with both the human and Eliza so we can run faster.*

Her words were like a cold shower, one I very much needed. I was panting after Killian in the middle of a wildfire. That was *not* smart for either of us.

My heart constricted. *What about Heather?*

Rosemary and Levi will come back to retrieve her body and meet us off the mountain, Sterlyn said.

Though I hated to leave her behind, they had a plan. The ones who were alive took priority, but at least they'd made arrangements to ensure we were able to bury her instead of abandoning her in the woods like a wild animal.

"Come on," Killian said, and motioned for me to go in front of him.

Not wanting to argue with him anymore, especially with so much at risk, I took off, leading the way to the car. Now that I was more attuned to my surroundings, I could hear someone catching up to us.

I thought we'd taken down the humans in the woods. *Someone's charging toward Killian and me.*

It's probably Griffin and me. We're close to where I ran into you earlier, Chad replied.

The men came into view, easing some of my fears. *I see you.*

Good. Now run! Chad gestured with his hands.

The four of us sprinted through the woods, but I kept an ear out for the enemy. We made good time, and soon the fire roared once more as we approached the thinning trees that revealed the Navigator.

Bulky was still there, along with the ten people who'd been examining the fire. They had our vehicle surrounded, and they'd armed themselves to the max with multiple handguns and tranq guns.

Tears of frustration filled my eyes. Rosemary couldn't drop off Eliza and Savannah until we'd secured the area. This close, I couldn't communicate well with anyone except Sterlyn and Chad.

How were we going to get out of this?

CHAPTER FOURTEEN

THE DIRENESS of the situation made the heat of the flames seem more sweltering. Every time I thought things couldn't get worse, I was proven wrong. I wasn't a big believer in a higher power, but I was beginning to develop a complex. With all the horrible stuff that had happened, something had to be working against us.

Or I was being melodramatic—but I'd never been that way before.

A familiar rough hand took mine, sending another jolt through my arm. I looked at Killian as he tugged me toward a huge red cedar.

Chad, I linked, not wanting to be separated. He stopped and turned, noting where Killian was taking us.

My skin buzzed, and I wanted to resist, hating the effect he had on me. Every time he touched me was more intense than the last, and that aggravated me more after our confrontation a moment ago. But if we kept fighting, it would only fracture us further. We needed to stand together to overcome this common enemy.

And these assholes had to be taken *down*.

Heather.

My heart constricted. Yet another person I'd lost. Another person I hadn't protected. Chest aching, I wasn't sure if I'd ever find my way back to the person I'd been before Dad had passed. Between losing several other beloved pack members and Heather, and Mom's disappearance, my world had been ripped apart.

Griffin pivoted and headed deeper into the woods.

Since Griffin knows where you three are, he's coming to meet me and bring me to you, Sterlyn linked. *It'll be faster than trying to use our connection to locate you.*

At least she was able to connect with every shifter here due to her mateship and the strange alpha respect bond thing Killian had with her and Griffin. Communication would still be more time-consuming, but we had a way to make it work.

When the three of us got situated behind the tree, Killian didn't release my hand. Instead, he held it tighter as if he thought I might slip away.

The pleasurable frisson mixed with my anguish and anger, turning me into a basket case of emotions. I wasn't sure which sensation was strongest, but I damn well knew which one I wouldn't be holding on to.

Chad slid between us, forcing our hands apart, and the enjoyable sensation dissipated. My wolf yearned to touch Killian again, but I wouldn't allow it. We had more serious matters to deal with.

Why were you holding his hand? Chad asked, glowering. Thankfully, he hadn't included Sterlyn in this conversation.

I didn't have a good reason, but I wouldn't admit that to him. *He tugged me over here and probably thought I might run off and attack the group on my own to avenge Heather.*

Though I would never be that foolish, Killian didn't know that.

Chad furrowed his brows. *Why would he think that?*

Because when I helped fight the two humans back there, he accused me of being reckless. As soon as I'd said it, I wanted to take it back.

Chad tensed even more. *What did you do to make him say that?*

He'd heard the words *fight*, *reckless*, and *me* in the same sentence. He didn't focus on the fact that I'd helped. I gritted my teeth. *Nothing. I did nothing to warrant him saying that. Now, let's focus on the problem.* I needed to take out my frustration and anger on the enemy.

We're coming up on you guys, Sterlyn warned seconds before the prickling sensation of awareness flowed through me. My wolf had picked up on their arrival, and I glanced over my shoulder just as she and Griffin slid in beside us.

Eyes burning, I turned back toward our enemy and watched as they talked with hand gestures. I couldn't tell what they were saying, but they kept pointing in our general direction. They suspected where we were, but I doubted they expected us to be this close.

The best thing we can do is wait until they disperse, Sterlyn linked. *Some of them will go deeper into the woods so we won't have to fight all eleven at one time. That will reduce our risk and eliminate the need to hurt more of them than required.*

That was a sensible plan. I'd worried that when I came back to the pack, I'd disagree with my new alpha's decisions. Seeing as I had no desire to be in charge or leave my pack, I knew I'd be forced to learn to deal with it, but that worry had been in vain. So far, Sterlyn hadn't made a single decision that I wasn't happy with. In many ways, her decisions were close to what Dad would've done.

Chad fidgeted. *If we wait, more backup could come.*

I glanced at him. *True, but they have more ammunition than we do. We're at a clear disadvantage.* Supernaturals, especially strong males, tended to be arrogant. They believed they were invincible, making them more vulnerable. The worst thing *anyone* could do, whether human or supernatural, was overestimate their abilities.

Exactly, Sterlyn linked as she placed a hand on my shoulder. *We need to mitigate the risks.*

But— Chad started.

I interjected, *Look at what happened to Heather.* Tears clouded my vision as the memory of Heather's lifeless wolf body flashed in my mind. I rubbed my chest, but it didn't relieve the agony.

He frowned, my words having the intended impact.

My wolf brushed against my mind, and my attention darted to Killian, only to find his focus locked on me. The scowl on his face indicated he either didn't like something I was doing or he'd noted the interaction between Chad and me. Either way, I didn't care.

We had an enemy to face.

I surveyed the people circling the Navigator.

A dark shadow appeared in front of us. A scream almost escaped me, but when I noticed the mocha eyes, I relaxed. At least I was getting used to being around a demon—something I'd never dreamed I'd say.

Sterlyn motioned to the eight men and three women around the SUV. Levi's shadow head appeared to nod, and then his eyes vanished as he turned around and soared across the opening toward the enemy.

It didn't hurt to have an invisible ally.

We inched toward the tree line, careful to remain undetected as Levi reached the enemy. Bulky Man stood at the driver's door of the Navigator and held his tranq gun at the ready.

Levi moved to the man standing by the passenger-side front door and jerked the tranq gun from his hand.

The guy stared at his hand, then at his rifle. He stumbled into the car and slammed into the woman beside him, who was leaning against the back passenger door. The woman glared at him, but Front Passenger Door Man was transfixed by his weapon.

I had to remember that to them, the rifle was hovering in the air.

Smacking the man's arm, the woman glanced at where the man was staring. She started to turn her head back toward the man again, then did a double take. Her mouth opened, and even through the roar of the fire, I heard her terrified scream.

She slammed into the man standing at the side of the hood on the passenger side, seeming unaware that she had. The man at the hood glanced behind, his eyes widening. Both he and the woman took off running into the woods across from us, the man by the passenger front door just a few steps behind them.

Bulky Man's mouth opened wide, yelling at them as they ran away. He glanced our way, his attention darting frantically along the tree line. He couldn't see us or the magically hovering rifle on the other side of the tall vehicle.

The other three on the driver's side of the vehicle and the man standing in front of the hood tensed and surveyed the area, trying to find what had scared their friends. Levi drifted toward the two enemies still close to him—a man on the passenger side near the back and a woman at the trunk.

Levi smacked the man's shoulders as he removed the gun on the man's other arm. The man spun around and then froze when he saw two rifles hovering in midair.

He stumbled back, winding up at the trunk with the woman and yet another man. They all stared at the floating guns, and then the woman and the man whose weapon had been taken ran off after their other three comrades, leaving the one man alone at the trunk. So now we had a woman and six men to fight immediately. The final man lifted his rifle, aiming at the air.

I stepped forward, desperate to help Levi, someone who was quickly becoming a friend, then paused. The alpha hadn't given the call. Just as I was about to tell her my plan, Sterlyn linked, *Move. Let's help Levi, then we'll get in from the passenger side once it's cleared. Griffin's focus will be on reaching the driver's seat and starting the car. Unfortunately, we can't leave the Navigator behind, or they'll figure out who we are from the registration papers inside.*

I tapped into my wolf speed and raced toward Levi. As I broke from the tree coverage, he shot the tranq at the man left by the trunk. The tranq sank into his leg, and the last man who joined the fight crumpled.

The five of us raced toward the Navigator, desperate to get in and move.

Bulky Man smacked the woman on his right and gestured at us. He aimed his gun at Killian, likely because he was at the end.

My wolf surged forward, and my skin tingled as fur sprouted all over my body. I hadn't meant to shift, but my wolf had taken control while I'd been distracted. She was *desperate* to protect Killian.

The final woman spun around, raised her rifle, and paused, watching my transformation. My clothes ripped from my body as it reformed, and I transitioned from running on two legs to four.

Just as Bulky Man pulled the trigger, Levi jerked the barrel away from us. The tranq exploded from the end and sailed ten feet clear of Killian.

We were maybe twenty feet from the Navigator, and my chest burst with new hope. We were going to make it.

J, what the hell! Chad chastised. *You get on me about intimidating the humans, yet you fucking shift.*

Bulky Guy tried to swing the rifle toward me, but Levi was there, moving it around. The remaining humans gathered on the driver's side of the vehicle, their attention centered on me.

That was why Chad was worried. In animal form, I posed a greater threat, and they would target me.

Chad tried to run in front of me, but since I was in wolf form, I was faster. I wouldn't allow him to take a tranq dart for me. I hadn't meant to shift, but I'd suffer the consequences of not keeping my wolf in line. I'd never lost control like that before.

Damn it, J, he threatened. *You're going to be—*

Griffin lifted his tranq gun and shot one man while Killian shot a tranq at one woman. Both darts hit their mark, leaving Bulky Man and three other humans to get past.

The way Chad hadn't completed his sentence bothered me. And then his connection to me began to feel sluggish.

Chad's hit, Sterlyn linked.

I spun around just as Chad fell forward onto the gravel. I glanced behind him to see the two who ran off into the woods aiming directly at us.

My lungs seized. Chad had been hit instead of me because I'd stubbornly run in front of him. Yet another person I'd let down.

Well, I wouldn't do that anymore. I hunkered down and charged at the women, ready to make them pay for what they'd done to my friend.

Jewel! Sterlyn connected, but I didn't pause.

One woman shot a tranq at me, but I dodged it. The dart hit the gravel and shattered as I ran past.

The other woman raised her tranq rifle at me as well, but I didn't flinch. I'd do whatever it took to protect Chad, and I had no problem going down with him.

A tranq sank into her shoulder before she could fire, and she stumbled back.

My attention went to the other woman. I was ten feet from her, if that. I reared onto my hind legs, prepared for her to fire again. This time, she would make sure her dart hit the spot. When she pulled the trigger, I dropped to the gravel, the dart sailing over my body.

I lunged onto her chest. As I landed on her, I bared my teeth, wanting her to feel the same terror I'd felt when I'd realized Chad had been shot. They'd shot him, and I shouldn't show her any forgiveness or mercy. What if he died like Heather?

The fear in her eyes made me hesitate. She was petrified, not full of anger or hatred. Everyone made poor decisions when terror ran rampant. Drool leaked down my mouth and onto her black shirt, and she cringed further. I was being cruel by lying on top of her and not ending her misery.

A hand touched my shoulder, and the jolt was stronger while I was in animal form. But that wasn't what bothered me the most. I was so transfixed by my anger and indecision that I hadn't noticed his approach.

I snarled, facing him. I wouldn't hurt him, but he needed to know I wasn't happy.

What I found in his expression fractured my resolve. His warm brown eyes were full of understanding, his face lined with worry or pain. There was no disgust or judgment.

Just as quickly as I read his expression, it hardened as he glared at the woman beneath me. He lifted his other arm, which held the tranq rifle, and without pause, he shot the woman in the leg.

She'd pass out in seconds.

As her eyes grew heavy, I climbed off, careful not to injure her. I glanced at her chest and realized my claws hadn't even cut through her clothes. Some threatening wolf I was.

I turned my attention back to Chad and cursed myself. How was I supposed to carry him while he was passed out and I was a wolf? I needed help.

Sterlyn helped Levi fight Bulky Man and another of the men while Griffin jumped into the vehicle. I watched as he started the Navigator so we could leave as soon as the enemy was neutralized.

Squatting beside me, Killian wrapped his arm around Chad's waist to pick him up. Those two had been disagreeing the entire time I'd been around, yet here Killian was, trying to save Chad. I couldn't make sense of him.

Watch out! Sterlyn linked, and my attention went back to the woods. Two more humans had come back, their guns aimed at Killian and me. Worse, they weren't aiming the tranq rifles.

Killian grunted as he slowly lifted Chad, not paying attention to our surroundings. He was focused on saving my packmate.

He was going to get shot.

CHAPTER FIFTEEN

I SLAMMED into Killian's side, toppling him over onto Chad as dirt exploded where he'd been standing.

Get to the Navigator now, Sterlyn instructed.

Something sharp sliced into my side, and pain exploded through my body. I whimpered and glanced down to find crimson spreading into my fur. *I'm hit.*

You two have *to move,* Sterlyn commanded, enough of her alpha will seeping through to make my wolf notice.

Levi raced toward Chad, not hesitating despite the danger.

But Chad. My heart splintered as another piercing pain shot through my other side. With both sides injured, my legs grew heavier, as if I might not be able to move them much longer.

Levi will take care of him, Sterlyn replied.

The last thing I wanted to do was leave Chad, but dying here wouldn't help him.

Blood poured down Killian's arm from where he must have gotten shot. But his attention was fixed on me, and he stepped in front of me.

Tell Killian to move! I linked to Sterlyn.

He's waiting on you, she replied immediately.

Butterflies took flight in my stomach despite the agony swirling inside me. It had to be nausea. I moved a few steps toward the Navigator, and Killian followed, blocking me from the gunfire.

I could never live with myself if he died protecting me. I quickened my pace, each step causing the pain to intensify. Vision blurring, I pushed through.

Sterlyn darted into the passenger side, leaned back, and threw open the back door.

Dirt hit my back leg where a bullet just missed me. Adrenaline pumped through me faster and muted some of the pain. I jumped inside the Navigator and hurried to the seat behind Griffin as Killian slammed the door shut. Blood soaked the front of his shirt, and my heart lurched into my throat. Both he and Chad had gotten hurt because of me. I'd been trying to do the right thing, but all I'd done was hurt more people.

I wished I could help Chad and Levi. *Please, gods, don't let them get hurt, too.* Though the enemy couldn't see Levi, bullets were flying in every direction.

Griffin peeled out as he reversed and spun the car to face the exit. The two humans were joined by the final man who'd run off, and they kept firing at us as Griffin stomped on the gas and blew past the parked Suburbans.

Wait! Chad! I turned back toward my window, my sides screaming in pain, but it was nothing compared to the agony of leaving him behind. *We can't leave him with them!*

Glass shattered, and something hard landed on top of me, forcing me to the floorboard. *Killian.* I realized the window by me had been shot out. The weight added to my agony while making it more difficult to breathe. I'd never been in such physical distress before.

We don't have a choice. Sterlyn's misery mixed with mine. *Levi was going to keep fighting so we could get him, but they all came out at once. We have to leave, or they'll capture us—or kill us.*

She hadn't asked about my pain, telling me she understood the importance of explaining her decision. *But—*

I know, she replied. *I don't want to leave him, either, but they weren't shooting at him since he's tranqed. They obviously decided they didn't need all of us. This is the best choice, given the circumstances.*

Every bump of gravel made Killian's weight that much heavier. After a minute, he must have decided we were far enough away because he slowly got off me.

"We need Rosemary!" Killian exclaimed as he ran his hands through my fur.

The jolt between us nearly took my breath away and numbed some of the pain, even though he was asking for another woman. I tried to turn my head to see him. It was difficult, but I couldn't ignore the frantic sound of his voice. Something was wrong.

When I finally mustered enough strength to turn his way, I wished I hadn't. Cuts covered his face, and his chest was soaked with blood. I couldn't tell how many times he'd been shot.

I whimpered, my wolf taking control. She *hated* seeing him this way.

Sterlyn touched Killian's shoulder. "Kill, you're both hurt, and we're heading to Rosemary now. Stay calm."

"Hold on," he whispered, rubbing his fingers through my fur. "We'll get you healed soon."

That was why he'd asked for Rosemary. From what I'd

learned growing up, angels had the ability to heal. The white glow I'd seen emanating from Rosemary's hands must have been that power she'd tried to use on Heather.

Heather.

The blows kept coming, and here I was, hiding in Griffin's Navigator. I couldn't imagine what Dad would think of me now.

I slowly sat upright, ignoring the shooting pain in my sides. The longer I lay there, the stiffer my body would become, and every bump was worse than the last. We were at the end of the gravel road, and the air wasn't nearly as smoky.

Killian's fingers dug into my fur as he stayed on the floorboard beside me. He rasped, "Don't push yourself too hard. You were shot multiple times."

As if I wasn't aware of that, but more importantly, so had *he*. He didn't need to push himself, either.

With each passing moment, air rushed in through the shattered window. My lungs screamed with more pain as the fresh air mingled with the smoke damage. If Killian hadn't been sitting beside me, I'd think he was still on top of me, crushing me.

The car ride was silent except for Sterlyn's and Griffin's coughing. Killian's touch, Sterlyn's concern and guilt, and my anguish were the only things keeping me company. My brain criticized me for allowing Killian to keep his hand on my neck. I didn't deserve comfort, only pain. But his touch was like the oxygen I needed, and I couldn't convince myself to make him move away. The reason had to be that he was injured, too. It wasn't like I had feelings for him.

My heart constricted, but I refused to analyze it. That would only cause more problems.

When we reached the bottom of the mountain, Sterlyn placed her phone to her ear.

"We're at His Majesty's restaurant, down on the right," Rosemary answered without a hello. "Park at the very edge of the lot, away from the front. We're in the back, hiding in the trees."

I had no clue what she was referencing, and I glanced out the window again. All I saw was a gas station and a few fast-food restaurants.

"Are you sure that's wise?" Sterlyn coughed and chewed on her bottom lip. "She could make a scene."

Rosemary chuckled darkly. "Surely the human knows better than to do something foolish, especially after she saw how we handled her friends."

She sounded confident, so she couldn't be aware of what had gone down after she'd left. Both Killian and I were not well off.

"You know I trust you. We'll be there in a few minutes." Sterlyn hung up and placed the phone on the center console.

Griffin cleared his throat. Beyond coughing, that was the most noise he'd made since we'd left the cabins. "Did she really call Burger King 'His Majesty's restaurant'?" He hacked as if the sentence had taken a lot out of him.

A shocked laugh escaped me, irritating my lungs further. If it weren't for the burning pain charging through me, I doubt I would've ever stopped laughing.

"You have to remember she's old. Though you were raised in Shadow City, just like she was, you grew up in more modern times, so fast-food restaurant names aren't foreign to you." Sterlyn smiled, but it looked sad.

Killian adjusted himself on the floorboard and winced.

"Just don't give her shit over it. We need her to focus on healing Jewel."

"And you, man." Griffin glanced in the rearview mirror. "You're all shot up, too. I don't know how Sterlyn and I got lucky."

Even if I'd wanted to contribute to the conversation, there wasn't much I could add. The longer I was away from Chad and Heather, the worse I felt, and not just the physical agony. I'd left Chad to be taken and Heather to never have a true resting spot. If Rosemary couldn't go back for her, either the wild animals would get her or the humans would cart her off and do gods knew what.

The car jerked as Griffin took a left into the parking lot. The change in direction jarred me, and I gasped. If I hadn't known better, I would've thought my body had been ripped in half.

Killian groaned through his own suffering, and I wished I could take away his pain. The desperate urge to protect him nearly pulled me under.

"Easy, man," he growled, his words almost indistinguishable.

"I have *no* control over the roads," Griffin grumbled. "I promise I'm not trying to cause you or Jewel any more pain."

I was pretty sure it couldn't get worse than this. *Wait... no...Gods, Fate, whatever higher power there might be, that wasn't a challenge.*

The car coasted to a stop, and Sterlyn opened her door. "I'll take Rosemary's spot with Savannah and Eliza so she can heal Jewel and Killian."

Every breath made me wheeze harder, and my lungs want to convulse. If it hadn't been for the pain, I'd be hacking up a lung about now.

The back passenger door opened almost immediately, and Rosemary's floral scent mixed with smoke filled the Navigator. She examined Killian and me, then frowned as white light flowed down her arms and into her palms. She reached for Killian, but he shook his head. "Jewel. Heal her first."

"You've got more wounds. I should—" she started.

But he cut her off. "Heal her *first*."

I wanted to argue, but I was limited in this form. Instead, I growled, voicing my displeasure the only way I could.

"I agree with the silver wolf." Rosemary exhaled but didn't argue further. Instead, she stepped back and disappeared from sight.

Then my door opened, and Rosemary appeared beside me. She inspected me without emotion, which was strangely reassuring. Her irises sparkled like a galaxy of stars, making her beauty more ethereal. She lifted her hands the same way she had with Heather and placed them on either side of one bullet wound. As soon as she touched me, her magic blended with mine. Her warmth was comforting, reminding me of when Dad or Mom would take me into their arms as a child. But as quickly as the warm comfort began, it went away.

"The bullets are still in there," she said through clenched teeth. "I can't heal you until they're out."

Fate must have taken my earlier thought as a challenge because once again, the situation had worsened.

Griffin banged on something up front. "We'll need to take them somewhere. If the bullets are still in her, they could be in Killian, too."

Bile burned my throat.

"I'll talk to Sterlyn." Rosemary shut the door and hurried off.

The vehicle became quiet, the only sounds Griffin's, Killian's, and my breathing. Normally, I found silence comforting, but not now. With my anxiety and pain almost at my threshold, I did the only thing I could. I played one of my favorite classical pieces, Mozart's Requiem in D minor, in my head until I passed out.

My body bounced, startling me from sleep. As soon as consciousness rolled in, the pain slammed back into my mind.

We're almost at the cabin, Sterlyn linked.

I opened my eyes to find Sterlyn in the passenger seat and the Navigator moving. The wind whipped through my fur, and Killian still sat on the floorboard beside me, his hand in my fur and his forehead resting against the seat in front of him.

My throat closed, and I whined softly. A small puddle of blood had pooled under his arm, and his face was pale under the soot.

He had to be worse off than me, which supported Rosemary's reaction.

The car stopped, and Griffin and Sterlyn got out quickly. Before I could take another breath, Killian's and my doors had opened.

Can you walk inside? Sterlyn asked from the passenger door as she placed her hands on Killian to help him out.

Yes. Call Griffin to help you with Killian, too. I'll be fine, I assured her. Killian was in this condition partially because of me. As a silver wolf, I would heal faster. He needed more help.

Griffin touched the door handle. "Jewel, if you change your mind, tell Sterlyn. She or I can be back here in a second to help you, too."

I nodded, wanting him to go.

When he was out of my way, I moved, glass cutting into my paws.

With as much speed as possible, I jumped down from the car. As soon as my legs hit the ground, pain exploded through my body. My vision blurred. If I'd thought the glass was bad, it was nothing compared to the agony of jostling my internal injuries.

When I could focus, I saw Eliza standing with the human, Savannah, in front of a one-story cabin that had seen better days. She flicked her wrists and said, "*Reserare ostium.*" The door swung open, and the witch turned to Savannah and murmured, "Get inside."

Rubbing her arms, Savannah entered the cabin, Eliza following.

It looked like one of the cheaper cabins in the Gatlinburg area that wasn't popular with tourists. That must have been how Sterlyn had rented it so quickly.

Movement flickered at the edge of the yard, and I saw Rosemary next to the woods, motioning for me to join her. I exhaled. Removing the bullets out here made sense. There wouldn't be a mess to clean up inside.

I hobbled over to her, trying not to whimper. Every step hurt worse than the last.

But when I was just a few feet away, Sterlyn frantically shouted, "Rosemary! Help!"

CHAPTER SIXTEEN

HEART STUTTERING, I spun around to find Killian on the ground between the Navigator and the cabin as Sterlyn's face turned as pale as the moon. Griffin leaned over his friend and placed a finger on his neck, checking for his pulse even though he should have been able to hear it.

"His heart's barely beating," Griffin said, voice cracking.

Rosemary's face scrunched with indecision. "But he said to heal—"

She wanted to honor Killian's request to heal me first. Well, there was one easy way to handle that. *I don't want her help until he's better. I may be in pain, but I'm not on the brink of death.*

Sterlyn parroted what I'd said.

Rosemary's shoulders relaxed, and her face smoothed. "I can't force you to do something against your will. I have no choice but to help him."

I exhaled, my sides screaming in response. Eyes stinging from the pain, I swallowed another whimper. I didn't want to distract them from Killian.

Rosemary's large black wings flapped as she flew the

short distance to him. She placed her hands on his chest, and a frown marred her face. "I will heal him enough so that his heart isn't as exhausted, but before I can heal him all the way, we will need to remove the bullets from his injuries, just as we'll have to do with Jewel."

The white glow raced down to her palms as if it sensed her desperate rush.

She placed her hands on his chest and glanced at Sterlyn and Griffin. "One of you, turn him onto his side and hold him up while the other digs the bullets out. There are two in his back and one in his front."

Griffin's eyes were the size of saucers. "Dig them out?"

"Just roll him over," Sterlyn commanded as she pulled her knife from her ankle sheath. "I need to sanitize this."

Rosemary shook her head. "We don't have time, and it doesn't matter. My magic will kill any infection that tries to grow before his healing kicks in."

Slowly, Griffin rolled Killian over as Sterlyn kneeled behind his back. She rubbed the edge of the knife on the grass, then grabbed the neckline of his shirt and sliced away the material.

His heartbeat grew slightly louder, and some of my worry eased. Rosemary knew what she was doing, and her powers were already improving his condition. Things would be okay.

They had to be.

As Sterlyn pulled the shirt away, the acid in my stomach lurched. Thankfully, I hadn't eaten in a while, so it was empty. Otherwise, I'd be vomiting.

Two bullet holes in his back leaked blood. Luck was on his side that one hadn't pierced his heart or lungs, but it had been way too close for comfort.

Sterlyn placed the tip of her knife inside one wound and dug.

I flinched as if she'd dug into my flesh. This was my imminent future. I stared at the woods, refusing to leave but unable to watch. God forbid I see his bare chest.

It was probably gorgeous, even full of holes.

"I got the first one," Sterlyn said with relief. "Working on two."

For the next few minutes, time stood still. Sterlyn was efficient, and soon, they rolled Killian onto his back so she could dig the final bullet out of his shoulder. The only good thing about the entire situation was that he was unconscious, though that meant he had been worse off than me.

Yet he'd been determined for Rosemary to help me first. My heart warred with itself, warming and then twisting and aching. I grimaced. He didn't get to be an asshole and a martyr. He needed to pick a personality and stick with it.

"Okay, done!" Sterlyn exclaimed as she stood.

Tears burned my eyes. Now that the operation was over, I moved to observe the rest. Blood oozed from underneath Killian, a stark reminder of how much he had lost. Anything that had been somewhat clotted, Sterlyn had reopened. With his shirt cut from his body, I could tell how pale he was, especially with the golden glow of the descending sun hitting him. Covered with soot, his face hadn't shown how wan he was.

Hands glowing even whiter, Rosemary poured her magic into him. She closed her eyes as the faint breeze blew her hair back from her face and ruffled her charcoal feathers. Even dirty, she was a vision. No wonder Killian had feelings for her.

Stomach churning, I tamped down the ugly emotion. These weird reactions around Killian had to stop.

Griffin placed an arm around Sterlyn's shoulder and pulled her to his chest. She nestled her head against him as they watched Killian the same way I was, waiting to see if Rosemary could heal him.

Rosemary at work was amazing. One of the bullet holes scabbed over in front of my eyes.

"There," the angel said as the white glow of her hands faded. "He's mostly healed, but I wanted to leave enough magic for Jewel and the rest of you, especially with all the smoke inhalation. With shifter healing, Killian should be back to normal when he wakes up."

Why isn't he awake? I linked to Sterlyn. My breathing turned ragged, flaring more pain inside me.

Sterlyn wiped her hands on the grass and repeated my question aloud.

"Because he has lost so much blood." Rosemary rubbed her hands on her pants, not caring that Killian's blood would stain them. "Now I need to heal Jewel, which will be more difficult since she's awake. You two will need to hold her down so she doesn't jerk from the pain while I cut out the bullets."

My heart thudded. Though I understood that getting them out was a priority, I dreaded it. I couldn't imagine worse pain than I currently felt, but I had a sinking suspicion I was about to learn how wrong I was.

I took a deep breath to calm myself. Fresh agony burst across my sides, defeating the *entire* purpose. Though I didn't make a noise, I winced.

"Take Killian inside," Sterlyn told Griffin as she moved toward me. "I think Jewel will be okay with just Rosemary and me out here with her."

"But—" Rosemary started.

Sterlyn cut her off. "If we need Griffin, I'll link with

him. We should take Killian somewhere comfortable so he can rest and finish healing."

Some of my tension eased. Maybe this wouldn't be so bad if Sterlyn thought she and Rosemary could handle me on their own. Dad had always believed a mindset could make a situation better or worse, and I chose to believe that Sterlyn thought this wouldn't be too extreme.

Her eyes glowed faintly. She had to be communicating with Griffin since Killian was asleep, Chad's bond was still cool, and she wasn't talking with me.

Rosemary hurried to me and gestured at the ground. "Lie down, and we'll work on one side at a time."

I wished I could sleep through the whole experience as Killian had. As I lay down, the pain was just as intense as when I'd gotten shot. With my silver wolf healing, it should've lessened a bit, but it had not.

I almost took a deep breath but stopped myself. I'd learned my lesson a few seconds ago. Only shallow breaths for me.

Griffin grunted as he picked Killian up like a princess. Griffin had one arm around his back and the other under his knees with Killian's face pressed to his chest. Griffin grinned and winked. "If he wasn't injured, I'd totally be taking his picture right now."

Mashing her lips together, Sterlyn arched her brow. "I'm surprised you'd be willing to take a picture like that. Sierra would have a field day."

His humor vanished. "She *would*. We will *never* mention this."

Rosemary tilted her head. "Why would Sierra run in a field for an entire day about this? I would think she would harass both of them about it past the point of everyone wishing she'd stop."

For a second, I forgot all about my pain. *What is she talking about? Doesn't she know what a field day is?*

She's very literal and doesn't understand many modern references. Sterlyn situated herself beside me, on the side farther from the cabin door. *Just like earlier.*

That felt like days ago.

"Do you need my knife?" Sterlyn asked as she held it to Rosemary.

"I'll use a feather." Rosemary pulled a wing toward her and spread a feather away from the rest. "I'll have better control that way."

Each feather was an extension of her, but I wasn't sure how the angel stuff worked.

Sterlyn placed her hands in my fur. My body stiffened of its own accord.

"Tensing will only make this worse," Rosemary said as she lowered herself so she was at eye level with the entry wound. "That's why I said we needed Griffin."

"She'll be *fine*," Sterlyn emphasized, and I almost wished she hadn't, because that informed me she was using the tactic of trying to ease my anxiety.

Though it was hard, I had to relax. I focused on the memory of Handel's *Water Music*. I reserved that piece for the worst of times, and I definitely needed it now.

I worried that Rosemary would tell me when she was about to go in, but then the sharp pain of her feather roared inside, catching me completely off guard. *How the hell is a feather that sharp?* I didn't know what I'd expected, but I'd thought it would be a lot softer than *this*.

Angel feathers have a sharp edge, like a knife, Sterlyn replied as both hands dug in, stabilizing me.

I must have been squirming.

"We need Griffin," Rosemary hissed.

The idea of someone holding me down even tighter had me tensing more. *Please, let me try one more time.*

"She's asking for one more chance. She didn't realize your feathers were so sharp. It shocked her," Sterlyn explained.

Rosemary tilted her head back. "They *don't* shock. I must have hit a nerve or something. I'll be more careful, but one more jerk, and Griffin is coming back."

I nodded, and a tear ran down my snout. Before she dug in again, I closed my eyes and focused on the soulful sounds playing in my head. This time, when the pain ravaged me, I only whimpered as I concentrated on the music harder, somehow making it louder.

The pain intensified as she pierced deeper inside me, and just when I thought I couldn't handle it, she pulled away. I kept my eyes closed tightly, waiting for the jabbing to begin again, but instead, the warmth of her magic flowed into me and surrounded the location. Within seconds, that side began to feel better.

The warmth left me, and I wanted to complain. There was something familiar, comforting, and safe about it. But I still had pain I needed her to heal.

"Let's switch sides," Rosemary said, bringing me back to the present.

Keeping my eyes closed, I focused on the music, and the stabbing pain of her feather in my injury nearly stole my breath again. At least I knew what to expect. As the pain became overwhelming, I clung to the knowledge that last time, she'd finished within seconds. Nausea racked me, and I tried to hold on to the music in my head, but it was useless. I needed something, *anything* to give me a sense of peace, and Killian's face appeared in my mind. Those warm brown eyes and sexy grin made my heart skip a beat, and not from my physical ailment. I hated that his face brought me comfort, but I'd cling to anything as long as it prevented Griffin and Sterlyn from holding me down like a prisoner.

When Rosemary's warmth entered me again, I tried to release the image of Killian, but it was burned into my mind, reminding me of when I was little and would stare at an image so hard that once I closed my eyes, the outline was still there.

Rosemary removed her hands. "There. You can let her go."

You did excellently! Sterlyn linked as she released her hold. "Are you feeling better?"

I climbed gingerly to my paws, waiting for that excruciating torture to rock through me. I felt a twinge more than anything. A bee sting hurt worse than that. I looked at one side where blood still coated my silver fur, but the bullet hole wasn't much more than a scab. *She's a miracle worker!*

Sterlyn smiled, some of the strain disappearing from her face. *Don't call her that. She won't understand what you mean.*

I hadn't thought of that, but Sterlyn was right. *I need clothes so I can shift back. I think Heather—* I stopped as a sob built in my chest. I'd lost someone else in such a short amount of time. Though she and I hadn't been close, we'd bonded during the past two days. It almost seemed like anyone close to me would soon be dead. I wasn't sure what I feared most: all of them dying or being left alone to mourn them by myself.

Tension seeped through Sterlyn. The small reprieve I'd given her, I'd quickly taken away.

"What's wrong?" Rosemary asked as she straightened, examining me.

"Nothing." Sterlyn headed toward the Navigator. "I'm

just getting the bag Sierra packed so Jewel can change. She wants to shift back into human form."

Though she'd used Sierra's name instead of Heather's, it didn't take away the pain. At least when I'd been in agony, all my brain could focus on was my physical pain...and Killian, though I'd like to pretend it was due to the anguish.

"I healed her almost completely but didn't want to use too much magic. I need to heal Griffin's, Eliza's, and your lungs. I'm already at half capacity." Rosemary rose to her feet and brushed off her hands. "Healing you three shouldn't take too much power, but with Levi following the humans, I don't want to pull from our connection or drain myself too low. The shifters we're looking for might need significant healing as well."

My blood ran cold, and I pawed at the grass. *Following the humans? So he couldn't get Chad out of there?* The urge to race back to the burning cabin surged through me.

"What do you mean, he's following them?" Sterlyn's hand stilled on the door handle to the back passenger side.

"He tried to drag Chad into the woods and hide him while they were distracted, but someone noticed and started shooting at Chad. Now they have three people watching him, so Levi's doing the next best thing—following them to learn their location, since they can't see him." Rosemary pursed her lips, and the skin around her eyes tightened. "I'm not happy about it, either, but it's better than either of them getting hurt. We can save Chad when we save the others."

Why was he dragging him? Picking him up and flying with him would've been a better option.

"I'm sorry, Rosemary. If I'd known—" Sterlyn sighed. *Demons in shadow form can't lift anything heavy. Their bodies have to remain weightless to fly.*

I hung my head. I'd been too quick to react and was letting that uncontrollable anger influence me.

My wolf surged inside me, ready to head back to the enemy. *Easy, girl*, I chastised her. Though we both wanted to run and save Chad and Levi, it would be foolish. If an invisible demon couldn't rescue Chad, then a wolf they were after surely couldn't. The best solution was for Levi to follow them, get the lay of the land, and let us know where they went.

"There was no other option. He told me how they were shooting at you. You did what you had to do. Otherwise, Heather wouldn't be the only one dead." Rosemary grimaced.

The physical pain I'd felt just minutes ago converted into emotion and stabbed my heart.

Sterlyn jumped out of the SUV with the bag on her shoulder. She headed over to me, unzipped the bag, and laid it on the ground. "Grab some clothes and change in the woods or in the cabin."

She didn't have to tell me twice. I needed alone time to sort through everything before I did something rash.

As I grabbed the first set of clothes I could find, Rosemary stepped in front of me. "Jewel, that didn't come out as I intended." She scratched her chin as her wings hugged her sides.

Tell her not to worry about it, please. I didn't want to keep talking about the loss. Thinking about it was hard enough.

Sterlyn informed her of what I was doing, so I rushed past them and ran deep into the woods. I didn't want to go inside the cabin yet because there were more people and potentially more questions. I just needed a moment to gather myself. This was why I preferred my own company most of the time. I could be myself even if that self was angry at the world.

Tuning everything out, I recalled Elgar's Cello Concerto in E Minor. It was easily one of my favorite tunes in the world, the music expressive in ways I feared to be. As my wolf receded, I found myself in human form and quickly dressed. The scab on my side was still there, but since it was mostly healed, I could shift without risking further injury.

The cool breeze lifted the floral skater skirt I'd chosen, and I attempted to tug down the sleeves of the burgundy quarter-sleeve shirt. This was definitely not an outfit I would normally wear, but the entire bag had been filled with skirts and dress pants. I was more of a jeans and T-shirt type of girl, always ready to fight. I'd thought Dad was paranoid when I was younger, but that was one thing I had listened to him about because he'd been adamant about it. It was more comfortable to dress like that anyway, and it worked for training.

As I made my way back to the cabin, Rosemary's floral scent was missing, replaced by Griffin's myrrh. I stepped from the tree line and found him standing there with his arms wrapped around Sterlyn. She leaned against his chest with her eyes closed, looking content in his embrace.

Killian flitted through my mind, and my heart panged. I stopped myself right there. I didn't need to continue down that train wreck of a thought.

Griffin's gaze landed on me, and he smiled. "It's good to see you back in human form."

"It's good to be back in it." Though I didn't mind being in wolf form, I didn't like being stuck in it. When injured like I had been, shifting could make matters worse because of the way the body contorted.

Sterlyn disentangled herself from Griffin and yawned. "Rosemary went inside to check on Killian and to make sure Eliza put up a perimeter spell for the human so she can't escape. We were waiting on you. Want to get some rest?"

Rest sounded amazing. Between the injury and the constant anxiety, fatigue had hit hard. My eyes burned, and not from the smoke. From the sound of Sterlyn's and Griffin's breathing, Rosemary must have healed them before going inside.

The three of us headed toward the cabin. With each step, my pace quickened. I wanted to check on Killian now that I was better and dressed, though I kept having to tug my skirt down. It felt like my ass was hanging out every time the wind blew.

Inside, the cabin was smaller than I'd expected. The kitchen and living room were one area with a door that led to the bedroom and likely one bath. Two brown pleather couches faced a television from the eighties. The entire place screamed out for an update, but that likely meant no one would be close by.

Killian was lying on one couch, his feet hanging over the edge. Rosemary stood in front of the other couch, hovering over Eliza and Savannah.

Eliza lifted a hand. "I'm telling you, the spell is set. You don't have to stand here and stare the poor girl down. She was just doing her job, and we'll make sure she can't get away to alert the others."

Crossing her arms, Rosemary arched an eyebrow. "Well, because of her and her *friends*, my mate isn't here, and another shifter is dead."

Sterlyn sighed. "We're all tired, and we need to rest while we can. Eliza and Savannah, you two take the bedroom. That way, Eliza will know if the spell slips, and she can handle Savannah. Griffin and I will sleep on the ground in here."

"I'll sleep on the ground in there." Rosemary lifted her chin. "If Savannah makes a noise I don't like, I'll know immediately." She flicked her finger toward the room. "Let's go."

Savannah jumped to her feet and scurried into the room. If Rosemary had wanted to instill the fear of gods in her, she'd done an amazing job. In truth, the angel sort of scared me, too.

On the rectangular table in the small, worn, maple kitchen lay a few pillows and sheets. I walked over and snatched up a pillow and thin cover before making my way to the spot on the floor underneath Killian, needing to lie close to him.

"Hey, you were hurt," Griffin murmured. "You can take the couch."

I shook my head. "You two are mates and like snuggling. You sleep on the couch. I'm fine on the floor. I'm so tired, I could sleep through anything." I put my pillow at the same end of the couch as Killian's head and bundled the covers where my body would lie.

You should— Sterlyn started.

Please don't, I cut her off. *I don't mean to be rude, but I'll feel better here. I got you all into this mess, and I need...* I trailed off. I'd almost admitted that I needed to be close to Killian. I didn't even want to admit that to myself, let alone anyone else.

Sterlyn tilted her head, staring at me. Her eyes widened, and then she patted Griffin's arm. "It's important to her. Let's just do what she asks so we can get to sleep faster."

Thankful, she hadn't pushed. I lay down on the blanket,

facing the couch, and focused on Killian's heartbeat and breathing. Before I even realized it, I was out.

I WASN'T sure how long I'd been asleep, but judging by the silver light shining into the cabin, the moon had to be high in the sky. I estimated it was around midnight, which meant I'd gotten an hour or two of sleep, max. My arm tingled, and I turned my head to confirm what I already assumed. Killian's arm hung from the couch, and his fingers brushed my shoulder.

Some of the weight on my soul lightened. He was doing well enough to lie on his side. Unable to stop myself, I leaned my head into his hand and pressed my lips to his skin. Whether I liked it or not, his recovery eliminated much of the turmoil inside me.

Lips tingling, I caught my breath. If that small touch felt this good, I wondered what his mouth would feel like. My body heated...and an odd sensation of being watched crept over me.

I darted my gaze to his eyes and found them open.

I jerked back as my face caught fire. I'd been careless and gotten caught acting like a creeper.

Oh, my gods. I needed the ground to open up and swallow me *now*.

"Hey," he murmured almost too low for me to hear.

There was no way in *hell* I could talk about this. I shook my head to warn him to drop it. I didn't trust myself to speak, and I definitely didn't want to chance waking Sterlyn and Griffin. I had to get out of here.

Slowly, I stood and inched toward the door, trying not

to wake anyone but desperate to be alone to think. I needed to come to grips with what I'd done.

Are you okay? Sterlyn's voice popped into my head.

Of course I'd woken her. She had better hearing than anyone else in the cabin. *Yeah, I just want to go for a walk. I'm a little restless.* I didn't bother turning around, not wanting to see the look on her face.

I can go with you, she offered.

She didn't like the thought of me out there alone. *No, it's fine. You stay there and rest. I'll stay close by and link you if anything feels off.*

Unease filtered through our bond, and she sighed. *If anything seems even sort of strange, you* have *to tell me.*

Promise. That was easy. *Besides, if anyone is coming, Rosemary will let us know.*

Our bond went back to its normal cadence. *You're right. But still.*

I smiled despite myself. She often reminded me of Dad. *I will.* I opened the door and stepped outside. The chill chased away the rest of my sleepiness, and I headed to the Navigator. The three-quarter moon shone down, putting my angel magic more at peace. I lifted my head and basked in the glow for gods knew how long.

The front door opened, and I tensed. *Please let it be Sterlyn.* I turned to apologize, but my words fizzled as my mouth dropped open.

Killian stood there—shirtless, chiseled, and damn delectable. He didn't look injured anymore; even his olive complexion was back to normal except for the soot that marred his skin. Dear gods, he was going to force me to address what I'd done in there. My legs itched to run away, but my heart tugged me toward him. I was a hot mess as usual when it came to him, but it was becoming progressively worse.

His attention was focused entirely on me as if nothing else existed. He walked straight to me, and his tongue darted out, licking his bottom lip. He cradled the hand I'd kissed to his chest, making his attention even more jarring.

My brain fried and stopped reminding me that being alone with him was a bad idea and that I'd made a fool of myself only moments ago.

"Why did you run out like that?" he murmured as he pulled me into his arms. "I couldn't run after you without Sterlyn asking a ton of questions."

Hundreds of jolts pinged through my body, his touch feeling that much more incredible. I tilted my head up and stared at him, unable to speak. His lashes were thick, his lips were full, and his sandalwood smell was mouth-wateringly tantalizing without a barrier between me and his skin. I stood on my tiptoes, so curious about whether his lips tasted just as good as I imagined.

His heart raced. I could feel every beat...or maybe it was mine racing in sync with his. Eyes locked on my lips, he gradually lowered his head toward mine as if asking for permission.

My head swam. I'd never been kissed before, and I knew that if he did kiss me, I wouldn't want to stop.

One hand caressed my cheek, and something sizzled between us. His lips were only inches from mine.

"Thank goodness I didn't lose you," he whispered.

Lose you.

Those words were enough to snap me to the present and out of my daze.

CHAPTER SEVENTEEN

IN THIS MOMENT of almost clarity, my brain screamed at me to move, but his lips touched mine before I could step back. My lips tingled as electricity coursed through my body.

I moaned from the pleasure thrumming through me. My wolf surged forward and howled inside my head, and instead of moving away, my hands landed on his bare chest, adding an inferno to the heat flaring within me.

If he were a drug, I'd happily become addicted.

His tongue slid across my lips, begging for entrance. I'd never imagined I could be connected to someone both physically and emotionally so quickly. It was as if he were my fated mate.

Fated mate.

The words stopped me in my tracks. *Oh, gods.*

Dad had said fated mates brought out the best in each other, but Killian hadn't done that. Instead, humans had kidnapped Mom and PawPaw and Nana because he'd informed the entire world about our existence. We *couldn't* be fated.

Feeling the change in me, he pulled back, his forehead lined with concern. "What's wrong?"

I laughed. I didn't know why, but it just bubbled out of me. I was beginning to feel crazy with both sides of me at war, adding to my exhaustion. "I can't do this."

His hold loosened, but he didn't release me. His irises darkened as he asked slowly, "Do what, exactly?"

Heart fracturing, I pushed the overwhelming agony aside and focused on what my brain was telling me to do. "Us. I *want* to, but I *can't*."

When he dropped his hands and stepped back, tears burned my eyes. I wanted him to argue and tell me I didn't have a choice...that I was his. It wouldn't change anything, but at least I'd feel as if he were willing to *fight* for me.

Maybe this was better. He'd turned cold and indifferent, and though it hurt, it would make it easier to remember why we couldn't be together even if he was my fated mate.

He opened his mouth, and I readied myself for the malice that was sure to come. He was an alpha, and I'd rejected him.

"Because I told the world about us, your mom, grandparents, and their pack have vanished." He winced, but he'd spoken the words with sincerity.

He made it sound so simple, but the swirling emotions inside me and the fading sizzle of our connection complicated everything. "Yes! I mean—"

"No." He lifted a hand and ran it through his short hair, his bicep bulging. "I get it. And Jewel, I'm so sorry. I never meant to cause anyone pain, *especially* you."

My body swayed toward him, and I wanted to close the distance between us. His kindness made holding on to my anger more of a struggle. I needed him to be an asshole. His sympathy made it harder to remember why we were a bad idea.

But what kind of daughter would I be if I gave in to the man who might have been the catalyst for my mother's abduction? I'd already lost Dad and abandoned my pack when they'd needed me to fight beside them. I couldn't disappoint another person and lose focus. "You didn't have the right to share our secret with the world." I wanted the anger to take control of me. I craved it. It would make it easier to walk away.

"I didn't, and I wish things were different." He placed his hands into his pockets. "But I promise we *will* save them. No matter what it takes." He tucked a piece of my hair behind my ear. "I won't allow you to have the same regrets that haunt me." He dropped his hand and moved away.

Grief consumed me. I didn't *want* him to leave.

"I'll go inside and give you space." He smiled sadly and licked his lips. "But just know, no matter what, I will always be here for you. Your happiness is the most important thing to me, and I'll do whatever it takes to make you smile again."

I closed my eyes to prevent the tears from falling. If I started to cry, I wasn't sure I could ever stop. Maybe once Mom and the others were safe, I would allow myself to be with him like my heart and body so desperately wanted. Until then, I had to keep my resolve. I'd left Mom while she'd been mourning Dad, and I couldn't let her down now.

No distractions.

Every remaining member of my family was in danger, and if something terrible happened while I was distracted by a certain tall, muscular, and delicious someone, that would haunt me.

The only sounds of the night were the raccoons and other nocturnal creatures scurrying past. Killian's scent receded, indicating he was heading inside as he'd said. In my short time around him, I'd learned he was a man of his word.

When the cabin door opened and shut, a tear escaped and slid down my face. I grabbed the hem of my short skirt and bent over to dry my eyes.

A dark chuckle made me freeze.

I yanked my skirt back into place and pivoted toward the sound of the laughter. A shadowy form loomed by a tree a few feet away. Then Levi flickered into view and rocked back on his heels with a smile that somehow widened. "And who said ladies have no class these days?"

My face heated yet again. "Well, I *thought* I was alone. Maybe you shouldn't go sneaking up on people in your demon form." I never used to embarrass myself like this.

"Then I wouldn't be here to tell you where Chad, your mother, and your grandparents' pack have been taken." He arched a brow, knowing he'd hit his mark.

"Where?" My pain and embarrassment were forgotten. We had a location.

The cabin door opened, and I turned to find Rosemary, Sterlyn, Griffin, and Killian coming outside to join us. Levi must have used his mate link with Rosemary to tell her he'd arrived. Griffin and Sterlyn held hands while Rosemary flew the short distance to Levi. The dark angel kissed the demon, and he pulled her into his arms...as Killian had done to me.

I averted my gaze, not wanting to watch their affection, but my focus landed on Killian. My heart seized in my chest. Everything inside me screamed to run to him, proving he was every bit the distraction I couldn't afford, no matter how badly I wanted him.

"Where did they take them?" Killian asked gruffly. He was struggling like I was, but there wasn't a damn thing I could do about it.

My heart chimed in about him being my fated mate, but I brushed it aside.

Rosemary disentangled herself from Levi, and they faced us together. Taking her hand, Levi winked at his mate, then focused on the four of us. "I followed the humans and Chad in the van for about an hour and fifteen minutes. I'm not familiar with the area, but I can take us to it."

That was more than perfect for me. "We need to break them out."

"Let's not get ahead of ourselves." Levi frowned. "I didn't do much scouting so I could come back quickly, but I figured we should keep an eye on the place for a couple of days. It's a large facility that seems very secure, with guards stationed outside."

This wasn't the news I wanted to hear, but I'd feared it would be the case. The humans who'd attacked us were trained in combat and had coordinated the takedown of an entire pack. Someone with significant money and power had to be behind it. I clenched my fists, enjoying the physical pain of my fingers digging into my palms—anything to ease the emotional chaos churning inside.

"Sounds like it could be government or military." Sterlyn rubbed her temples. "But I thought they'd attack Shadow City, or Shadow Ridge or Terrace. I hadn't considered an outside pack."

None of that mattered. "Can we have this conversation once we get there and get a layout of the area?" I wanted to rush there and go after the pack and Mom, but I wasn't reckless. If we didn't scope out the facility first, all we'd wind up doing would be handing ourselves over to them for testing or whatever the hell they were up to. I just wanted to make it there to at least start planning a rescue.

"She has a point," Killian said, gesturing to me. "We should figure out the guard rotation and go from there."

Warmth expanded in my chest. His support lent me strength.

Griffin released Sterlyn's grip and headed toward the door. "I'll wake Eliza and Savannah."

"I hope you don't expect me to carry them." Rosemary frowned. "Especially since there's room in the Navigator."

"They can ride with us," Sterlyn agreed. "Thank you for carrying them here safely."

My attention flicked to the vehicle in question. "I'll see what we can use to clean up the mess inside. There's glass and blood everywhere."

I hurried toward the cabin, needing distance from Killian...and something to keep me busy.

THE MOON HAD DESCENDED halfway in the still-dark sky as we pulled into a rural area on the outskirts of Lenoir City. Rosemary flew high to stay out of sight of humans, though I could see her faintly with my wolf eyes. Levi floated a few feet above us in his shadow form, leading us to the area.

On the way, we'd asked Savannah about the location and who she worked for, but she didn't know anything. There were different groups, one that had knocked out the shifters and one that had taken them away. The people who had performed the attacks didn't know the end location so that if anyone were captured, they wouldn't be able to give it away. Since her pulse didn't increase and the sulfuric stench of a lie never came, we had no reason not to believe her.

Killian and I sat in the back row of the Navigator on opposite sides. Eliza had cast a witchy spell to put all the pieces of the broken window back together. You couldn't even tell it had shattered, which made Griffin happy.

Every now and then, I placed my hand on the empty seat between us, hoping Killian would "accidentally" brush it. But no matter how long I kept my hand there, he didn't take advantage. I was both disappointed that he hadn't and furious with myself for even wanting him to touch me. But the anger I'd harbored for him when I'd met him had vanished, causing me to channel that rage at myself. Though he never touched me, every time he glanced at me, I felt it. And he paid a *lot* of attention to me, which was the only thing easing my mind.

The bond with Mom and Chad warmed in my chest but stayed on the cool end of normal—as if they were sleeping. They were probably sedated, and I wasn't sure whether that was a blessing.

Levi directed us into the lot of a small, closed gas station. The area was isolated apart from a few run-down restaurants on either side of the station and a white wooden antique shop across the street.

"Pull in and stop there," Sterlyn instructed from the passenger seat.

Griffin slowed the vehicle, and he turned into the spot. "It would be nice if I could see him, especially since I'm the one following him."

"I could drive," Sterlyn smiled serenely, already knowing what he would say.

He glanced at her as he put the SUV into park. "You most definitely *could*, but I like being in the driver's seat."

"Figures. Supernatural men are the same as human ones," Savannah grumbled, probably not aware we could all hear her.

"Oh, child." Eliza chuckled. "There isn't any difference between them except supernaturals can be over the top at times."

Face paling, Savannah gasped. "You *heard* me?"

"Just as if you had said it in your normal voice," Sterlyn answered with a smile as she rolled down her window.

Levi's shadow form appeared in her window. "The place is only a few miles from here."

My wolf stirred. "It's four in the morning. We can't check in anywhere yet. We should scope out the area." I didn't want to waste precious time.

Killian leaned forward between the mid-row seats, his shoulder brushing my arm and causing the jolt I'd been jonesing for. "She's right. Levi can lead Jewel and me to the location. We'll take first watch."

Sterlyn turned toward the back seat, her eyes glowing. When Griffin grumbled beside her, I realized she'd been communicating with him.

"I'll go with you as well while Griffin finds somewhere close by for everyone else to wait." Sterlyn faced forward again, kissed her mate's cheek, and opened the door.

Griffin's hands were so tight on the wheel. He didn't want Sterlyn to go, but they must have decided it was best for him to stay behind with Eliza and Savannah.

I edged past Killian, allowing the entire sides of our bodies to touch. I schooled my expression and suppressed a shiver, not wanting him to realize the effect he had on me, but I was certain he knew. I slid between the mid-row seats just as Eliza opened the passenger door and climbed out. She stepped out of the way so I could slide by her. Once Killian got out, the four of us moved toward the woods behind the gas station. Tennessee's rural areas were nice, the woods plentiful and easily accessible.

"Rosemary is doing a flyover and will meet us when we get close enough to keep watch," Levi said as he floated between a huge oak and a red cedar.

As I entered the woods behind Levi, the Navigator door shut, indicating Eliza had gotten back in.

My wolf surged forward, wanting to shift. Though we could move faster, we weren't set up to shift back in terms of clothing. Plus, we wouldn't be able to communicate with Levi and Rosemary, and I wouldn't be able to talk with Killian. I held my wolf back but tapped into her magic to run faster.

Sterlyn and Killian were doing the same, but Sterlyn and I moved more slowly than we actually could since Killian didn't have the power of the moon.

Raccoons and flying squirrels rustled in the woods, and the graceful flowing movement of trotting deer caught my attention. The transition from night to day was beginning.

In another situation, I'd have enjoyed the run in the woods. Though I would've preferred it in my animal form, running was freeing.

About another mile in, the scent of musk hit my nose. *A wolf pack must live nearby.*

I smell it, too, Sterlyn replied. *But since we're just passing through, we should be okay.*

I hoped she was right. Most packs left other wolf

shifters alone if they were passing, but some could be terri-torial. Either way, it was too late now to backtrack.

We continued on, and soon, through the leafless branches, a massive building came into view. It was shaped as three conjoined rectangles, the center larger than the two on either side. Flat concrete roofs topped the structure, which had glass windows in front. A black asphalt parking lot allowed for about fifty parking spaces. For a building this size, I would've expected ten times that number, suggesting that most of the space was for items that weren't leaving. Unfortunately, I was sure "items" meant what the humans considered the captured wolf shifters.

Guards stood at the corners of the building, two on each side, and those were just the ones we could see. There was no telling how many were within.

Our group stopped a few feet shy of the tree line, not wanting to chance anyone noticing us. We could see every-thing from this position.

The sound of wings drew my attention skyward. Rose-mary landed beside Sterlyn, who stood on Killian's other side. A frown marred the angel's face. "I couldn't make out anything more than what you can see from here."

Sterlyn's jaw clenched. "That's because they don't want anyone to know what's going on in there."

A lump formed in my throat.

"Then we wait." Killian strolled over to an oak tree and leaned against it, facing the building. "And note everything we can until we have enough intel to go inside."

There wasn't anything more to add. That was our best option, so I found a clear spot on the ground and sat, ready to observe everything.

Two hours later, we hadn't learned much. Levi arrived and sat with Rosemary to keep watch. The guard change was still probably a couple of hours out, but the guards standing outside looked tired. We needed a whole hell of a lot more than that to go off of before we made our move.

Sandalwood filled my nose as Killian squatted beside me. My heart pounded at his nearness, though I couldn't fathom what he wanted to say to me. My palms sweated as butterflies took flight in my stomach. *Please be a dick*, I chanted in my head.

He said, "Hey, I've got a granola bar we could split, if you want."

Of course he was being kind and considerate. Damn him. "Thanks, but you need your energy. You almost *died* not even twelve hours ago." My voice broke as my emotions slipped through.

"True, but you were horribly injured, too." He pulled out a flattened bar from his back pocket. "I'd feel better if you ate."

I snickered. The bar had conformed to his ass, and if he'd been anyone else, I'd be disgusted. I wasn't sure what it said about me that I wanted to eat it more.

The chocolate color of his eyes turned a shade lighter. "I like the sound of your laugh, though I'm a little concerned that offering you food is so funny."

My body turned to him of its own accord, and all I could do was stare at this amazing guy beside me. I leaned closer to him, wanting to taste his lips. He didn't move away, and that was all the encouragement I needed. I was helpless to keep my distance from him.

Paws pounded in the forest. I jerked away as his forehead wrinkled with confusion.

He couldn't hear them yet.

"Incoming," Sterlyn said from her position a few feet away at a red cedar she was using for back support. "That has to be the local pack." She jumped to her feet, turning toward the sound.

We had no place to run or hide. We had to face them... and pray they weren't here to fight.

CHAPTER EIGHTEEN

FOLLOWING STERLYN'S LEAD, I stood beside my alpha. Though I would listen to her instruction, I needed to be ready to fight if she gave the order.

Maybe I should've eaten some of that granola bar.

Rosemary and Levi flanked Sterlyn's other side as Killian moved to stand next to me. He was so close that our arms touched until he took a slight step in front of me.

"There are at least fifteen of them," Rosemary said as she spread her wings. "With five of us here, that would mean we each take three at a time. Not ideal, but we've faced worse odds."

The guilt formed a hard knot in my stomach. Though I'd been there with the human fighters, I didn't have as much experience as the others. Even earlier, I hadn't fought three at one time by myself, and this would be vastly different. Yet another stark reminder that I hadn't been around to help my pack when they'd needed me most.

Killian's body tensed even more, and he inched farther in front of me.

I gritted my teeth as my anger bubbled. Though Killian

was making it clear that he was just as nervous as I was about me fighting, it still flustered me. "You do know I've trained for battle my entire life, right?"

He glanced over his shoulder. "With your heritage, I have no doubt whatsoever, especially after having had the honor of knowing your father."

The air was knocked out of my lungs. Of course he'd met Dad. For some reason, I hadn't put the two of them together. Dad had mentioned Sterlyn having a best friend— and it was Killian.

As I opened my mouth to ask why, then, was he hovering in front of me, I realized the other wolves were almost right on us. Red-hot anger swirled inside me, and I swallowed my question with difficulty. I didn't want the strange pack to think we were arguing and use that against us.

Rosemary glared at me, and her nose wrinkled with disgust. She must not like the way I'd spoken to Killian. My blood heated even more. She had her mate, and she needed to keep her nose out of *my* business.

He isn't trying to belittle you, Jewel, Sterlyn linked. *He's protective of those he cares about, and that includes you. But I need you to focus on the potential threat at hand.*

Her words were the equivalent of a slap to the face, though she hadn't meant them to be. It just proved how irrational I was being. Like Mom.

I lifted my chin, countering the urge to hide my face. I had to get my emotions under control.

Five wolves became visible through the branches. They were the usual shades of wolf: gray, dark red, brown, cream, and a fawn with a black dorsal stripe. They raced toward us, attention locked, but showed no signs of aggression.

The five of us stayed in a somewhat straight line, except

for Killian, who still stood slightly in front of me. I wanted to grab his hand and tug him back, but his touch would distract me worse than my annoyance with him did.

Though only five were visible, I could hear at least nine other wolves fanning out around us. They were hoping we couldn't determine their numbers, but with Sterlyn's and my exceptional hearing, we could make out four spreading to our left and another five to the right. They were prepping for battle, though I hoped we could prevent a fight from happening. We were still missing one wolf I thought I'd picked up on when they'd been running toward us.

There are fifteen like Rosemary said, right? I linked with Sterlyn.

She nodded. *Yes, though one seems to be missing.*

Human footsteps headed our way, and some tension left my body. One of them must have shifted into human form. That was a good sign—it meant they were willing to communicate.

The five wolves stopped ten feet away, spread out among the oak trees, and a naked woman a few years older than me stepped from behind a red cedar. Her ash-brown hair cascaded down her shoulders, stopping a few inches above full, round breasts that emphasized her beautiful beige complexion. Thick lashes surrounded aqua eyes that were locked on Killian.

A low growl rattled in my chest.

He retreated a step so his back brushed my arm, the now-familiar jolts taking hold, but not even that could appease me. She needed to look away and get some clothes on *now*.

Frowning, the woman turned her attention to me. That irritated me worse, like she was afraid he might be with me.

Though her essence wasn't evil, something was off about her.

To our left, another set of human footsteps approached us. A man in his mid-twenties stepped out from behind a massive oak, completely naked as well. He had the same hair color as the woman, but his was longer and more gorgeous. His eyes were more of an emerald, but his complexion was almost identical. They had to be siblings.

Neither one of them was uncomfortable in the nude, which wasn't uncommon among wolf shifters. Our pack was more modest than most, but that mainly had to do with most of the men and women being mated. Once you found your mate, you didn't like anyone to see them naked or permit them to look at anyone else that way.

The man examined us, and when his attention landed on me, Killian stepped completely in front of me, blocking me from his view.

Oh, hell, no. That girl hadn't even looked away from him. If anyone needed protection, it was him from *her*.

Sterlyn cleared her throat, forcing the man and the woman to look at her. Making sure her eyes stayed above the man's waist, Sterlyn said, "I'm sorry if we concerned your pack. We aren't here to cause any trouble."

The man turned his attention to Killian and answered, "We smelled three wolves, so we didn't think you were a threat, but we didn't expect to find an angel and...whatever he is." He gestured at Levi.

Of course the man assumed Killian was the alpha. It didn't matter that Sterlyn emanated stronger alpha magic than Killian—she was a woman. Most packs were still sexist when it came to leadership positions.

This would have been the perfect opportunity for

Killian to hurt Sterlyn's credibility, but he remained quiet and didn't take advantage of the situation.

"My name is Sterlyn. The wolf at the end is Killian, and the woman between us is Jewel. The angel is Rosemary, and that's her fated mate, a demon named Levi." By introducing us, Sterlyn was showing them that we weren't here for malicious reasons. Bad guys didn't usually give their names. "We have no intention of fighting over your pack or territory." Sterlyn motioned to the large building behind her. "Our friends were taken into that building against their will. We didn't know the area and accidentally crossed onto your territory. We'll be sure not to make that mistake again."

"What kind of friends?" The man's brows furrowed, but he sounded concerned. Unlike the woman, his essence was all good. Okay, hers wasn't bad, but I had a bad feeling about her.

"An entire wolf pack." Sterlyn's voice broke. "And two members of my pack are with them."

The girl gasped and raised a hand to her mouth. "No."

My anger at her nakedness evaporated as icy fear took over.

"What type of place is it?" Rosemary asked, her wings spreading out wider behind her.

"It's a testing center, but we have suspected they also handle viruses and other biohazardous material." The man took a few steps toward us.

Killian scowled at him, making it clear that he didn't like him moving closer.

"Why would you say viruses?" I stepped up beside Killian and looped my arm through his, hoping to calm him. Jolts coursed down my arm, but I focused on the siblings, wishing they'd brought clothes to change into. Killian relaxed enough to intertwine our hands.

The woman frowned at the gesture.

"They routinely bring in metal briefcases and large containers with biohazard symbols on them." He shrugged. "It's an educated guess."

"Maybe we'll finally get some answers," the woman said hopefully. "We haven't interacted with them—we don't want them to know what we are or that we're near."

Now I really didn't like her, and it had nothing to do with her being naked in front of Killian and everything to do with her sounding happy that our wolves had been taken instead of her pack. "I'm so glad that their capture will provide you with some much-needed clarity."

Levi chuckled humorlessly. "They aren't even my friends, and I wholeheartedly agree with Jewel's sentiment."

Even the demon didn't appreciate her comment.

"Ruby didn't mean it like that." The man lifted his hands in surrender. "She's been the most intrigued by what goes on down there, more so than our father."

That confirmed they were siblings.

"Thanks for speaking on my behalf, Birch." Ruby rolled her eyes and crossed her arms, making her breasts more pronounced. "But like these women, I can speak fine on my own."

"Even with my newfound emotions, I hope I never become that irrational," Rosemary scoffed, and glanced at Sterlyn. "Please tell me if I ever do."

Sterlyn grinned. "I don't think you have anything to worry about."

"Do you know *anything* else about the place?" Killian asked. "Are there normally guards outside?"

Birch shook his head. "That's new. There aren't that

many vehicles in the lot this early. We can't be any more help than that."

So the humans had increased their security measures. Though I'd wager they'd contained the shifters adequately, they weren't sure of our strength, speed, and abilities. Not only that, but they'd also want to make doubly sure that no one unauthorized could get in.

"Thank you. That's more than we knew a few minutes ago." Sterlyn smiled sadly and exhaled. "In the future, we'll try not to encroach on your territory. We know where part of it is now, and we'll be more careful."

"Y'all staying close by for a little while?" Ruby twirled a piece of hair around her finger, her attention settling back on Killian.

If she wasn't careful, I might punch a bitch. I could barely control the fiery rage swirling inside me like never before.

Even though her attention was glued to Killian, he didn't budge from my side, and his attention was on anything but her. That was the only thing keeping me from lunging at her.

"We will have to monitor their activity for a few days and bring in reinforcements." Rosemary rubbed her hands together as if the motion were in tune with her mind. "But we will be *here*, not close by. We have to be able to see the building."

Levi chuckled endearingly. "You're so damn adorable. I love you so much."

"I love you, too, and thank you for the random compliment, though I prefer to think of myself as beautiful," Rosemary said as she squeezed his hand.

"A fellow confident woman." Ruby tossed her hair over her shoulder. "See, brother, it's not a bad thing."

Despite my severe dislike for her, I couldn't argue with that.

Birch rolled his eyes, and then they glowed faintly. Eventually, he said, "I spoke to Dad—he's the alpha of our pack—and I told him what we've learned. Once you get settled, why don't you come by tonight for dinner, and we'll see if our pack can help you."

Maybe they were a good pack of wolves after all. Many packs liked to keep to themselves and not become involved with other people's issues.

"We wouldn't want to impose." Sterlyn thrust her hands into her pants pockets. "Or cause problems for you."

"If they're taking wolves, it could be our problem soon." Ruby raised a hand.

The last thing I wanted was their help, but we didn't know the humans' numbers or what we were up against. One thing was certain: the humans had weapons.

"Okay. What's your address?" Sterlyn removed her phone from her back pocket and plugged in the coordinates.

Within a few minutes, arrangements were made for us to arrive there at six, and the pack headed back to their homes.

As soon as Ruby disappeared, I removed my hand from Killian's. My heart screamed at the loss of contact, but the longer I stayed plastered to his side, the harder it would be to resist the draw between us. The corners of his mouth tilted downward, but he didn't try to force me to remain. Instead, we resumed our positions and were rewarded by a view of the changing of the guards.

Ten hours later, I woke up in the guest bedroom of a house Griffin had rented for the next two weeks. It was on ten acres of land and only a few miles from the building where the pack was being held hostage.

After Birch and Ruby had left us, we'd stayed for a few more hours to watch the guard change. During the day, there was one guard at each corner of the building, but at least fifty guards had entered the building, along with about the same number of people wearing white lab coats, which added merit to the bio-testing/virus theory.

I stared at the white popcorn ceiling, trying to make my mind rest. Even in my sleep, I had dreamed of the fire, fighting, and Mom and my grandparents being experimented on.

My hands clutched the paisley comforter as the peach walls closed in on me. I could now add claustrophobia to my ever-growing list of issues. Lovely.

A faint knock on the door signaled that my alone time was up. "Jewel, we need to head out to meet with *Birch's* pack," Killian said.

Smart man. He knew to use the man's name and not Ruby's, though he clearly didn't enjoy saying it.

I exhaled and threw off the covers. Luckily, there wasn't a mirror in the room. If I saw my reflection, I might refuse to open the door. The more time I spent around him, the harder it was to stay focused on saving my family.

After yanking on the uncomfortable skirt, I marched over and opened the door. As soon as his attention landed on my face, Killian's expression softened and twisted with concern. His fingertips brushed my cheeks as he murmured, "This will be over soon."

I looked as bad as I feared, but it didn't matter. Nothing mattered except saving the others. "Let's hope so."

Not wanting to spend more time alone with him, I

pushed past him, though my feet were difficult to move. I walked down the light brown hallway to the living room.

Sterlyn and Griffin sat on the long, dark coral couch, which rested in front of the double windows and across from the television. Rosemary and Levi sat on the matching loveseat perpendicular to it, their backs to the entryway I'd passed through.

"Are you ready?" Sterlyn asked, then yawned. She wore another black shirt and jeans. Even she had dark circles under her eyes. My grandfather's pack being taken was affecting her as much as it was me.

I nodded. I wanted to go to the local pack and see if they were willing to help.

"Then let's get moving," Griffin said as he stood and headed to the door.

"What about Eliza and Savannah?" Kilian asked from behind me.

Pulling her wings into her back, Rosemary climbed to her feet. "Eliza spelled the house and is staying behind with the human. Sierra, Alex, and Ronnie are on their way to help stake out the area, so we'll have more people to alternate shifts with. She'll let them in when they arrive."

That was for the best. The local shifters hadn't seemed comfortable with Rosemary and Levi, so adding a witch to the mix might make them more hesitant to help.

"I know we discussed that we didn't want a large number of shifters here since we're using another pack's territory to get there and back, but I want some of my own pack to attend when it's time to break the captives out." Killian stood tall and strong just like the alpha he was.

My heart warmed, and I tried to tamp down my emotions toward him. He was just being a good guy. That was all.

"We have to be careful and plan accordingly." Griffin opened the door and waved us out. "Let's roll. We need to get to the spot before the guards change again."

We headed outside, and I paused when Rosemary opened the car door and climbed in to ride with us.

She and Levi think it will make the wolves feel more comfortable if they appear more human, Sterlyn linked.

Good idea. I nodded and climbed into the middle row behind Griffin. Rosemary and Levi had taken the back. Of course, Killian took the spot next to me, and my pulse thudded harder.

Soon, we were pulling out of the gravel road of the rental property and heading toward the pack house.

"Remember, we don't tell them anything about who we are," Killian said as he stared out his window. "We don't need them giving us any trouble and refusing to help us because we're from Shadow City and the Ridge."

"Technically, I'm not." Levi laughed. "For once, being from Hell might benefit me."

"You'd better watch it, or you'll be living there again very soon." Rosemary gritted her teeth. "You live in Shadow Ridge with me and the wolves now, so you are one of us."

"Oh, Rosey. I was teasing," Levi said, and I heard a kissing noise. "Just trying to lighten the mood."

Griffin glanced in the rearview mirror. "To Killian's point, we stick to what they need to know: the Gatlinburg pack was taken. That's it. They can assume what they want from there."

"Understood," I said quickly to prevent Levi from trying to be witty again. I didn't want to hear anyone kissing.

I pressed a finger to my mouth, remembering the feel of Killian's lips on mine.

The oaks and red cedars thinned as a neighborhood of cottages came into view. The houses were various shades of blues, greens, and yellows with an asphalt road running through it all. Each house abutted the woods.

We pulled up to three clothed men waiting at the entrance to the neighborhood. Birch stood next to a man with a similar complexion. He was taller and bulkier though smaller than Killian or Griffin. His dark brown hair was cut short, and his jade green eyes narrowed at our vehicle.

The man I assumed was Birch's father motioned for us to stop and get out.

I didn't blame him. Though we hadn't been threatening earlier, it was clear we were in a desperate situation. I'd also want to check out the visitors before letting them enter my pack territory.

"The first sign that something is wrong, jump back inside," Griffin instructed us as he opened the door.

Sterlyn turned to us. "We'll be fine. They're just being cautious. I didn't feel any ill will from them earlier."

Worst case, we had the car and an angel and demon on our side. But they weren't trying to be threatening. They just wanted to make sure we didn't pose a risk to their pack.

But by the time our group was all out, the alpha's face had turned as red as a tomato. He sneered at his son, then bellowed, "Why the *hell* did you bring *them* here?" He pivoted toward us, his face twisted in disgust. "Don't you realize *who* they are?"

CHAPTER NINETEEN

THE SMALL AMOUNT of hope I had burst like a popped balloon. They recognized Killian. Even though I didn't like Ruby, I'd hoped their pack would help us. I hadn't been in a ton of battles, but I knew that not all the wolf shifters could leave Shadow Ridge to help save Mom and the others because that entire area was still in turmoil.

"What are you talking about?" Birch glanced from his father to us.

The third man, who was in his thirties, shook his head, causing his shaggy reddish-brown hair to fall into his russet-brown eyes. "Think about what's been on the news on repeat for the past three days."

Sterlyn pointed at Killian and said, "If you could at least hear why he did it—"

"*He* isn't the only one to blame for this mess," the alpha spat as he stood straighter. "That angel and the two of you were on television, too. Yes, he may have said the words, but you are all to blame."

"Now, listen here," Griffin growled. "You don't get to talk to her or any of us like that."

I grimaced. Griffin needed to keep his temper in check before things got worse.

"If you don't like it, leave," the alpha said through gritted teeth. "In fact, just leave."

Killian hung his head, and I wanted to rush over and comfort him.

Wings exploded from Rosemary's back as her eyes narrowed.

I hated speaking out of turn since this was a situation my alpha should handle, but I was the only one here who wasn't involved in the scandal. *I hope this doesn't upset you,* I linked before saying, "I felt the same way as you, and in some ways, I still do."

Griffin's head snapped to me. He opened his mouth, then closed it promptly.

No, this is good. He'll connect with your honesty, Sterlyn replied with a little relief. *You're the likeliest to get through to him since you weren't there.*

Though her words were kind, they still stung. Yet another reminder that I hadn't been there to fight alongside my pack. The guilt was so heavy in my stomach that I feared the weight would topple me over.

I took a step but couldn't stop myself from glancing at Killian. His face was twisted in anguish, though I couldn't be certain why.

"You're here with them," the alpha said. "Why should I believe you? For all I know, you were one of the wolves on television."

He had a point, but he also should have known better. I straightened my shoulders, unwilling to cower in front of the man. Though I wasn't an alpha, I was a silver wolf and stronger than any of the men standing before me, especially since it wasn't a new moon. "I wasn't with them during the demon war, and more than that, you'd know if I were lying. Unless you're telling me you're weaker than an average shifter?"

The alpha frowned, not liking my insinuation, but I refused to be bullied, and part of his attitude was because I was female.

"Dad has a point," Birch interjected. "If you blame them, why are you with them?"

I walked past Griffin to the hood of the Navigator. The three men were only five feet away, but I wanted to be close so that if I lied, they could easily smell it.

"Sterlyn is my alpha." I nodded at her. "And I had no one else to turn to." I also didn't realize Killian was their friend at the time, but that wouldn't have mattered. My options were limited.

The reddish-brown-haired guy snorted. "There's no doubt she's telling the truth."

That was what I'd been going for, though Griffin was snarling behind me, and I was pretty sure if I glanced at Rosemary, her feathers would be sticking out everywhere. I'd never seen her that way before, but the image seemed fitting.

Now that they believed me, it was time to rein things back in. "They're doing everything they can to save my mom, grandparents, and their pack. That counts for something."

"Maybe to you, but not to me." The alpha scowled and crossed his arms. "They're helping you because you're part of their pack. If you were anyone else, they wouldn't be here."

Levi strolled to the other side of the hood. "That's not true. In the short amount of time I've been part of this group, I've seen them help acquaintances and strangers without hesitation. Everything they do is for good reason—usually the greater good—even when dealing with their enemies. I've seen them forgive old enemies in the hope that they can change for the better."

Rocking back on his heels, Birch placed his hands behind his back. "Dad, if they're willing to share their reasons for informing the world of our existence, maybe you could reconsider?"

The alpha turned his stony glare on his son.

"Why do you think they'd consider telling us?" The third guy chuckled. "I seriously doubt there was any logic to the decision."

"There *was* logic, and we have no issues with sharing the reasons." Sterlyn lifted her chin and shut her door, showing she was more than willing to stay. "If you give us the opportunity to explain, you'll find out we put a lot of thought into the decision."

My heart hammered. This was important. We'd already met one pack that was unhappy with what Killian and the others had done—there was no doubt we'd run into more. This essentially indicated how willing others would be to listen to their story, and I hoped they chose to. Even I hadn't heard it. If Sterlyn said they had reasons, I wanted to hear each and every one.

"Fine," the alpha growled. "But we'll talk in our home. I don't want to involve any more pack members until I make my decision." He turned to the reddish-brown-haired man. "Astro, go keep an eye on things while Birch and I listen to their story."

Astro's shoulders sagged, but he nodded. "If you change your mind—"

"I won't. Go, do as I say." The alpha puffed his chest.

It took every ounce of self-restraint I had not to roll my

eyes at the overly macho persona the alpha was presenting. Astro was just curious like I was, but the alpha didn't like being questioned.

Thank gods Sterlyn wasn't like that.

Killian came around the Navigator and stopped beside me. His attention was locked on Birch, and the alpha heir arched a brow at the attention.

"Should I pull the vehicle inside?" Griffin asked as he kept a hand on his door.

"Not necessary." The alpha flipped his wrist. "I don't want you pulling into the neighborhood and making my pack curious. Leave it here—no one will be coming or going any time soon."

I'd think more people would be curious about why we *didn't* pull in, but if that made the man happy enough to hear Sterlyn out, so be it. I wouldn't look a gift horse in the mouth.

"Follow me," Birch instructed as he turned on his heel and headed toward the section of cottages on the left.

The alpha stood stationary, likely wanting to follow us to ensure we weren't up to anything fishy.

"Come on," Killian murmured, and touched my arm, tugging me to walk next to him, right behind Birch.

The jolt shot through my arm and into my soul. Each touch was more intense than the last, and my head swam. His scent filled my nose, adding to the effect.

The Navigator turned off, and Griffin's door shut. The scents of musky freesia and leather and myrrh swirled on the breeze as he and Sterlyn walked behind us, and I assumed Rosemary and Levi were in the rear.

Each cottage had about an acre of land around it. I couldn't tell how large the entire neighborhood was, but it went on a ways. The road curved slightly about half a mile in the distance, and I assumed it led to more houses. Most pack neighborhoods had only one way in and out to prevent outsiders from having other ways inside. It limited traffic and reduced the risk of someone causing trouble and escaping.

Birch walked up to the first cottage and ran up the two small steps onto the tiny porch. The white house looked recently painted and well-maintained. He opened the door and entered the living room.

A woman sitting on a cream loveseat jerked her head up, her sparkling aqua eyes focusing on us. Her mouth formed an O as a few tendrils of her light ash-brown hair fell from her messy braid. Ruby sat next to her and grinned when she saw Killian.

Bitch.

We shuffled into the living room and lined up in front of a gray stone fireplace. There weren't many places to sit, just two loveseats perpendicular to each other.

The woman glanced at Killian, then back at the television to our left, and back at him again. I turned my head and found Killian on the screen. It was the same segment Heather and I had seen right after arriving at the Gatlinburg pack homes.

"Birch! Jeremiah!" The woman jumped to her feet and stuck a shaky finger at Killian. "What in the world is *he* doing here?"

At least I had a name for the alpha now.

"Calm down," Jeremiah said as he shut the door. "I didn't know these were the visitors who were coming. Everyone, this is my mate, Dawn."

"How did you not *know*?" She gasped and placed a hand on her chest. "His face is everywhere."

"I'm sorry." Birch rubbed his temples. "Ruby didn't

recognize them, either." He glanced at his sister. "Tell them."

Ruby beamed as she leaned back in her seat. "Of course I recognized them."

Why was I not surprised? Killian clearly intrigued her. Though I didn't blame her, she needed to back the hell off.

Birch's mouth dropped. "And you still let me invite them here?"

This was way too much drama. All I was hoping for was extra help in saving Mom and the others.

"A wolf pack was taken. Isn't it in all our best interest to help them?" Ruby placed her arm on the back of the loveseat.

This was a bad idea, I linked with Sterlyn. *Maybe we should go.*

Let's see if they're willing to help. The more allies we have, the better our odds of getting everyone out with limited casualties. If it doesn't go well, we'll leave without wasting too much time, she assured me. Sterlyn cleared her throat, gaining their attention, and said, "I understand that you're upset, but like we told you out there, we had reasons for telling the world about us."

"Maybe because you allowed someone to videotape you!" Dawn lifted her hands at the television. "Why would you do that?"

"That's what we're trying to tell you." Griffin's nostrils flared. "We didn't set that up. We were in a war with demons, and they were terrorizing humans. The humans fled our towns en masse before the vampires could erase their memories. In all the chaos, humans released video evidence. We didn't know cameras were recording everything!"

Mom had told me about all the chaos. That was why

seeing Sterlyn, Rosemary, and the others on television hadn't been that shocking.

"Look, if you're going to be mad at anyone, it should be me." Killian stepped forward. "I got on camera and informed everyone. Not Sterlyn or Griffin. *Me*."

Sterlyn's earlier words echoed in my mind. *He's protective of those he loves.* Had he done everything so the hatred was channeled toward himself and to shelter everyone else? *Please don't tell me that's why he did it.* I had to hang on to my anger, or everything I'd said and done would be in vain.

"Fine." Jeremiah stood at the door, one hand on the knob, ready to force us to leave at any moment. "I'll blame it entirely on *you*, but that doesn't help matters. I will not help anyone aligned with the person who created this problem. I can't put my pack at risk by associating with you."

"This is *just* like Shadow City," Rosemary scoffed. "People are so self-righteous that they don't give a feather about listening to anyone's voice but their own."

Sterlyn's shoulders shook with soundless laughter. "That issue is a worldwide problem."

"You come here with a self-inflicted problem, asking *my* pack to help you, then make digs at me when I don't give the answer *you* want. You revealed a secret that had been kept longer than any of us can comprehend." Jeremiah's face reddened. "Hell, I didn't even know about that damn city until three days ago when you decided to ruin everyone's lives! Did you think the humans would be okay with us? They fear *everything*. I've heard enough. I hoped your reasons would make things better, but they've only made things worse, and I don't care to hear any more. Your presence is putting my entire pack at risk. You need to go. I sincerely hope you find a way to save your pack, and we won't stop you from trying, but we will *not* risk our necks and have those people find out about us."

And there it was.

"Daddy, helping them could be a *good* thing." Ruby leaned forward, her arms extended.

"Oh, you better shush, child," Dawn rasped while giving her daughter the mom glare. "You will respect your father and alpha, and you have a lot to answer for as soon as they're out that door."

"If you would let us explain, there were people who wanted to distort the message for their own political—" Sterlyn started.

"Like I said, I've already listened longer than I should have. I never should have allowed you to enter my house, and now you're staying past your welcome." Jeremiah's irises glowed. "I said *leave*, or we will make you."

CHAPTER TWENTY

MY HEART HAMMERED. We needed to salvage this situation, but I wasn't sure how. The alpha clearly meant it when he said *leave*.

Rosemary spread out her wings. "I understand you don't want to help, but—"

"It's best if you stop right there," Jeremiah snarled as he lifted a finger. "If I have to tell any of you to get out one more time, I'll call my pack to assist in your departure." His eyes glowed, indicating he was already communicating with at least one person, if not the entire pack.

"Daddy, we don't have to hide anymore!" Ruby shrieked as she jumped to her feet and stomped. "That's a good thing!"

The urge to slap the wench nearly overrode my self-restraint. She appeared to want to "help" us, but she was only escalating the situation. Now her father wasn't only angry at us but also at her for meddling.

"You think it's a *good* thing?" Jeremiah's face turned pink as he parroted the words back. "Tell me how, Ruby? Is it because the humans will want to question every wolf they see and always fear that one of us is trying to harm them? Look at what happened to these people—the humans took an entire *pack*. Before, if a human saw something they didn't understand, they had nothing to blame and brushed it off as impossible. Now, *everything* they don't understand will be blamed on our kind."

Though Killian had become the spokesperson for a reason other than narcissism, I couldn't help but agree with Jeremiah. Outing our entire existence hadn't been a strong solution; rather, it was one that would cause intense problems now and weeks, months, and years down the road.

"Oh, please." Ruby rolled her eyes. "We couldn't stay hidden forever, and Killian did an amazing job on television. He was down-to-earth and pleasant. No one could be scared of him." She bit her bottom lip as she stared at him.

I inched closer to him, fighting the urge to pee on him. Since we weren't mated, that was the closest thing to claiming him I could do.

Even though no one had heard that thought, I winced. I'd never before had the urge to pee on anything in wolf form unless it was a tree. Killian wasn't bringing out the best in me—not like Mom and Dad had in each other.

Killian placed a hand on my waist, and my traitorous body warmed.

"I swear, Dawn. You'd better get her into her room before I do something I regret." Jeremiah pinched the bridge of his nose. "She needs to learn her place."

Head jerking back, I held in a scoff. There was a hell of a lot more going on here than just him being flustered with us.

Birch stepped toward his sister. "I can take her back there so you two don't have to hear her complain all night."

Placing a hand on her hip, Ruby glared. "Nice of you to

point that out since you're a boy and next in line for alpha, even though you're younger than me. You have a place all to yourself while I'm stuck here with them until I find a mate." Her attention flicked to Killian, and I stepped toward her.

Killian's grasp tightened on my waist, bringing me back under control. Going after the alpha's daughter in his own house while he was trying to get us to leave was the worst thing I could do. I had to remember this was about saving Mom, Chad, and the pack, not about whatever connection was brewing between Killian and me.

"She's right." The words rubbed my throat raw. "Though it was less than ideal, Killian had no choice but to share the news, and he handled it better than anyone else could have." I couldn't look at Killian, but I could feel him vibrating with tension.

Jeremiah's hands shook. "*She* is my daughter and part of my pack. You are not and need to go." The light in his eyes glowed brighter. "I've asked you many times, and now you've forced my pack into action."

Head dropping, Ruby submitted to her father.

I'd made the situation worse. I hated leaving without their help, but overstaying our welcome had escalated the tension. I just hoped this pack wouldn't prevent us from watching the facility. I linked with Sterlyn, *What do we do? We need access to watch the building*.

As if to reinforce my point, Griffin's hands clenched, making the atmosphere more volatile.

I'll handle it, she told me, and placed a hand on her mate's shoulder. She continued out loud, "You're right. You've allowed us inside your home against your better judgment, and we've shown disrespect, though that was not our intention. Shadow City is notorious for not having an open mind and not being willing to listen to others, so we assumed the same was going on here, and we've insulted you."

"You weren't far off here, either," Ruby muttered, crossing her arms and flinging herself back onto the loveseat. Her actions were those of a petulant child, which seemed fitting for the situation, but she didn't continue to run her mouth.

Dawn glared at her daughter, but it was Jeremiah who spoke. "You've done enough."

"I'm not a child—" Ruby started.

Her mother cut her off. "Then don't act like one."

The continued disrespect was appalling. I'd never talked to Dad that way, and Jeremiah did seem like a decent alpha. He was protecting his pack, though I disagreed with his methods. That was the luxury of not being an alpha—no one criticized your decisions, thinking they knew better.

Levi cleared his throat and took Rosemary's hand. "We'll leave now."

Rosemary frowned. "But..."

Eyes glowing, Levi used their mate bond to discuss it further. The angel didn't want to leave, but we couldn't push this alpha too far.

Killian's large, warm hand touched my wrist, and a familiar jolt shot up my arm. He nudged me toward the door, positioning me in front of him so he was the last one to go, and said, "I'm sorry my decision to inform everyone upsets you, but I promise, I had the purest intentions even if it didn't come across that way."

"Well, intentions don't mean much when it puts everyone at risk." Jeremiah exhaled, some of his anger gone. He sounded more frustrated or fatigued. "Please go."

Killian placed his other hand against my lower back, and a pleasant buzz nearly took my breath away.

Birch stepped onto the tiny porch and held the door open for our group to exit. He remained silent but nodded toward the Navigator.

"Come on, Rosey," Levi murmured as he led her outside after the alpha heir.

Her feet stayed planted until Levi glanced over his shoulder at her. She huffed, her displeasure clear, but made her way outside, hugging her wings around her body so she could fit through the door easily.

The four of us followed closely behind them.

Jeremiah followed Killian and me outside. He and Birch were making sure we walked directly to the SUV, and I didn't blame them. They didn't know anything except that we weren't above causing drama.

They had a right to feel that way. The news had broken only a few days ago, and humans had already kidnapped and isolated an entire wolf pack. Though my grandfather's pack wasn't as strong as the silver wolves, they were still some of the strongest in this area.

As Jeremiah had promised, several of his pack members arrived in wolf form. Twenty wolves stood a few feet from the house entrance, ten each on the left and right, giving us a clear path through the center. They were going to watch us the entire way into the vehicle, and if there were twenty in sight, I guessed there were just as many out of view for backup.

Birch walked through the center, leading us to the car. The twenty wolves were hunkered down, ready to sprint into action. As Killian walked past the first one, the wolf snapped at his ankle.

My blood warmed as my eyes cut to the dull gray wolf who had tried to bite him. I stepped toward him as Killian´ wrapped an arm around my waist, holding me back.

I tried to get past him, my attention on the coward who had tried to hurt Killian while he'd been preoccupied. "Why don't you try that when someone is ready to fight you?"

"I'm fine," Killian said, just as the wolf lunged at me.

The wolf aimed for my arm, and my training kicked in. I spun out of Killian's grasp and leaned into my leg, kicking the wolf in the snout before he could bite my arm. His head jerked back, and he landed a few feet away on all fours.

Snarls rose around me as the other wolves closed in. We never should've come here.

"If you're going to hurt someone, hurt me." Killian stepped in front of me, taking a protective stance.

No, I was protecting *him*.

The irony that I was most upset about *this* wasn't lost on me, but I could be ashamed about it late, after I finished what I had set out to do.

"That's enough!" Jeremiah shouted from behind us.

The wolves either weren't listening or couldn't hear him.

Two wolves jumped at Killian, and more snarls came from behind us. I turned to see three more approaching.

My chest puffed out. Good, I got the most. See? I was protecting him. My chest deflated just as fast. Holy shit, I had *three* wolves to fight on my own.

As the three wolves sailed toward me, I noted they were focused on Killian. Everyone here was targeting him, which *was* probably why he'd agreed to be the face of the supernaturals. He'd planned to take the brunt of their anger and protect others. I'd suspected as much from his earlier comment, but seeing these wolves aim their anger and aggression at him confirmed it. He hadn't done it for power or influence but to protect everyone he loved.

He was a damn good guy.

Bastard.

Well, now he had someone to protect his back, even if he didn't want me to.

"Get a handle on your pack, or we'll be forced to fight," Sterlyn bellowed as she ran toward us. "We were leaving amicably."

A wolf redirected its attack at me. She wanted to distract me so the other two could hit their mark. Chad had trained me for this situation. Whether Dad had liked to admit it or not, most wolves disregarded me as a threat and focused on the males. I'd trained on how to deflect and protect.

As Chad had taught me, I crouched, ready to strike. When the two wolves leaped at Killian's back, I jumped, forcing my body to spin, and kicked the female wolf in the face as I sailed between the two large wolves and wrapped my arms around their necks. Once my forearms were secured under their chins, I jerked my body back, halting their forward motion, and we tumbled to the ground.

I released them, and the two men turned their anger on me and went for my arms. Pain sliced into my right forearm, and I braced myself for the same pain in my left. It never came. Forcing myself not to overthink it, I punched the wolf that had bitten me in the snout. He whimpered, and his jaw went slack.

"I said enough!" the alpha shouted, his alpha will lacing into his voice. Every pack member froze in place.

"What the *hell* is wrong with you?" Griffin shouted from in front of Killian.

Holding my arm to my chest, I stood, not wanting to seem weak. Sterlyn stood beside me, releasing her headlock on the wolf who'd been attacking me on that side. Killian had claw marks on his arm, but he had a wolf held down by the throat while Griffin was straddling the back of an unconscious wolf. He must have knocked him out with a punch or cut off the wolf's oxygen.

Levi was flickering back into human form next to a wolf that appeared to be knocked out next to Rosemary, who was lowering her wings as she stared at the remaining wolves.

Note to self: never piss off an angel or a demon. I might be part angel, but I didn't have the same fighting skills.

"I didn't intend for this to happen when I called for reinforcements, but surely you can't be surprised by our reaction to your group." Jeremiah rubbed a hand down his face, seeming both flustered and embarrassed. "I will handle my pack, but this should serve as a reminder that people will react strongly to what you've done."

He was right. I'd felt that strongly, too...at first.

Rosemary wrinkled her nose. "You mortals are strange. You say Killian shouldn't have informed the world of our existence because it would incite violence against our kind, yet in all my years, I've seen more violence on the supernatural side. Violence is already running rampant, and instead of working together, we continue to let this tear us apart and form a wider divide."

"It won't be the humans who destroy us," Sterlyn added, climbing to her feet to stare each wolf, followed by Birch and Jeremiah, in the eye. "We will. Shadow City's history will repeat outside of its walls unless you learn from our fall and the secrets that were exposed as repercussions."

There it was again. *Repercussions.* It sounded like they hadn't wanted to share the news. I needed answers from more perspectives instead of letting my anger drive me and blur my end goal.

"Maybe, but for now, you need to go." Jeremiah flicked

his wrists. "Birch, get them out of here. I have a pack to deal with."

Not wanting Killian to see my injury until it had more time to heal, I hurried to the vehicle. I trusted that the alpha would deal with his pack.

The six of us climbed into the car. I opted to sit behind the passenger seat so my injury would be out of view, and Killian sat beside me.

Before I could shut my door, Birch stepped up and gently took my arm. He murmured, "I'm sorry that happened. Dad didn't expect it, and by the time he realized what was going on, you'd already gotten hurt."

At least Jeremiah hadn't planned it. I only wished he'd alpha-willed his pack sooner. "Will your pack give us trouble while we monitor the building?" My voice cracked. I was afraid of the answer.

"Dad meant it when he said he hopes you get your pack back." Birch pressed his lips together. "You'll be fine, and make sure you clean that when you get home." He stepped back and shut the door.

I almost wished he hadn't. I could feel Killian's gaze boring a hole into the side of my face. I didn't need to look at him to know he wasn't happy, though I wasn't sure about what—Birch checking on me or the fact I'd gotten hurt protecting him.

He had no right to be upset.

The ride back to the farmhouse was silent. Killian stared at me the entire way. My body buzzed from the attention, which frustrated me.

Back at the house, a luxury sedan was parked out front. That had to be Ronnie and Alex. Though I hadn't met them, they were the only people we were expecting.

We all got out of the SUV, and I headed to the front door.

Killian hurried around the vehicle and stepped in front of me, blocking me from going into the house. "We'll catch up to you all in a minute. I need to talk to Jewel alone."

He hadn't even asked. Just told me what to do.

Part of me liked it, which made the other part furious. I focused on my fury, though that was the exact thing I always tried *not* to do.

CHAPTER TWENTY-ONE

KILLIAN'S IRISES darkened to dark chocolate as they locked on my injured forearm. I lifted my chin, feigning defiance. The truth was, I was exhausted and didn't want to fight anymore. "I'd rather go inside."

The door shut, leaving us alone...and the noise was deafening.

He smiled sadly. "Don't worry. I won't keep you long."

I hated how his words tugged at my heart. All I wanted to do was rub my body all over him. The need was growing so strong that it took all my willpower to keep my distance from him. I feared what would happen if I allowed one ounce of weakness. He commanded so much of my attention now that if I let him consume me, Heather's life would be for naught, and my goal of saving my family would be forgotten. "I should go. When I'm around you, I sometimes forget that my family and Chad are in danger, and I can't—" I stopped the words, but the damage was done. The truth had slipped from my lips, but worse than that, I'd revealed the depth of my obsession with him.

"You underestimate your strength, but I would never

want to do anything to make you feel as if you're letting your family down. That's a burden I don't want you to live with." His voice deepened as if he were haunted by something...or someone.

My heart squeezed uncomfortably, and I wanted to ask him to share his pain. Dad had said that sharing your burden with someone you cared for made things more bearable. But that was the thing. Every moment I spent with him, I was seeing the *real* Killian, not the one I'd built up in my head and hated. My urge to be with him...just to be near him...had increased tenfold. It was best for me to wait until Mom and the others were safe. "Why did you want to see me alone?" I breathed.

The question hung around us. I had meant it innocently, but the weight of the words was hard, even for me. I wanted him to slam me against the SUV and kiss me, but I also wanted him to be an asshole. I'd learned that neither option would be the one he took because he was sincerely the most wonderful man I'd ever met.

"That's a loaded question," he murmured as he stared at my lips. "There are so many ways to answer it."

My body warmed, and my breath caught. My heart begged for him to close the distance between us.

"But the real answer is I wanted to thank you." His focus flicked down to my injured arm. "I hate that you got hurt because of me," he rasped. "But if you hadn't been there, well, I'd hate to think where I would be. Bart trained you well."

Bart.

Dad.

A lump formed in my throat, and I couldn't swallow. "Thanks." Though I'd tried to say it quickly and strongly, the word broke. I missed Dad so damn much, but hearing

Killian say that made me feel like Dad would've been proud if he'd been alive.

The thought pierced my heart with devastating pain.

"I'm sorry you're going through this," Killian murmured as he tucked a piece of hair behind my ear.

Somehow, I managed not to lean my head into his hand. I exhaled and snorted humorlessly. "It'll be mostly healed by morning." I raised my forearm to show him that the bleeding had slowed.

"I didn't mean your wound, though I wish it never happened." He dropped his hand back to his side. "I meant the conflicting emotions I caused by telling you that Bart trained you well. It's the worst sort of bittersweet feeling that only someone who's gone through the same thing can understand."

Darting my gaze to the grass, I blinked as my eyes burned. I didn't want to cry, especially outside the house where there were two people I'd never met before. "Sometimes, it feels like he's still alive, and I reach for my phone to call him. Then I remember. It's like losing him all over again, but at the same time, I'm afraid the pain will stop coming." I rubbed a hand down my face. "I sound insane."

"Not at all," Killian said as he stepped closer to me. "My entire family died while I was at a *party*." His face morphed from the kind man I knew to a snarl full of contempt and disdain. "A party I thought was more important than assessing a potential threat that a bear shifter had identified while running through the woods. I blew it off, thinking the bear was messing with us.

"At the time, the shifters were more divided than before Shadow City fell. But the bear shifter had been right, and my entire family died while I was celebrating my senior year.

"Each time I walk by Olive's room without feeling any pain, it petrifies me. I already let them down once, and in a way, walking through the house without a hint of remembering them feels like I'm letting them down all over again. Every time people tell me I'm the alpha my dad always saw in me, it's like they're ripping open a wound, especially since their deaths are on my hands. So I understand a little bit of what you're going through."

Unable to stop myself, I raised my uninjured hand and touched his chest. I wished I could take away his pain. He carried such a heavy burden, one that wasn't his to bear. "I won't try to mitigate your guilt." In a way, he and I were the same. Similar situations haunted me. "Because I *understand*. If I'd been with the silver wolves to help in the battles, maybe more would be alive. If I'd stayed with my grandfather's pack instead of going into town with Heather, maybe they wouldn't have been taken. Just know, if you need someone to talk to, I'm here."

He inhaled sharply. "I won't try to stifle your guilt, either, though you've done nothing wrong."

"That's attempting to stifle." The corners of my mouth tipped upward. Though we were both hurting, baring my soul to him felt right. Of course he'd be the one person who understood me, though I hated the reason. Every inch of me wanted to take his torment away. "And I could say the same to you." However, it would be pointless. Neither one of us believed it. All we could do was try to rectify how we'd let down everyone we loved.

He chuckled, though pain reflected in his eyes. "Being with you makes the hurt more bearable. You're the rainbow after the storm."

Stomach fluttering, I moved closer to him. I'd never thought I'd be the type of girl who turned to mush for a man, but here I was. The sincerity of his words and feelings was undeniable. His sandalwood scent filled my nose, and the energy between us jolted into my soul.

He was the only thing I could focus on.

"And that's why I'll respect your wishes. Because I understand the importance of putting family first." He placed his forehead against mine. "I would never want to do anything to add to the burden you carry. I'll be right beside you the entire way, and when you're ready for something more between us, you'll know exactly where to find me."

At first, I didn't understand his meaning, but reality crept into my mind. My face burned with shame. Just like I'd feared, being around him had made me forget. How could I have a moment of happiness when Mom, Chad, and my grandparents were in trouble?

"Hey," he whispered as he ran his fingers through my hair. "It's okay."

I shook my head and stepped back. "No, it's *not*. I lose focus when I'm near you. It's both magical and infuriating. But if something happens—" I cut off, unable to continue.

He gently pulled me against his chest, careful with my injured arm. I'd never felt so safe before, and guilt crushed me. Mom and the others weren't safe. I didn't have the right to feel this way.

The front door swung open, followed by a groan. "Seriously! Even Killian finds someone before me. Come *on*!" Sierra exclaimed.

Stomach lurching, I wanted to bury my head in Killian's chest. Instead, I disentangled myself from his arms and put distance between us.

Sierra frowned deeply as she glanced between us. Then she stomped her foot and sighed. "Ugh, sorry. That was me being a jerk, but my gods. *I'm* the hopeless romantic of the group, yet here I am, the last to find someone."

"Maybe if you learned to stay quiet every once in a while, Fate would show you more favor," an unfamiliar voice said from inside. He had a not-quite-British accent—I couldn't determine where it might be from.

Sierra glanced over her shoulder. "I can't help it that your old ass can't keep up with my modern wit."

"You do realize my soulmate is a woman close to your age." The man sidestepped Sierra and joined us outside. "And I, for one, am glad if Killian has found someone." The man was a tad shorter than Killian and handsome in the opposite way. His angular features emphasized his pale blue eyes. His sun-kissed brown hair was brushed to one side and contrasted with his fair complexion. He wore a white button-down shirt with black slacks, and his stance was regal. This had to be the vampire king.

"You do obviously like them young." Sierra smirked, her gray eyes lightening with mirth. "And Ronnie has a *thang* for men older than her grandparents."

I wished I were as brazen as Sierra. I wasn't the silent type, but I definitely didn't go around poking at people's weak spots.

"Oh, Sierra." A woman with gorgeous copper hair wrapped an arm around the spunky girl. Her emerald irises twinkled. She was several inches shorter than Sierra, making her around five and a half feet. "My grandfather was a prince of Hell, and Alex is nowhere close to his age."

"Touché." Sierra wagged her finger. "It's amazing how Alex grunts and groans at me, but you're just as witty."

"*Wit* isn't my concern with you. It's more your constant babbling." Alex rolled his eyes and focused on me. "I'm sorry to meet you in this fashion. I'm Alex, and this is my wife, Ronnie."

Mom had told me about the vampire-demon hybrid vampire queen, but I hadn't expected someone with such a strong demon heritage to be so compact.

Great, now I was stereotyping people by their size, the very thing I criticized so many—especially men—for doing. "Mom told me all about you."

"Well, she spoke about you often." Ronnie smiled and closed the distance between us. Her attention flicked to my hand. "That must be the injury Sterlyn mentioned when telling us what happened with the local pack."

I moved my arm behind my back, hating that I'd been injured. Not that I wanted others to have been hurt, but it again reinforced that I didn't have the battle experience of everyone else. "It's nothing. It should heal quickly."

"Don't be surprised if either Rosemary heals you or Mom doctors you up." Ronnie lowered her voice in warning. "They take care of every one of us when we're injured. Granted, blood heals me now, but they always have their hands full, taking care of the injured."

"You all get hurt often?" Every one of them seemed fierce. Indestructible.

Killian laughed as he stood beside me, so close that our arms touched. "You did see me almost die yesterday."

My blood ran cold despite the warm jolt of our connection. That seemed like forever ago, but he was right. It was just yesterday. The memory of his pale complexion and the sound of his weakening heart would always haunt me. "But that was because you were protecting me." If he'd died, that would have been yet another life lost because of me.

"Most of us have been constantly on the brink of death this past year," Alex said as he walked behind Ronnie and placed his hands on her shoulders. "That's what we do. Protect one another."

Killian turned his gaze on me. "Kind of like you protected me."

He had me there. My natural instinct was to protect him, and I didn't regret it one bit, even with my arm still throbbing from the bite.

Suddenly, my connection with Mom warmed in my chest, drawing my focus inward. The sensation was similar to a pack member waking up, so it should've been comforting—except it wasn't. If she was awake, I wasn't sure what that meant about what they were doing to her. *Mom*, I linked.

Jewel, Mom replied, her panic slamming into me. My heart raced. *Did they catch you, too?*

No, they didn't. My eyes blurred. At least she was coherent enough to speak.

The jolt of Killian's and my connection increased, making me focus outward as well.

"Jewel!" Killian said loudly with panic. "What's wrong?"

"Mom. She's awake." I blinked, causing tears to fall down my cheeks. "I wasn't expecting it, and I'm not sure what it means."

Sterlyn, Griffin, Rosemary, and Levi joined us. Killian must have linked with them.

Then we must be close to the cabins, Mom connected again. *I didn't expect us to be close enough to communicate, but they probably don't know how it all works.*

When I replied, I added Sterlyn to the link. *No, you aren't close by. I got Sterlyn and a few others, and we came back to locate you. The humans burned down the cabins, and it was a trap.* I left out the news about Heather's death. We had enough to contend with. *They captured Chad, but Levi followed them in his demon form, so we were able to locate you.*

They have Chad. Mom's connection warmed to normal, as if that had startled her awake. *Sterlyn is with you?*

Yes, I am, along with Griffin, Rosemary, Levi, Killian, Eliza, and Sierra, Sterlyn replied as she pushed calm through the connection. *Once we know what we're up against, more pack members will come.*

No, we can't risk it, Mom linked, unaffected by the calm Sterlyn had sent. *These humans knew what they were doing when they attacked. They took out the wolves who were doing a perimeter check. Dad felt them go unconscious and was about to go look for them when the house was flooded with gas that put us to sleep.*

That was why they hadn't connected with Heather and me. They'd been knocked out. But how would humans know that we could communicate like that? That shouldn't be common knowledge, especially given the short time between the world learning about shifters and these humans taking the pack.

You all need to leave. Mom's concern filled the bond. *I can't risk anything happening to Jewel.*

Normally, I obeyed my parents, but something had been changing in me ever since Dad's death. Now, with Mom being taken, I couldn't be the obedient daughter any longer. *And I can't risk anything happening to you, Chad, my grandparents, or anyone else there with you. Do you hear what you're asking me—what you're asking us to do?*

I just want you safe. Mom's guilt washed over me, making it hard to breathe.

We both carried demons. *And I couldn't live with myself if something happened to the pack.*

She's right, Mila, Sterlyn interjected. Her lips mashed together as she nodded. *None of us are leaving. The humans won't stop with you. You're pack and family, and we always take care of our own, which includes your parents and their pack.*

A strange combination of emotions came from Mom, and I sensed she wasn't sure what she was feeling. That was one thing about the bonds—unless you actively shut it down, the pack experienced your emotions.

Those flowing through to me changed to straight terror.

My palms became sweaty, and the hair on the nape of my neck rose. Someone was watching her. *Mom, what's wrong?*

CHAPTER TWENTY-TWO

THE SECONDS CREPT BY, but it felt like an eternity as I waited for Mom to answer.

People are dressed in white scrubs, Mom linked. *They're coming toward my cage.*

Cage.

They'd crated her like a fucking dog?

Can you fight them? Even as I asked the question, I already knew the answer. She was in a heavily guarded building with an entire pack locked up and under control. Even if she tried to fight them, she likely wouldn't get far. Freeing her would take a coordinated effort, and unfortunately, she couldn't pack link with the others.

Sterlyn rushed to me and placed a hand on my shoulder. Even though she was trying to provide comfort, the world closed in around me.

Mom was in danger, and here I was, unable to do a damn thing. This was how I'd felt when Dad's link faded after he'd taken a bullet for Sterlyn. I'd been safely tucked away and nowhere nearby when his life had been stolen from him.

What if the same thing was happening to Mom?

I pivoted on my heel. I had to get to her. Staying here helpless was no longer an option.

I raced toward the woods, ready to head back to the spot that overlooked the building. The other pack wouldn't help, so the best option we had was to observe and find out how to break them out of that prison. That had been the original plan, anyway.

They aren't letting me out, Mom replied. *They're taking my blood, and whatever they injected me with is making me sleepy.*

There was no telling if they were sedating them to keep them restrained or if they were knocking her out to move her. And I wouldn't learn the answer here at the farmhouse, distracted by a sexy-ass man who made the world seem right despite everything being wrong. I had to get there and save them.

"Jewel, rushing into battle is never advisable," Rosemary said as she landed in front of me, her wings spread out, blocking my path. "Impulsive actions will likely lead to your capture and possibly that of everyone else here."

I'd never been on the receiving end of a scolding like this before. I was usually so cautious, needing to ensure my anger didn't influence me. Still, I wouldn't apologize for worrying about the people I loved. "I'm not rushing to the building. I just want to scope it out. We wasted time asking that pack to help us."

She scanned me and must have found whatever she was searching for, because her wings lowered, and she nodded. "Levi and I can go with you."

"Me, too," Killian rasped as he moved up beside me. His presence eased some of my worry, frustrating me.

"That's a horrible idea." Rosemary furrowed her brows.

"The local pack just attacked you. Do you think it's wise to risk provoking them now?"

She was right. I wanted him close—things didn't seem so dire with him near—but split up and without Jeremiah around, that would only risk another attack. On top of that, my attention would be divided.

"But—" Killian pouted.

Ronnie flanked me and said, "Alex and I will go. That way, Alex can stay close while Levi and I change into demon form and slip inside. Rosemary can fly over and keep an eye on the local pack."

My chest expanded, but I tried to hold back my hope. "Won't they hear the door open? They saw Chad's body move when Levi tried to pull him away."

"We can fit through small crevices, so no door opening is required." Ronnie winked.

I exhaled, a weight lifting from my shoulders. Maybe our situation wasn't as dire as I feared. Though we were outnumbered, Levi and Ronnie could give us a clear picture of what was going on in there.

Still, freeing a pack of nearly two hundred shifters was a huge undertaking, so we needed every advantage we could find.

Alex patted Killian's shoulder and said, "I'll keep an eye on her. You have my word." His lips mashed into a straight line.

Nodding, Killian sagged. "If anything seems weird—"

"Oh, gods," Sierra moaned as she waltzed over and slid her arm through Killian's. "You act like you won't see her again."

He glared at her, and she tensed.

All I could focus on was my irrational desire to yank Sierra away from him by the ends of her hair. I inhaled deeply, trying all over again to calm my insane need to pee on him. They were friends, nothing more, but red still filmed my vision.

"I do believe a certain someone is attempting to start a catfight." Levi snorted as he waggled his brows.

My face burned. Obviously, I wasn't concealing my jealousy well.

"Where?" Rosemary looked around, her wings spreading. "I don't sense panthers nearby."

"No, love." Levi closed his eyes, though his face lit up with adoration. "It just means that—"

Rosemary lifted a hand while her wings lowered. "If it's another modern saying that doesn't make sense to me, just stop. I thought you were warning us of another threat."

"Gods, how I missed her." Sierra giggled but wisely detangled her arms from Killian's.

Sterlyn waved us on. "You five, go. Griffin and I will get some rest and relieve you in a few hours. We'll schedule a rotation so we don't become too exhausted to keep an eye on things."

Though I hated to leave Killian, I had to find out what was happening with Mom and the missing pack.

We took off, ready to survey the area for the night. With each step I took away from Killian, my stomach churned more strongly. My wolf whimpered, growing frustrated with my stubbornness, but even if it was a mistake, it was mine to make.

It was approaching ten, and I rubbed my hands together to diffuse some of my nervous energy. I winced as the sting from the wolf bite coursed through my arm.

Though it was already halfway healed, it still hurt when I put pressure on it. If I'd slept, I would've healed faster, but this stakeout was more important.

Alex seemed content with silence, which boded well for me. I didn't know him and doubted we had much in common. He seemed nice enough, but I wasn't the most comfortable with non–wolf shifter supernaturals.

"Are they okay?" I whispered. I hadn't seen Rosemary for a while, and Levi and Ronnie still hadn't come back. A sense of helplessness surged through me.

We were sitting on top of a hill hidden by trees, watching the facility, and gods only knew what was being done to them right this second.

Alex glanced at me and sighed. "They're checking out the inside and getting a feel for what's going on. So far, they've seen three large rooms filled with cages. The pack has been divided into men, women, and children. All the wolves are sleeping, but the humans have blood samples and are doing tests."

Blood was better than body parts, but there was no telling why they were examining their blood. My stomach revolted at the thought of it.

I got up and paced between the trees, sporadically checking on the guards in each corner. "I hope nothing happens to them in there. It's not like we can do much."

"Oh, I'm aware. I'm feeling the same concerns as you." Alex smirked, though it didn't hide the concern lining his face.

Adding to my misery, I could now add *asshole* to my ever-growing list of qualities. "Ugh. Of course you are. Ronnie's your mate. I didn't mean to be insensitive."

"You weren't. I'm glad you're concerned for their well-being. You wouldn't be a true silver wolf if that weren't the case." Alex leaned against a tree. The slightly more than half-full moon still shone brightly enough to add more paleness to his complexion. "That's what you're bred to be—a protector. Something Killian will have to come to grips with."

My breath caught, and I stared at him. "What do you mean?" I wasn't sure why he'd brought up Killian, but just hearing his name had butterflies fluttering in my stomach.

Alex placed his hands in the pockets of his slacks. "Just that—"

The sound of approaching footsteps cut him off. My heart pounded as I pivoted toward the woods.

Now I wished I'd asked Rosemary to heal my arm.

"Stay right here," Alex murmured, and blurred from view.

Damn vampire speed. I couldn't even object to him leaving before he'd vanished. Not wanting to abandon him to his own demise, I hurried after him. No one else would die or be injured alone.

Tapping into the magic of the moon, I ran, and Alex came into view with Birch and Ruby a few feet in front of him. Fur sprouted on Birch's arms as his wolf surged forward, and Ruby sneered as she crouched. Things were about to get out of hand.

"Guys, wait," I said as I pushed my legs to move faster. "Stop!"

The three of them were focused on each other as if nothing else existed.

"Rosemary!" I said a little louder, not wanting to scream this close to the building. Though I doubted the humans would hear me, I didn't want to chance the sound carrying down from our higher elevation.

Birch's clothes ripped from his body as he changed from

two feet to four paws. Ruby's hand formed claws as her wolf also surged.

Fangs extended from Alex's mouth, and his once blue eyes turned crimson as his vampire bled through.

Even though I was only feet away, it might as well have been a mile. Birch lunged at Alex as Ruby swiped at his side.

I couldn't stop them.

Alex blurred back, avoiding Birch's lunge and Ruby's swipe, but they were already reorganizing. That bought me time to reach them and force my way into the center.

As I ran between them, Ruby swiped at Alex again as fur sprouted from her arm. Her shift was imminent.

Alex blurred, but Ruby had anticipated the move. She changed the course of her hand, and it was clear she could connect.

Something black barreled down from the sky, grabbing Alex a split-second before impact. He hissed loudly, taken by surprise.

The scent of peony rose told me it was Rosemary. She must have heard me call for her.

When Ruby hit air, she shook her head and blinked.

"He's with us!" I said through clenched teeth. "Don't attack him."

Ruby's focus swung to me, and the fur on her arms receded. She blinked and glanced at where Alex had been moments ago. "We were coming to see if any of you were out here, and we found a vampire lurking. They don't hang out in this area, so forgive us for attacking. We didn't realize your group was so diverse."

In her defense, most supernatural races stuck to their own kind. They must have already found it strange that we were allied with Rosemary and Levi; now we'd added a vampire to the mix.

Birch's head tilted. Then he changed back to human.

"I'm grateful that you saved me from her claws, but I prefer my feet on solid ground," Alex said as Rosemary carried him over to me. When she placed him on the ground, Alex pulled at his white button-down. He glared at the now-naked Birch and Ruby. "You just attack people without making sure they're a *risk* first?"

Rosemary laughed, the sound beautiful. Everything about the angel was damn alluring. "I find that joke rather funny."

He cut his almost normal blue irises to her. "It wasn't a joke."

"How could that not be a joke? You and Matthew used to attack people all the time without provocation." Her brows furrowed as the mirth vanished from her face.

She was quite the literal person. I'd never met anyone so straightforward, but it was refreshing. I always knew exactly what she thought.

"I'm not like that *now*." Alex winced. "Not since Ronnie came into my world six months ago."

"I'd normally say that isn't enough time for a person to change, but Levi has taught me otherwise." Rosemary brushed her hair over her shoulders and arched a brow at the wolves. "I don't like them, but I can't blame them for attacking someone they don't know. Though it would've been more strategic to ask questions first."

The corners of my mouth tipped upward. I loved how Rosemary had put them in their place. "They're on edge. We all are." I didn't want to stand up for them, but they'd come here for a reason. I didn't want to piss them off before they informed us why.

"He was racing toward us," Birch growled as he tensed. "What were we supposed to think?"

"It doesn't matter. He's with us." I placed my hands on my hips and lifted a brow. We needed to get back and monitor the building, not stand in the woods, bickering. "Why were you looking for us?"

"We—" Birch started.

Alex cut him off as he snarled, "My wife is on her way. You need to put clothes on before she gets here."

"Uh...why?" Birch looked down at his naked form.

My eyes followed his gaze, and I closed them immediately. Normally, nudity didn't bother me—it was part of being a wolf shifter, after all—but it felt wrong to stare at him, even though it wasn't with lust.

"Because the only person my wife sees naked is *me*." Alex patted his chest. "So go put some clothes on, and then we can talk."

Birch's mouth dropped.

"He doesn't have spare clothes, so either tell your *wife* not to come, or deal with it." Ruby rolled her eyes and focused on me. "Where is TV Guy?"

Of *course* that was the first question she'd ask. The urge to throat-punch her nearly overwhelmed me.

"TV Guy?" Alex rubbed the back of his neck. "What is she talking about?"

"Killian." His name made my throat raw, and I snarled at the end.

Birch shook his head and leaned back on his heels, making things bounce that shouldn't have been capturing my attention. He was well endowed, though I hated acknowledging it. "Ruby," he warned.

"What?" She gestured at me. "I figured he'd be sniffing around wherever she is."

"Of course he would be." Alex's attention locked on me. "Aren't you and Killian together?"

I inhaled, pressing my lips together. That was the loaded question. I wanted to scream *yes*, but it wasn't true, and the sulfuric stench of a lie would reveal the truth, anyway. But I didn't want that bitch to know.

Okay, I did know why. She was into him. I suspected it was because he *was* TV Guy...and also happened to be the most delicious man I'd ever seen. *Opportunist* might as well be written on her forehead.

Rosemary fluffed her feathers. "Not yet, but they will be. I'm certain they're fated mates."

I froze. I'd put aside the possibility of us being fated mates earlier, disregarding it because I had enough to deal with. But her words confirmed what my wolf already knew.

My heart warmed toward the angelic woman. Though I never disliked her, I'd been wary of the way Killian had felt for her at one point.

"All I heard is that they aren't together." Ruby beamed before she forced her expression into one of indifference. "And I'm sure if they were fated mates, they'd be together by now."

"Not considering how stubborn the women in this group are," Alex muttered, rubbing his chin as he stared at me.

I did not like where this conversation had gone, and I wanted Birch to leave and take his sister with him. I tried playing one of my favorite musical pieces in my head, but even that calming technique was failing me. "I'm assuming you came here for a reason?" I snapped.

Blowing out a breath, Birch said, "I just—"

Ruby cleared her throat loudly and glared at him.

"*We* just..." He trailed off and karate-chopped his hand

at her before continuing. "We wanted to apologize for how everything went down. If Ruby had told me who you were, I would've never invited you over, and the attack wouldn't have happened."

"Seriously!" Ruby exclaimed, and stomped her foot. "I thought Dad would want to help save a pack of wolves, and I...well, I didn't know that I *needed* to share. I mean, *they* didn't."

Unfortunately, she had a point, though I would never admit it. "You didn't have to come all this way to apologize. We understand where your dad was coming from. He did what he thought was best for the pack."

"Still, I hate what happened, and I wanted you all to know that I truly am sorry." Birch kicked at the ground, making the whole naked thing even more uncomfortable.

"You came and apologized. Good deed officially accomplished." Alex moved his hands in a shooing motion. "Now you can find some clothes."

He was possibly more ill at ease with Birch's naked state than I was.

"Normally, I'm not uncomfortable with nudity, but since being mated, I have to agree." Rosemary shrugged. "But is there anything else you want to discuss?"

"No, we'll go," Birch said as he took Ruby's arm. "You guys have a good rest of the night."

The two of them walked off, and Alex grumbled, "I'm just glad I told Ronnie that everything was okay before she could get here."

For some reason, his possessiveness was endearing instead of assholey. That was the thing about fated mates—protectiveness was ingrained in the bond, and it had nothing to do with trying to dominate each other.

Rosemary took to the air. "I'll keep an eye on the

surrounding area. If you need me, call out for me again. I was able to hear you just fine."

That was comforting. I hadn't been sure how well angels could hear.

Sighing, I headed back to the cliff with Alex to keep an eye on things.

As PROMISED, Sterlyn and Griffin showed up around midnight to relieve us. Ronnie came back and informed us of everything she'd seen, which wasn't much. All the wolves were sedated, while the humans continually took blood and tested it without talking much.

Levi and Rosemary were going to stay behind to see if anything changed once the third shift headed in, so Ronnie, Alex, and I headed back to the farmhouse. The moon was still rising, and nocturnal animals rustled all around us.

Eliza and Savannah had prepared a meal and had leftovers waiting for us, and my stomach rumbled in anticipation.

It wasn't long before the farmhouse came into view, and some of the tension in my body began to recede. Killian was near.

The smell of overly sweet perfume that young girls wore, thinking they smelled good, hit my nose, followed by a high-pitched giggle.

"Oh, Killian," Ruby murmured, and giggled again loudly. "You're so funny."

Hell, no. She'd run over here as soon as she'd learned we weren't together?

My hands clenched as fury burned in my chest, hot and wild.

The smart thing to do was go inside. Killian *wasn't* mine. I kept pushing him away and had no right to be upset. But my feet had a mind of their own, and they marched toward the voices. When I turned the corner of the house and took in the view of a swinging bench hanging next to a round table and chair, I almost came unglued.

It was worse than I'd imagined.

CHAPTER TWENTY-THREE

MY HEART FRACTURED as I watched Ruby, sitting next to Killian on the rocking swing, place her legs across his lap. The bench faced a towering grove of red cedars and oak, and the starry sky was clear and definitely romantic.

That should be *me* there next to him. Not *her*.

My nails bit into my palms, and I took a deep breath to calm the raging inferno inside me. How the hell did she even know where we were staying?

My feet stopped moving. Ruby must have followed my scent through the woods. I'd led her straight to him.

Killian pushed her feet from his lap. "I just said it was a pretty night and that I was tired and needed to head inside. There was nothing funny about it."

"I love it when a man plays hard to get," Ruby cooed as she leaned over to him and ran a finger across his chest. "It makes the capture that much more rewarding."

I growled, unable to hold it in. Those breathing exercises Dad had drilled into me were not helping me *one bit*. He'd sworn that breathing would clear my head, but I decided it only gave me crystal clarity on all the ways I could kill her and bury the body so she'd never be found.

Huh...maybe that *was* rational. The thought definitely had merit and eliminated all my problems.

Killian pushed her off him and stood.

Maybe if he'd done that earlier, Ruby wouldn't have gotten her scent all over him.

He smiled at me. "You're home."

My heart flipped, pissing me off even more. He didn't have a right to look at me that way after he'd let her touch him. "Disappointed?" I sounded sour to my own ears.

Ruby smirked as she climbed to her feet and stood next to him, watching me.

She really was a bitch.

Alex chuckled as he and Ronnie paused on their way to the front door. "Thank gods we're over that part."

"I agree. Their beginning might be even rockier than ours was," Ronnie replied, and took his hand, tugging him toward the door. She paused to look at me. "Do you want me to stay?"

The longer I stayed here, showing my anger, the happier *Ruby* would be. The best thing I could do was go inside. Killian and I weren't together, and if he wanted some smelly, overly ripe female rubbing herself all over him, well, I didn't have a right to be upset. He'd done nothing wrong.

So why did it *feel* like he was cheating?

A sharp pain stabbed my heart and didn't relent. If anything, it intensified. My wolf whimpered, adding to my agony. The pain was worse than anything I'd ever experienced, which was saying something. This was why I was trying not to be *with* him. He overwhelmed me, and we weren't even together. I couldn't imagine if I gave in to the desire.

"I'm going in, too." Staying out here with Ruby making advances on him would drive me to let that anger take over. He'd said he would wait on me, but I was the one pushing him away. He could do anything he wanted.

Part of me wondered if he would even want me after Ruby got her claws into him. She might be annoying, but she was beautiful.

Killian took a few hurried steps toward me, leaving Ruby behind. "I was just telling Ruby I was going in as well."

Those words should've comforted me, but instead, they infuriated me. He'd been sitting out here alone with her under the sparkly sky while I'd been watching over a building where my family were prisoners, accompanied by a vampire king who'd grumbled about Birch's nudity the entire time. This situation was beyond not fair.

"But Killy..." Ruby pouted.

She had a *fucking* nickname for him? And here I'd thought I couldn't hate her more.

My wolf inched forward, wanting to take a bite out of her, and I was afraid she'd do far worse if I let her out.

"*Killian*," I seethed through gritted teeth. "That's his *name*."

"Killy's a nickname I came up with while we spent some time together." Ruby flipped her hair over her shoulder and moved up to Killian's side.

I clenched my jaw. How much *time* had they spent together?

"Oh, boy," Ronnie murmured. She hurried past Alex and took my arm. "You said you were coming inside, so let's do that."

When she first tugged, I resisted. I could easily break Ruby's nose so it would heal crooked. That might make her look more homely. Or I could rip out a chunk of her hair. Actually, the combination would be better. There were so many tantalizing possibilities.

Ronnie yanked harder. "Come *on*, Jewel." She lowered her voice so only I could hear with my silver wolf ears. "Before you do something you can't take back."

My head snapped away. I was letting the rage I'd always feared get the best of me, and Ronnie was right. If I hurt Ruby, I might enjoy it in the moment—gods, I would enjoy it in the moment—but I'd seen what happened when Mom gave in to her anger and the intense guilt she carried afterward. I couldn't be like that.

No. I *refused* to be like that.

Giving in, I allowed Ronnie to pull me away. I hadn't known this woman long, but she was already a friend and had prevented me from doing something stupid.

When I'd heard that our pack was integrating back into society, I'd been concerned. I wasn't used to being around any supernaturals besides silver wolves. But being with this group was easy. The differences I'd expected to divide us weren't an issue, and our varying abilities were a strength. We were working together toward a common goal.

Maybe Sterlyn had it right.

"Ruby, thanks for visiting, but it's time I walk you home," Killian said.

He was going to *walk her home*? My rage became all-consuming. I might not ever feel sane again. My vision hazed, and my breathing turned ragged.

I was a complete and utter mess.

"Actually, *Killian*," Ronnie said, "Alex and I will walk her back. You said you were tired, so you should go inside."

"Sounds great," Killian said, at the same time Ruby said, "No, he can walk me."

"I *insist* we be the ones to escort you to your territory line," Ronnie replied. "Right, Alex?"

Alex groaned. "Yes, and she can point out areas we should avoid. Just please tell me there won't be any *naked* people walking around. There's only one person I ever want to see naked again, and if you aren't clear on who that is, I can assure you it is not *any* wolf."

Under any other circumstances, I'd find his discomfort funny, but not now. Not with *her* so close to Killian.

Releasing her hold on my arm, Ronnie hurried over and grabbed Ruby similarly. "Let's go. We don't need the wolves hunting us down and trying to attack my husband again."

"But—" Ruby tried to plant her feet on the ground, but Ronnie kept pulling until they'd moved past me. The wolf shifter tried again, saying, "Let me tell Killy—"

That was it. I was going to beat her ass.

I started after her, but a familiar large hand took mine. The jolt shocked my system, and I went still, trying to catch my breath. The mixture of pleasure, pain, and hope swirled inside me, making me feel insane.

"Goodnight, Ruby." Killian sighed. "Just...please talk to your dad like you said you would."

Ruby glanced over her shoulder, giving him a dazzling smile. "I will." She wasn't even fazed by him holding my hand.

Now I wanted to hurt him. My free hand fisted, and I got ready to punch him in the face. He'd just given her a reason to visit him again.

Maybe that was what he wanted.

I told myself to let go of his hand, but I couldn't bring myself to do it. I needed an anchor, and unfortunately, he was it. And as much as I wanted to punch him, I also wanted to kiss him. The split personality inside me went to war once again.

After the three of them had vanished into the tree line, my wolf stirred restlessly. Normally, she would've been appeased, but she was as riled up as my emotional side. I jerked my head toward Killian and snapped, "Why did you *do* that?"

He stared blankly. "Do what?"

"Offer to walk her home!" My voice rose, though I hadn't meant for it to. I found the power to yank my hand from his as I glared. I was acting like a child, but I couldn't help it.

"It's dark, and there's a warehouse full of trapped wolf shifters nearby." He lifted his hands. "I didn't want anything bad to happen to her."

A pang of betrayal coursed in my chest, and I rubbed it. "So you *are* interested in her." I held my breath, ready for him to destroy my entire world.

"What?" He took a step back and stared at me like I'd grown a second head. "*No.* Why would you think that? I've made it clear that I want you, or I thought I had."

Stomach fluttering, I let all the conflicting emotions wash over me. This mixture of desire, anger, pain, and adoration was not normal. I waved a hand at the hanging bench. "You were sitting outside alone with her for gods know how long, then you wanted to walk her *home.*"

"First, I was out here waiting for you. I came out when Sterlyn and Griffin left to relieve you. Second." He held up two fingers. "She got here a few minutes ago, and I didn't want to be rude. And last, though I have no particular feelings for her, I still don't want her, or anyone else, to get hurt. I'd have felt the same about Birch."

"So you would've walked Birch home?" I squared my

shoulders and held his gaze, knowing the answer.

Killian hung his head. "No, but...Ruby's not like you or Sterlyn."

I jerked back as if I'd been slapped. "Is that supposed to be an insult?"

He ran his fingers through his hair and closed his eyes. "Not at all. I just meant she's not strong and capable like you and Sterlyn." He exhaled. "I swear, every time I'm around you, I get tongue-tied and mess things up. You're so damn caring and the most beautiful girl I've ever laid eyes on. I would never want you to think I was insulting you."

Pulse quickening, I swallowed hard. "You think I'm the most beautiful girl you've ever seen?" Out of everything I should have focused on, *that* was what I'd come out with?

"There's no question about it," he rasped as he opened his eyes and stared into mine. "There is absolutely nothing you need to worry about with Ruby or anyone else."

At those words, my world righted itself, and the pain receded.

He gestured toward where Ruby had vanished. "It's good that she came, though. She told me she'd talk to her dad again about helping us."

Anger slammed right back into place, knocking the breath out of me. "And you *think* she'll be able to do that?" I chanted internally, *Please don't be that stupid.*

"My parents always listened to Olive and me." Killian shrugged. "Maybe he does the same thing with his kids."

Of course his parents had been good people, because he was an outstanding person. The fact he thought she could sway *her* father was laughable. "Were you there with us when we visited their pack and got attacked on our way out?"

"You know I was." His forehead wrinkled. "Why in the

world would you ask that?"

"Because if you think she has any influence on her father, maybe a demon or an alien took over your body." I wasn't sure if aliens existed or if demons could possess people. They probably couldn't, but their shadow forms could seep into small places, so I'd go with it.

He laughed. "No, it was me, and I do agree with you. But it doesn't hurt to have her try, does it?"

Ugh. I needed him to fight back, not understand. That just pissed me off more. Then add in the fact that she'd be back time and time again to see him?

My wolf howled in protest.

He was *ours*.

Before I could think about the consequences, I'd closed the distance between us and placed my lips on his. There was one clear way to stop her from coming back and rubbing all over him.

Make him *mine*.

He took a quick breath as I swiped my tongue against his full lips. I hadn't tasted him last night, but I was changing that now. He opened his mouth, allowing my tongue entrance, and his faint citrus taste, combined with his delicious scent, made me dizzy.

This was better than anything I'd ever imagined.

Lips buzzing, I pushed him backward toward the swinging bench. I needed to make him mine *now*.

He moaned as he threaded his fingers into my hair and didn't fight where I was leading him. I slowly guided him to the bench, and when the back of his legs hit the seat, I pushed him down and climbed onto his lap, straddling him.

His hands clenched my waist as his tongue danced with mine, but I needed more. I needed *all* of him.

I rocked against him, shivering as his hardness pressed

against me and he grabbed my hips. My body heated, and the scent of his arousal wafted into my nose. He groaned, "Jewel, you gotta stop. You're going to kill me."

I lifted back a little. "You don't like this?" I blushed. I'd never done anything like this before, so maybe I was doing something wrong.

"I *love* this—" he started.

That was all I needed to hear. I cut him off with a kiss as my hand inched toward his jeans. Maybe if I touched him, he would like it better.

I reached the button and moved both hands to unfasten it, but he caught one wrist in his strong grip. "Not like this."

"But you said you liked it." My eyes burned, and I had to fight the urge to hide my face. I had no clue what I was doing, but it *felt* right.

He shook his head, and a tear trailed down my cheek.

"Oh, baby." He wiped it away. "I didn't say I liked it—I said I *loved* it, and I do. But this needs to be done right."

"This can be right. We need to do this *now*." I didn't want Ruby touching him, laughing with him, being near him ever again. I needed to claim him.

His brows furrowed. "Why? We have eternity."

"Because *she* needs to know you're *mine*," I growled. "She needs to back off."

"That's why you're doing this?" He arched his brow and grinned. "You're worried about Ruby?"

The warmth left my body, and I leaned back, putting distance between us. "Why is that funny?"

"It's so damn sweet. You want to claim me to make her back off, and part of me wants you to," he said as he brushed his thumb against my cheek. "But I can't do that. Our relationship deserves better than that, and allowing you to do it will only hurt *us* in the long run. I will only claim you when you're truly ready, not because you and your wolf are jealous."

My vision blurred, and I struggled to my feet. Out of every man in the world, I felt safest with him, yet here he was, rejecting me. "You said you'd wait until I was ready."

"Yes, until you're *ready*." His face twisted with regret. "This isn't you being ready. You told me yesterday that you weren't. To make this choice because some foolish girl wants to use me to prove something to herself isn't right for you or us. You're *it* for me, but only when you're ready for me to be *it* for you."

I couldn't meet his gaze. Cheeks hot beyond measure, I climbed off him and ran for the door. I couldn't stay out here with him alone. Not after this. My heart shattered into a million pieces.

Killian called, "Jewel!" but I didn't stop. Once the tears started falling, I wasn't sure when they would end.

"Just leave me alone, please." I rushed inside, needing to find the closest thing I had to a bedroom since everything else had been taken from me.

Days passed in a blur. I avoided Killian, not wanting to talk to him after I'd made such an ass of myself. He, of course, obliged me by giving me space—which pissed me off and provided relief.

The lab techs continued their tests, but this morning, more guards had arrived. They were preparing for something. I sat at the base of the large oak tree I favored. It was a clear day, not a cloud in the sky, but I couldn't enjoy the midday warmth.

Sierra was with me, rambling about a movie she and

Savannah had watched last night. Surprisingly, the human had taken to Sierra, but we still couldn't risk her escaping. or she might lead her people to us. We had to wait to release her until the pack had escaped.

With a whoosh of wings, Rosemary descended, and her peony rose scent swirled around me. Levi was inside the building, trying to learn what had brought more guards on board.

"Any news?" I asked, not bothering to look at her.

"More techs are coming tomorrow." I sensed her standing beside me. "We need to make our move tonight. I'm about to head back to the farmhouse and thought you might like me to ask someone to take your place so you can get your affairs in order."

Now she had my attention. I looked up and met her gaze. "Are you threatening me?"

Her eyes widened. "Why would you ask that?" Rosemary pursed her lips. "If I were threatening you, there would be no question."

"Girl, people get their affairs in order before they die." Sierra snorted. "That's why she asked if you were threatening her." She stood from her spot under a red cedar and sashayed toward us.

"Death is unpredictable, so you should always have things organized." Rosemary shook her head. "Mortals are so strange, especially as their days truly are numbered."

Sierra wagged a finger at the angel. "*Not* reassuring."

Pinching the bridge of her nose, Rosemary turned to me. "I'm not trying to scare you. I'm saying from experience that it's asinine to fight the connection with the one Fate has chosen for you. Believe me, if Levi and I had put all the effort we'd used to fight our connection into completing the bond, it would've prevented so much pain. Killian is a good man, and the pain you're putting the both of you through is pointless. So simply be brave and put your fears of committing to him aside."

I wanted to say I'd tried, but Killian had been right. I hadn't approached it with the purest intentions. And boy, was I thankful he hadn't taken advantage of my vulnerability. He deserved the sort of claiming that showed the person Fate had chosen for him *wanted* to be with him. Each day I stayed away from him, I became more certain I needed him. I was just too embarrassed to face him. But he was the best person I'd ever met, and I'd be so lucky to have him in any capacity, especially as my mate. Even when I'd acted jealous and hurt, he'd never gotten angry or frustrated with me. He hadn't judged me. He'd let me be myself, and he was so damn patient. He was the person I needed.

"What if he changed his mind?" I glanced at the ground, hating my insecurity. Ruby had been coming around, and I'd been avoiding him. I'd given her the perfect opportunity to gain his attention, especially since my actions had proved I didn't deserve him.

"Girl, he hasn't." Sierra cringed. "All he talks about is how he might have messed things up with you, and he won't share what he did to think that." Her eyes sparkled. "But you can give me the deets. I wasn't going to bring it up, but Rosey did, so here we are. My opening complete."

Rosemary glowered. "Only Levi calls me Rosey."

But all I could focus on was that he hadn't told a soul about what had happened. I hadn't expected him to, but I'd been wrong before. "There's nothing I want to share."

"Oh, come *ooon*," Sierra drawled.

Before I had to answer, something flickered inside me.

My connection with Chad went from a sleepy state to one of pure terror. *Chad, what's wrong?*

CHAPTER TWENTY-FOUR

THEY'RE—

He cut off as horror switched to something else.

Pain.

It shot through the bond, and my stomach dropped. Though it was a faint echo of what Chad was feeling, the sensation stole my breath.

He didn't answer. I clenched my fists. I should have been the one in that building, suffering, not Chad. I'd exposed my brother to this. I'd asked Sterlyn and the others to help me, and Chad being locked in there was my fault.

An arm wrapped around my waist, and Rosemary's scent brought me back to the present.

"What is wrong with you?" Rosemary gritted out as her arm tightened around me. "I said to make things right with Killian, not sacrifice yourself for no good reason. You won't make it down the hill without being spotted and captured. We'd be down one person to storm the building when the time comes and have one more person to save. They're on higher alert already, making it more difficult to get inside."

Shit. She was right, but Chad's pain had blinded me.

"They're *doing* something to him." I rubbed the throbbing spot in my chest near my heart where my pack links were located.

"Doing something?" Rosemary sounded confused. "I don't know what that means."

Bewildered, Sierra snorted and said, "Don't look at me. I don't, either. Remember, I'm not part of their pack."

I went still and played "Moonlight Sonata" in my mind. I had to remain logical, or I'd only add to our group's problems. "I don't know what they're doing to him. He's in so much pain, he can't think straight." I made myself sick, imagining the worst.

"Are you good?" Rosemary asked, her arm like a tight cocoon around me.

"Yes. Thank you." I breathed deeply and concentrated on how the piano sounded, trying to calm my racing heart. "I didn't mean to be rash. It's just...he's hurting."

"Unfortunately, I understand that now. Emotions can make us do asinine things, but you need to be aware of that to counteract it." Rosemary released her hold but stayed close.

I appreciated the bluntness of her words. They were what I needed to hear to keep my head level. My vision swam, and I forced my lungs to work. "I won't be stupid again."

"Don't make promises you can't keep," Sierra sang behind me.

Under normal circumstances, I'd have found her charming, but this wasn't a laughing matter. Someone was hurting Chad.

Sterlyn linked with me, *Was Chad able to tell you anything?* Her worry flooded me. Normally, I got calm and reassuring vibes from her. Now, her concern intensified my own panic.

The urge to run toward the building again surged through me, but it didn't take me by surprise. I dug my feet solidly into the ground. *He started to but got cut off.*

Of course she'd felt his pain. In fact, she'd be experiencing it worse than me because of her alpha connection with him.

That must be why he hasn't responded to me. We have to wait until he can, unfortunately, since Mila is still asleep. Cyrus is gathering a larger group to help with the breakout tonight.

My shoulders relaxed marginally. We were working on a plan. The past week had been hard, even beyond the tension with Killian. Just sitting close by, watching the building the people I cared about were housed in, was agonizing. All I could do was sit and wonder what was going on inside, and my skin crawled every time Ronnie and Levi reported back that the wolves were asleep and the lab techs were testing their blood. They were gearing up for something, and the time had arrived.

Griffin and I are heading your way to take over, Sterlyn informed me.

Okay. Usually, I'd complain. I had an hour left on my watch before they relieved us for lunch, but I needed to move and clear my head.

Sitting here and doing nothing was unbearable.

Chad's pain started to ebb, and I connected with him. *Are you okay?* Clearly, he wasn't, but I wasn't sure what else to say. The only thing that reassured me was that his link was still warm. He wasn't dead, but there were fates worse than death.

Forced...to...shift, he replied slowly before his connection went dormant, as if he'd fallen asleep.

Sweat pooled under my armpits. I'd never been forced to shift before, and thinking of how the humans might have done it made me sick. At least Chad was asleep, which hopefully gave him a reprieve from his torture.

I inhaled and moved a foot forward, trying to work out some of my anxiety.

Rosemary's hand clutched my shoulder. "I thought you weren't going to do anything stupid."

She thought I'd been about to run toward the building again. I couldn't blame her. "I'm just antsy, and you were right behind me."

I spun around to face her.

She bit her bottom lip but didn't remove her hand.

I stared despondently at Rosemary. Rather than the burnt orange color she favored, she wore white. She'd said it helped her blend in with the clouds on brighter days. Today, she looked more like the angel I'd met, the dark circles under her eyes gone. When angels depleted their magic, it took a while for it to fully recharge. I hated that I'd been part of the reason she'd been so drained.

"Chad says they made him shift." My words broke out of me, though I hadn't meant them to. It had been so hard to hear he'd been tortured like that. Worse, I suspected he wasn't the only one. PawPaw and Nana popped into my head, and I wondered if they'd been tortured as well. Since I couldn't connect with them, I wasn't even sure if they were alive.

Eyes burning, I blinked to keep tears at bay. Having a breakdown would only lead to fatigue, red eyes, a stuffy nose, and a horrible headache. Oh, how much I'd learned since Dad had passed.

Sierra's eyebrows lifted. "How?"

I gripped the ends of my hair and tugged. That was better than lashing out at her, especially since her question was valid. I was just frustrated that I didn't have the answer. "I don't know. He passed out before he could share." Maybe, in a way, it was best he hadn't. Possibilities rushed through my head—injections, torture, gas...gods knew what else.

"We have no option but to infiltrate the building tonight." Rosemary dropped her hand and pursed her lips. "We all suspected something had changed, but this confirms it. Their testing will only escalate."

Smacking Rosemary in the arm, Sierra growled, "Not helping."

Rosemary caught Sierra's wrist and leveled a steady gaze at her. She said in a low tone, "Do *not* do that again. I may seem more mortal now, but I *am* an angel and won't tolerate being beaten."

I mashed my lips together, trying to hold in a laugh or a noise of terror. I wasn't sure which. Rosemary scared the hell out of me, and her wrath wasn't even directed at me.

"Okay." Sierra's mouth dropped. "It's just that she's still upset, and I was trying to get your attention."

We didn't need animosity among our team, especially now. "It's fine," I said. "We're all tense, and Rosemary was being honest. I do appreciate your concern, Sierra, but we need to move. Sterlyn and Griffin are on their way, and Cyrus is pulling a group together to join us tonight."

Rosemary lowered her wings to her sides. "We could use the help. When we get inside, the fight will become harder once the humans realize they're being attacked."

And they had weapons. Rosemary hadn't said it, but we were all aware.

"Did Levi see anything?" I'd forgotten he was in the building.

Rosemary shook her head. "No. When you told us something was wrong, he tried to find Chad. He's still looking, but he'll let me know as soon as he locates the men."

Even though Levi might not be able to determine what the humans had done to the shifters, he could check that no one had died. As far as we were aware, all the shifters were still alive. Ronnie and Levi didn't know the pack the way I did, though, so it was hard to say. The humans had been keeping the wolves unconscious and feeding and hydrating them through an IV.

Heart aching, I moved back to my tree and sat down to wait for Griffin and Sterlyn. I closed my eyes, focusing on the sun warming my face, and played soothing music in my head.

This would all end tonight.

———

As I WALKED through the last bit of trees that led to the farmhouse, Ruby's overly ripe scent assaulted my nose. She'd been coming here every day, and I'd been giving her all the time in the world alone with Killian. I couldn't face him after making such a damn fool of myself.

Though it was agonizing to know she was there with him, I'd managed to hold myself together. But I couldn't now. Not after hearing Chad and knowing these humans were now tormenting others. I was barely hanging on.

"I'm going to head back to the others. Are you okay?" Rosemary asked, inching away.

Even though I wasn't, there was no way I'd try to get her

to stay. I took a deep breath, making sure my words sounded steady. "Yes. Go back and help them."

Without hesitation, she nodded and shot into the sky, heading toward the large hill that overlooked the building. With the threat imminent, she'd decided to stay with Sierra, Sterlyn, and Griffin and gather more intel from Levi to begin forming a solid plan. Though we'd been planning, we weren't sure we had enough information to act on. Now we had no choice.

I stood at the edge of the woods alone, trying to pull myself together. When my feet finally moved, my eyes were drawn toward the side of the house. As expected, Ruby was behind Killian as he leaned over the table, talking to Eliza and Ronnie. The three of them were in deep conversation, and Ruby squatted next to Killian's black chair and placed a hand on his knee.

My blood boiled, and I snarled as Killian knocked her hand away.

Though his reaction should have eased my anger, it didn't, and when Ruby smirked at me, my wolf tried to surge forward. I held her back, but I wasn't sure how long I could contain her.

"Please don't stop her advances just 'cause I'm here." I should've kept my mouth shut. I had no right to be upset with him. I was the one who kept pushing him away. But my gods, I couldn't control my emotions around him.

"What? I didn't." Killian jumped to his feet. "I mean...I don't want *her* advances."

"Killy..." She pouted. "After all our time together—"

Ronnie slammed a hand on the table, fracturing the wood, and stood. "You need to *stop*. You know he's not into you, yet you come here every night to take advantage of his good nature."

"No, I would..." She trailed off, and her gaze flicked around as if she were searching for an answer. "He's an alpha. Why should he waste time over a girl who avoids him and doesn't give him the time of day?"

Rubbing her temples, Eliza leaned back in her seat and looked at Ronnie. "I'm so thankful you and Annie didn't act like that."

"Why does my status as alpha matter?" Killian asked Ruby. "You know Jewel holds *all* my attention. So why are you trying to start something with me when you know it's a lost cause?"

"It's not a lost cause." Ruby gestured at me. "You aren't taken. That means your mind isn't made up."

Though I wanted to yell at her that she was stupid and needed to go, she *was* right. He and I weren't mated. In theory, he could choose a mate and break the fated-mate connection between us. Ignoring Fate was never ideal, but he *could* choose to be with someone else.

"Ruby, I made my decision the first time I saw her. Hell, Fate made the decision, too." He made his way to me. "Jewel is it for me. Whether I wait months or years, *she* is the one I want to be with when the time's right."

My stomach fluttered, and guilt swept in close behind. Why should I be allowed to be happy when people I loved were at risk? This was why I'd put off being with him for so long.

"But—" Ruby's bottom lip quivered, and she crossed her arms, emphasizing her cleavage in the V-neck of her black sweater.

"You're a smart woman," Killian said.

I growled. I didn't like him complimenting her. He'd told Ruby he wasn't interested in her, but I didn't like how nice he was about it. At the same time, I knew that was *him*, and it was one of the things I loved most about him.

Wait.

Loved?

A grin slipped onto his face as he took my hand, and instantly, my anger thawed. Without missing a beat, he said, "And you're nice and kind when no one is watching you. It's like you put on this façade for the world."

"That's because none of my pack takes me seriously, so why bother trying when they'll just ignore me anyway?" Ruby hung her head and lowered her arms. "You and this group are so supportive, kind, and strong. It's something I'd like to be part of."

My chest tightened, and the rest of my anger disappeared. She wanted Killian because he was the only unmated man in a group she was desperate to join. I understood feeling alienated; I'd experienced that often since our pack had always been separated from both humans and other supernaturals. I'd struggled with it during my teenage years, and that was with Chad, Theo, and Emmy by my side.

"There's one thing I've learned, child." Eliza leaned across the table and patted Ruby's arm. "You don't have to be mated to someone in this group to become part of it. They're welcoming of just about anyone, as long as you're a good person and don't continually make trouble."

Laughing bitterly, Ruby's eyes glistened as she looked at the sky. "In other words, I've already fu—er—messed up."

"If I'm part of this group, anyone can be." Eliza climbed to her feet and smiled sadly. "I made a much bigger mistake than you. One I'm not certain *I* could have forgiven. But they did. So I think you have a good chance if you quit your games and try to be a friend to *everyone* here." She glanced over her shoulder at Ronnie. "Let's go in and check on Savannah. She got Alex started on vampire heritage before we came out here, so she might need some saving."

Ronnie snickered. "I don't know. She actually seems very intrigued by all the supernatural stuff she's learned." Her attention landed on me. "Wanna join us?"

It was probably better if I went inside. I'd made a big enough fool of myself—again. But when I took a step toward Ronnie, Killian tightened his grip on my hand.

"I want to talk to her alone before Cyrus and the others get here," Killian rasped. "Chaos will ensue once they do."

Ronnie looked at me, and I nodded. If Killian wanted to talk to me alone, he deserved that.

She then looked at Ruby and arched an eyebrow.

"I need to head home. Don't worry." Ruby scoffed noisily. "Dad is pissed that I've been hanging out with you guys." She headed toward the tree line but paused in front of Killian and me. "I'm sorry for being self-centered. If it makes you feel any better," she said as her attention cut to me, "I knew I didn't have a chance."

My heart raced again as some of my anger returned. She'd meant it as a compliment, but she'd been pushing my buttons for the sake of upsetting me. I chose not to respond, knowing anything I said would only undo any goodwill.

She kicked at the ground, then cleared her throat. "I guess I'll see you guys later." She took off, leaving Killian and me alone.

I kept my attention on the bench swing, not sure where else to look. I'd come damn close to showing my ass yet again, and I was sure he wanted to talk about it.

A goldfinch and robin landed on the swing, and I wondered what it would be like to be fully animal. My human side was as much a part of me as my wolf, but if that human side had been missing, how different would I be? Would I be standing here, uncomfortable, next to my mate, or would I be confident enough to embrace him?

"I've been worried about you," Killian said as he tugged on my hand, indicating he wanted me to face him. "How are you holding up?"

Facing him was the very thing I wanted most, but I was worried about what I would find. He'd bared his heart in front of Ruby, Eliza, and Ronnie after I'd acted so coldly. I turned my body toward him but stayed focused on a spot of brown grass at his feet. "I'm..." I trailed off, not wanting to finish the sentence. He'd know the lie as soon as the word *okay* left my lips. "I'm safe, and they aren't."

"We're going to do something about that." He placed his finger under my chin and tilted my face up to meet his gaze. "Believe me when I say we've all had people we love in danger, and we had to take time to ensure we were ready to save them." His face lined with concern, and kindness warmed his eyes.

My throat dried. "It just feels wrong."

"If I could do anything to make this easier for you, I would." He twirled his finger in my hair.

"You *do*. That's the problem." I hadn't expected to be so honest with him, but the words tumbled out. He'd just confessed his devotion to me; it was the least I could do in return. "You make the burden feel less heavy, and at times, I forget the people I love are in danger. What does that say about me?"

"That you're with the person who was made for you, giving you balance." His other hand intertwined with mine. "The world is full of horrible things, and there's always a reason not to be happy. But misery disregards all the good things in the world, too. We're trying to rescue your loved ones. You're not out partying or trying to forget about them. It's okay to laugh at a joke or feel content in the sun. It's not all or nothing."

His words sat heavily on me. I'd always seen things as either good or bad with nothing in between, but he was right. This world had a *lot* in between. In my view, if Mom was upset, I should be, too. If Dad was frustrated with the pack, I needed to fix it. I'd always let the state of mind of others dictate how I should feel or react, which sometimes made me so damn angry.

"Just know I will *always* be here for you, whether you're crying or smiling." He cupped my cheek and kissed my forehead.

The jolt between his lips and my skin shot straight to my soul. Between his words and our connection, for the first time, I truly believed I was being foolish.

He dropped his hand. "And when you're ready for me—for *us*—you'll know where to find me."

He released me and turned to head inside, and my wolf howled inside me.

CHAPTER TWENTY-FIVE

THE FARTHER AWAY KILLIAN MOVED, the louder my wolf howled, and the more my heart ripped into shreds. Every wall I'd put around it shattered.

He was right. There would always be a reason not to be together. And what if something happened tonight? Though I hated to consider a negative outcome, I couldn't dismiss it. We were outnumbered.

Shouldn't we have a chance to be together, even if only for a few hours instead of a lifetime?

"Killian," I called out desperately, loudly, afraid he'd vanish from sight. "Please don't go."

He stopped but didn't turn to face me as he said, "I thought you wanted to be alone."

I wasn't sure how he knew that. I was pretty sure I hadn't said those words to him. "I did, but not anymore." I bit my bottom lip. "Unless you don't want to stay out here—with me." I'd never force him to do something he didn't want to do, including spending time with me.

"There's nowhere else I'd rather be." He slowly turned but didn't move closer.

I wrung my hands, fighting the urge to grab him. I couldn't act hastily, or he might think I was reacting again and push me away. He deserved better. "Want to go for a walk?" That would give us a chance to talk and ease my nervous energy.

"Sure." He came back to me, facing the woods opposite the facility we were watching.

Good idea. Sierra would likely be coming back for lunch, and I didn't want to run into her while trying to spend time with him.

We walked past the swinging bench toward the oak and red cedars on the other side. The rental place had once been a farm, but it hadn't been active in quite some time.

Killian stayed quiet, matching my strides, letting me choose whether we talked or remained silent.

Though I felt safe with him, I'd never been good at confessing my feelings. Coming right out and saying that I loved him would be *way* forward, especially after I'd been pushing him away, but saying I liked him wasn't strong enough.

How did people have these types of conversations?

I rubbed my sweaty palms against my jeans. This was ridiculous. He'd told me he'd wait for me and that I was the woman he wanted, but I couldn't figure out how to tell him how I felt.

Instead of saying anything, we walked for a while in silence. The scents of the woods and fresh air soothed me, and I tipped my face toward the sun.

Skin tingling, I became aware that he was paying attention to me. He had to be able to hear my heart racing, but he didn't say anything.

The attention had sweat pooling in unpleasant places.

So I went with my gut. "I'm sorry."

His eyebrows furrowed. "What for?" He faced me more as he ducked under the branch of an oak tree.

"Pushing you away." Honesty was easier for me than feelings. I rolled my shoulders, trying to relax. "I...was afraid, but you were right. There's always going to be a reason for us not to be together if I look for it."

I moved faster, going deeper into the woods. The trees were getting closer, and we had to be half a mile from the farmhouse now. The soft padding of hooves told me deer were nearby, which meant Killian and I were pretty much alone.

More so than ever before.

My heart raced. There went the bit of composure I'd found.

He increased his pace, catching up to me. A slight smile spread over his face. "There's nothing to apologize for. But are you trying to leave me behind?"

Ugh, great. It did look like I was trying to ditch him. I kept running hot and cold around him. Oh, my gods, I was like the typical *man* in this relationship. "No, I...just don't know how to say it." I stopped in my tracks.

After a few steps, he halted and pivoted toward me. "Jewel, you don't have to say *anything*. You have nothing to apologize for. Things have to be right on both sides before we wind up together."

"But that's the *thing*." I swallowed loudly. "I *do* want you. More than I want oxygen." Thank gods Sierra wasn't around. If she'd heard that, she never would've let me live it down, saying it was romance-movie-worthy. I'd known her for a little more than a week, and I'd already become *very* aware that she was a romance-aholic.

He chuckled. "I kinda need you to keep breathing so we *can* be together when the time is right."

There it was again—when the time was right. He wasn't picking up on the hints I was dropping. He was going to make me say it. I cleared my throat as my face heated. "What I'm trying to say is...I'm ready."

His head jerked back, and he reached for my hand but stopped. "Ready for what, exactly?"

My throat closed, and my body stiffened. Maybe now that I was ready, he'd changed his mind. I wanted to laugh and act like I was just joking, but I couldn't muster up the gumption. If he had changed his mind, I *needed* to know. "Us...now. That is...if you still want me, too."

Belly laughing, he beamed. "I just told you less than half an hour ago that you're it for me. You think I changed my mind in that short amount of time?"

I refused to avert my gaze, though I *really* wanted to. Even if he had changed his mind, I was still a strong wolf in my own right. "Well, you just reached for me and stopped."

"Because if I touch you, thinking you're ready to be *mine* and I somehow misunderstood, it would be all the more crushing," he rasped as he snared my hand and pulled me to his chest. He placed his finger under my chin, tilting my face up again.

I loved that gesture. With that action, he seemed entirely focused on me, and nothing else mattered.

"Ever since that night you came to my house, my heart has beat only for you. My entire world shifted. Finding out I was part of what happened to your loved ones was unbearable."

"It wasn't your fault," I tried to reassure him.

"Just listen, please," he asked softly.

How could I say no to that? I nodded, my voice gone after taking in his tender gaze.

"I became the voice of supernaturals because Sterlyn,

Griffin, Alex, Ronnie, Rosemary, and Levi were mated. I did it to protect them in a way I couldn't do for Dad, Mom, and Liv." He blew out a breath. "Then, within days, *you* appeared, my fated mate, and I was the reason your family was taken."

My head spun from his sandalwood scent. "Why are you telling me this?"

"Because if we're doing this, I want you to know everything. Once we're bonded, there's no way you'll *ever* get to fucking back out," he growled. "You need to know the truth before you tell me you're done waiting again. I planned to tell you everything after we saved your mom, Chad, your grandparents, and the rest of the wolf shifters."

That was fair, though there was no way I would change my mind. "Okay. Why did you feel the need to announce the existence of supernaturals?"

"Because some vampires who lost their humanity escaped Shadow Terrace, along with demons who chose evil. They wanted to expose us." Killian sneered as he glanced at a nearby tree. "The princes of Hell arranged to have humans witness heinous acts and take videos to leak."

My eyes filled with tears. All this time, I'd judged him so harshly, but the group had made a huge decision with the best information they'd had on hand. Killian had tried to protect his friends. "So you volunteered to become the target?"

"Had I known you would show up..." His face softened. "I don't know what I would've done, but I wouldn't have been so eager to volunteer. At the time, it felt right, especially since Mom, Dad, and Liv died because I'd chosen to go to a party instead of going with them to investigate a threat."

"I used to think it was, but now I know that this *wasn't*

your fault." He was carrying a burden that wasn't truly his to hold. "If you'd gone with them, you would've died, too." My heart constricted. We hadn't even cemented our bond, but I couldn't fathom a world without him in it. The thought terrified me. "You don't have anything to make up for."

"Yes, I do. That's how I know I'm not *worthy* of you." His irises darkened as his arms circled my waist. "But I promise...no, *promise* isn't a strong enough word." He licked his full bottom lip. "I *vow* I will spend every day making things up to you and to my family's memory. That is, *if* you still want me."

"Of course I do," I whispered. Nothing would ever change my mind about him. He was such an amazing man and the kind of person I strove to be—patient, kind, loyal, and understanding. Every quality I didn't possess.

His lips met mine, sealing the vow he'd made me. His tongue slipped into my mouth, filling it with the faint citrus flavor I now associated with him.

Though my wolf howled, I pulled back, breaking our kiss.

His forehead lined. "What's wrong? I thought—"

"You confided in me, so now it's my turn to confide in you." He wasn't the only one with flaws.

"There's nothing—" he started.

"Nuh-uh." I lifted a hand between us and wagged a finger. "It's only fair since I heard you out."

He took a step back, giving us space, and chuckled. "Then please, convince me there's something wrong with you."

"Oh, there's plenty." I hadn't confided in anyone. "When Dad died, my world shattered. He was my best friend, my confidant, and then he was just *gone*. Instead of coming with the pack to be led by Cyrus, I left, needing time to mourn."

I paused, waiting for his judgment, but he remained silent, so I continued, "You see, there's this anger inside me. It's similar to my mom's. It's like...when something happens to someone I love, I want to destroy the world. I...I wanted to lash out, so I left. I abandoned my pack when they needed me most. And while I was gone, Mom was captured, and so many of my pack members *died* because I was a coward." There it was, my dirty confession.

"Jewel, you were *brave*," he said as he took my hands. "You felt anger that you could've taken out on your pack like Mila did. But *unlike* your mother, you recognized you needed time to heal instead of causing more drama and problems within your pack. You took care of yourself, and your pack was stronger for it."

That was a nice way of spinning it, but I wouldn't let him see me with rose-colored glasses. "Killian, the point is, I have hot rage inside me. Sometimes, I feel like I might explode. I don't want to be that person."

"You get angry whenever someone is hurt, right?" he asked.

"True, but—"

He arched his brow. "Now it's my turn to finish. We all get angry when someone we love or care about is hurt, whether it's physically, emotionally, or spiritually. You're a *silver wolf* and a born protector. That's your instincts coming out, and you, unlike your mom, are self-aware enough to know when you need time. Anger is natural. To not feel it is to be numb, and if you want to talk to anyone about feeling that way, then Rosemary is your girl."

For the first time, someone had made me feel as if I might not be broken. "I never thought of it that way, but it's a problem, so you might want to reconsider." The last thing I wanted was for him to choose to be with me and then discover I made him miserable.

Tightening his arms around my waist, he pulled me flush against his chest. "Let's see. Do you want to be with me because Ruby's been hanging around me?"

"Well, I won't lie. It wasn't fun to watch, but no, not this time." The past several days, knowing she was likely hovering all over him, I'd been tossing in my bed. "And I'm sorry—"

He kissed me again, cutting off my words. "Then I have no hesitations."

When his lips touched mine again, I didn't stop him. We'd confessed what we felt the other needed to make an informed decision, and we were standing here in each other's arms. I snaked my hands around his neck and threaded my fingers into his thick hair, deepening our kiss. I never wanted to stop.

Our tongues mingled, and my body warmed, soaking in his smell, his taste, and the jolts coursing through me everywhere.

I didn't know how long we stood there kissing, but it would *never* be long enough. My hand was inching toward his waistline when he snagged my wrist.

Not this again. Maybe he had changed his mind.

"We should go back to the house," he murmured. "Maybe go to your room."

My body blazed, and my heart felt lighter. He wasn't reconsidering. "No. Our friends will hear, and we've waited long enough." I stood on my tiptoes, kissing him once more.

He tried to back away again. "But—"

"Unless you don't want to claim me, there is no other

place I'd rather do this." Being outside was perfect. We were part animal, and we were attuned to nature.

I removed my wrist from his hand, and this time, when I slid my hand downward, he didn't stop me.

"Dear gods," he moaned, and picked me up.

I wrapped my legs around his waist as his hand cupped my breast. When he gently caressed my nipple through my shirt, I almost came unglued. No one had ever touched me this way, and the fact that my first time was with him made it more perfect.

He set me against an oak tree and placed my feet down. He tugged the edges of my shirt up, and I helped him remove it from my body. I reached behind me, unfastened my bra, and tossed it to the ground.

My wolf surged forward, eager for our bond to be completed.

"Gods, Jewel. You're more beautiful than I imagined," he rasped as he drank me in.

His words embraced me, and I yanked on his shirt. "You imagined me like this? That's funny, because I've thought of you completely naked." I pulled the shirt over his head, and his abs contracted as I stared at him. Dark hair patterned his body. Not too little and not too much. The perfect amount, which was a common theme when it came to him.

"You're going to kill me," he growled as his head lowered, his mouth capturing a nipple.

My body lurched backward as heat and dampness enveloped me, and his tongue worked magic with friction and velvety roughness I'd never experienced before, the sensation addicting.

As warmth exploded through my body, I found his jeans button and unfastened them. I wanted him naked. I wanted him to be *mine*.

We pushed his jeans and boxers down together, and Killian kicked them off. Then he eagerly removed my jeans and underwear. We were desperate not to have any barriers between us.

For a moment, we stood and just...looked at each other. My eyes widened, and I tried to decide where to touch first.

His mouth returned to worshipping my body, and I eagerly took him in my hand and stroked, hoping to the gods I had some idea of what I was doing.

He groaned, giving me confidence.

His hand slid between my legs and stroked my folds. I gasped at the onslaught of pleasure coursing through my body. When one finger slipped inside me, a guttural growl emanated from his chest.

He pulled away, a breathtaking smile on his face. "You're a virgin?"

I nodded, cheeks flushing hotter. "Does that bother you?" I knew he had...more experience. My wolf snarled at the thought, and I told her to stand down.

"Gods, no. It's fucking hot as hell. And...I'm...also possessive as hell." He held my gaze for a beat, looking for something, and when I smiled, his mouth went back to my breast, and his fingers continued to work me.

He swayed his hips as I stroked him, and soon, the fire inside me was raging, and my wolf was growling in impatience.

It was time.

"Killian, please. I need you," I whimpered. He'd caressed my body into a quivering mess, and I needed the final act to make us one.

"I want to make sure I don't hurt you," he said as he leaned forward, pressing his forehead gently to mine.

"You won't. I just—"

He cut me off with a long, sensuous kiss and positioned himself between my legs. "I feel the same way." His hands grabbed my ass, lifting me, and I instinctively wrapped my legs around his waist again. The tree trunk dug into my back, but all of that was erased as he slowly edged inside me. Once he filled me, he remained still as my body adjusted to him. "Did I hurt you?"

"No. More," I moaned, moving my hips. I needed friction, the kind only he could provide.

"Oh, gods, *Jewel*." At first, he moved slowly, each thrust better than the last. I wrapped my arms around his neck and fused his mouth to mine. Then he was moving quickly, and the friction inside me was about to ignite.

I pulled away slightly, the urge to set my mouth on his neck taking over. I kissed him where his pulse beat under my lips and paused.

"Do it, please," he groaned.

That was all I needed. I bit into his neck, and my power poured into him. A sizzling, euphoric sensation coursed through my shaking body, a feeling of utter rightness. I released his neck and tilted my head back, ready for him to do the same to me.

He kissed down my jawline and neck to the base of my throat. Unlike me, he didn't pause, likely because I'd already initiated the claiming.

His teeth nicked my skin, and he latched on. A molten spot flooded in and settled inside me. It was larger than Sterlyn's link or any connection to my other pack members.

An orgasm crashed over us. His pleasure blended with mine, pulsing through us, making the ecstasy that much more amazing. He thrust inside me harder as we sailed over the edge.

I love you, I linked. Those were the first words I wanted him to hear me say through our link.

Warmth like never before spread into me. *I love you, too.*

When he stilled, my head was still fuzzy. Then I noticed something different. My pack links were gone, and instead, around three hundred bonds filled the same spot.

I trembled, absorbing the change and sorting through the new connections. I'd joined his pack, since he was an alpha. I hadn't even considered that this would happen.

"Damn it," he growled as he pulled back and kissed my lips. "The silver wolves are freaking out. They felt your connection vanish."

"It's because we mated. You need to tell Sterlyn." The haze of sex and completing our bond was already fading. "I didn't think—" I wouldn't be able to link to my mom. Or Chad. "I really didn't think this through."

"Neither did I. I'm talking to her now." Killian placed his forehead to mine and pushed his love into me. "I hate that our moment was interrupted, but they thought something was wrong. It's hard to get upset with them over that."

He was right. If they hadn't been concerned, it would've meant they didn't care.

It was so strange, not being able to talk to Sterlyn. Killian could, so why couldn't I? I didn't like it, but the strength and love coursing through me empowered me.

Killian tensed. "We have to get back to the house. Now."

CHAPTER TWENTY-SIX

AS KILLIAN PEELED his body from mine, I caught myself pouting. The time we'd spent together had been transcendent and sweet but way too short. I hated that I'd wasted so much time this past week pushing him away, but I hadn't been ready. If we'd rushed things, I wouldn't have felt as great as I did now.

The missing links to my mom and Chad were an issue, though. I hoped they hadn't been too freaked out and that Sterlyn had reassured them quickly...if they were awake.

I blew out a breath and bent to grab my clothes scattered among the dead leaves of the oak tree. It was a beautiful late fall day, and I appreciated the cool air after the heat that had wafted between us. The Tennessee late fall was upon us, and the air was crisp but not cold enough for it to be slightly uncomfortable for a shifter to be naked outside.

As I fastened my bra, Killian growled, "It's a damn shame you're covering up."

I smirked. "I could channel Birch and Ruby and change back into my birthday suit."

His nostrils flared. "Not funny. Say something like that again, and I might be forced to spank you."

Laughter bubbled out of me. "Is that a promise?" I hadn't felt this happy in such a long time, not even before Dad had passed.

Mouth dropping, Killian raised his eyebrows so high they almost reached his hairline. "Keep talking like that, and we won't make it back to the house."

Though he was teasing, the urgency of the situation washed over me again. People were worried about me, and I didn't have my phone. I needed to reach out to Emmy so she didn't think I'd been captured like—

My blood ran cold.

Mom.

My heart grew heavy. Though Killian was right about there always being a reason not to be together, I couldn't keep the guilt at bay. Even in this short amount of time, my soul had connected with Killian, and I didn't regret the decision, but Chad had been tortured, and just an hour later, I was having the best sex of my life—the *first* sex of my life—while claiming my fated mate. That somehow seemed...well, part of the issue was it didn't seem *wrong*. Which was wrong!

"Hey, what happened?" Killian asked as he touched my arm.

The pleasant jolt shot right into my soul, bringing me back to the present...back to him. "Sorry. I can't connect with Chad and Mom anymore. I just...didn't think that through—"

Sierra's voice popped into my head. *A little birdie just explained to me why I felt a new wolf enter the pack within link range.*

Of course she'd choose *now* to link with me. Somehow,

though, the timing was perfect. Here I was, missing my former pack mates, when a new one I was already fond of could link with me. *I'm assuming you mean Sterlyn and not Rosemary.*

You'd be right, though you have a point. Rosemary is definitely more birdlike than Sterlyn, she replied, and her amusement tickled my chest. *I can't wait to use that analogy with her. I can't believe I didn't think of it before.*

I suspected Rosemary would not appreciate it, but there was nothing I could do about it.

"In fairness, I didn't think it through, either." He cleared his throat as his cheeks reddened. "I lost all sense of anything beyond you when I realized you were ready to complete the bond."

His worry weighed on our connection.

No, we would not be having a moment like this before we made it back to the others. I kissed his lips sweetly and pulled back, then put on my shirt. "I did, too. We still have the walk back to enjoy each other's company, so let's push off dealing with anything heavy until we can address it with the others."

"Okay," he said, but didn't move away.

This would become a problem soon, since he was still naked. I was already struggling not to climb him again. I took a few seconds to appreciate how breathtaking he was. Handsome, strong, alpha male...and all *mine*.

"Just...I hope you don't regret it." He bit his bottom lip as his face twisted in agony. "Because—"

"Never." I placed my hand on his chest where I could feel his heartbeat against my palm. "I will *never* regret it. You're my everything, and I'm sorry." I winked and focused entirely on him and this moment. "There aren't any takebacks."

He exhaled and lowered his forehead to mine. He linked, *Thank gods.*

Communicating with him through our mate connection was more magical than I could've imagined. It was different from a pack link. Stronger. More vivid. I could sense how he was feeling, and when we'd opened ourselves to each other, I almost hadn't known where I ended and he began.

Though I hated to shorten our moment, other people that I loved were in danger. *We should go. Do you know why they want us back so urgently?* I forced myself to step away from him and put on my underwear and jeans.

Cyrus, Darrell, Annie, and some others have arrived. He followed my lead and dressed.

They were here already. I glanced at the sky and noted that the sun had begun its descent. We'd been out here longer than I'd realized. The sun would be setting within the next hour.

We had a lot of planning to do.

Then I guess we'd better hurry, I linked, and took his hand. Despite walking back into our harsh reality, this time, it would be different. This time, Killian was by my side. My heart swelled with a love I'd never thought possible. The organ grew so full, it could possibly explode.

Hand in hand, we headed back to the house. But we were walking toward a future together instead of me fighting to push him away.

As THE SIDE of the house with the bench swing, table, and chairs came into view between the leafless oak trees, I saw that almost everyone was outside, including Savannah. At the corner of the house, Darrell, Sterlyn, Cyrus, and Annie stood deep in conversation, while Eliza, Circe, and two women I'd never seen before sat at the table.

A woman about my age with long bronze hair that cascaded over a sky blue shirt stood behind Eliza. Her chestnut eyes were locked on the man standing beside her and behind Circe. The man had his hands on Circe's shoulders and was leaning forward, talking to the group. His long jet-black hair emphasized his pale skin.

Rosemary stood in front of the bench, glowering at another angel. The new angel had long golden hair that hit her lower back, and dark blue eyes were narrowed on Rosemary. She was slightly shorter than Rosemary, and her beige wings appeared almost white next to Rosemary's dark charcoal feathers.

Savannah sat awkwardly on the bench, trying to avoid whatever was going on.

"I don't understand why you're *here*." Rosemary lifted her hands. "I thought you were helping Mother and Father with the city and the *humans*."

The new angel lifted her chin in defiance. "You know Yelahiah likes to do things her way, and Zagan thought I could help fly injured wolves away from *these* humans if needed."

There was history between the two, and I found myself thankful that I wasn't on Rosemary's unfavored side. Although it had been touch and go for a while—she and Killian were close friends. *What's going on there?* I rubbed my chest, sensing five other links besides Killian and Sierra warming. I'd been so smitten with Killian that I hadn't noticed until now.

That's Eleanor, Killian explained. *She resented Rosemary for a long time and has taken several cheap shots at her during their long lives together. Then Rosemary found out why Eleanor hated her and, after regaining her emotions by bonding with Levi, sympathized with her. She's trying to be the bigger person by involving Eleanor in angel decisions, but she still doesn't trust her.*

And how long have their long lives been? I had no clue how old Rosemary was. From what Dad had taught me, I knew angels and vampires were immortal. I knew Alex was about three hundred years old because Sierra brought it up every chance she got. He had older mannerisms, but Rosemary's were even older.

No one knows how old she is. Killian chuckled. *She doesn't share, but let's just say I'm fairly certain she's a lot older than Alex.*

Why would you say that? I'd been so focused on my own pain and anger that I hadn't gotten to know more than superficial stuff about Rosemary and Levi. They tended to stay in their room when they were here, and that wasn't very often. Rosemary always needed a task to focus on.

Every time Sierra jokes about how old he is, his attention immediately goes to Rosemary if she's around. His shoulders shook. *Then she'll glare, cutting him off.*

When we reached the edge of the tree line, Darrell glanced at us. His blood orange eyes lit up, and he pushed his long, dark brown hair to the side. "Well, well. If it isn't the first silver wolf to abandon our new little pack. Thank gods Sterlyn called to let everyone know what happened."

"Oh, I...uh..." I choked and stammered. In many ways, Darrell was like a second father to me. He'd been my dad's beta and was my best friend's father. When I wasn't at my house, I was at theirs. "I'm sorry if I scared you...I didn't think about how my links would change."

Sierra walked around the corner of the house with three men and two women behind her. She quipped, "I'd say thinking was the last thing you were doing," then waggled her brows.

Oh, dear gods. I wanted to avert my gaze to the ground, which was unacceptable. If I reacted, she'd keep goading me. I lifted my chin defiantly, but I couldn't prevent my face from heating.

"Shut it down, Sierra," Killian growled. "Or I'll make you."

"You know she's our alpha's mate." A girl with stunning blue eyes and hair that reminded me of sunshine tossed her glossy locks over one shoulder. "And Killian is already protective of the people he holds dear, so he'll be more extreme over her. If you keep poking at her, you'll be in for a rude awakening."

Sierra pouted. "Luna, I love you. After all, you saved my life—which means you're supposed to take *my* side."

The girl—Luna—lifted her hands in surrender. "Killian took my ass in even after all the horrible shit I did, so I'm on *both* sides and trying to be a friend." She turned to me. "And I'm just glad he found someone who makes him happy and that we now have a super-strong alpha mate."

A man a few years older than me whistled. His pecan-brown hair was pulled into a low ponytail, and he scratched the chocolate-copper scruff on his chin. "Fate was kind to you, man."

This time, I couldn't stop my gaze from falling to the dead grass under my feet. I still wasn't comfortable around large groups, especially around people I didn't know. This past week, I'd gotten comfortable with everyone here, but now we had over ten new people at the house.

Killian clenched his free hand. *I'm sorry that Lowe and Sierra are so rude.*

It's fine, I assured him as I touched his arm. *They're just teasing you.*

"Dude," said a man who was around six feet tall with sandy blond hair and light brown eyes. "You don't talk about someone's *mate* like that, especially the newly mated."

"Listen to Scott!" A girl with a short pixie cut smacked Lowe on the arm and narrowed her dark green eyes at him. "Killian's already about to come unglued."

"At least April and Scott understand how things work," Killian gritted out. Despite still being annoyed, he relaxed his shoulders. "Jewel, I'd like to introduce you to some of our pack members. You know Sierra, and unfortunately, you now know which one is Lowe. The girl next to Sierra is Luna, who, until now, was the newest member of the pack, and then April is the other girl. Scott is the smart man who told Lowe to watch his mouth, so that leaves Collin." He gestured to a super-muscular man about my height. If I hadn't known better, I would've thought he took steroids, but some wolf shifters worked hard to push their own strength.

Unsure what to do, I forced a smile, praying I didn't look crazed or constipated. I'd never wanted the alpha position, but being an alpha's mate had responsibilities, too—more than I'd ever anticipated having. However, for Killian, I'd do anything and learn to be the strong mate he deserved.

Eliza stood and gestured at the table. "Since we're introducing people, we might as well do the witches, too. You already know my daughter and priestess, Circe. The girl standing behind me is her daughter, my granddaughter, Aurora, and the man behind Circe is Aspen, her Blessed Mate." Eliza waved her hand at Circe, indicating she should introduce the rest of the women.

Circe placed a hand on the arm of a woman with gorgeous ruby hair and ominously intense onyx eyes. "This is Herne." Then she gestured to the golden-skinned middle-aged woman across from her. "And that is Cordelia."

Cordelia smiled, her charcoal eyes kind. The breeze ruffled her curly midnight hair. "It's very nice to meet you, Jewel."

"Nice to meet you." Fortunately, I sounded sincere. These people had all come to help save Mom, Chad, my grandparents, and the others. My eyes teared up, and I blinked steadily, hoping I didn't break down from gratefulness.

After a pause, Eleanor stepped forward. "And I'm Eleanor. I've had the same warrior training as Rosemary."

I wasn't sure how to respond. "That's...great. Thank you for coming." I smiled when she nodded back.

Annie hurried toward me and gave Killian and me a hug. "Congratulations! Though I hate that we lost a pack member, I'll let it pass since it's to one of the best men in the world."

Now it was Killian's turn to look awkward. Our bond pulsed, and goosebumps rose over my skin from his discomfort.

As she pulled back, I stepped closer to Killian. "I'm sorry if I worried you all. I didn't realize I would switch to his pack." I took turns looking from Annie to Sterlyn to Cyrus to Darrell.

"I should've warned you. I knew this was imminent—I've been there." Sterlyn smiled. "But we've been so consumed with staking out the facility and learning the routines so we can get the pack out. All the silver wolves before you, Emmy, and me were men, so we never ran into this issue before." She placed a hand on her chest. "Dad thought about it when I was a child, and he cautioned me about the non-alpha silver wolf women in our pack finding mates, noting we might have that problem. That was back when we were hiding entirely and it was a potential exposure concern. I never thought much about why he'd told me until now. If Killian wasn't an alpha, he would've become part of the silver wolf pack, but since he is and has such a large pack, you became part of his pack. I'm sorry I didn't think to talk with you about it."

We did have a lot going on, but in the end, it wouldn't have changed anything. It would've just been one more reason for me to justify not completing our bond. "It's not your fault. But why can Killian link with you and Griffin and I can't?"

"Because I acknowledged them as stronger alphas, and it's a rare bond that only alphas can do with one another. It was a personal choice." Killian squeezed my hand. "And one you can't make, unfortunately." *I'm sorry if that upsets you.*

That burned, but it proved there were benefits to being an alpha. *Not at all. It's a good thing you can communicate with them. You'll just have to fill me in on...all the things.*

Promise. His eyes twinkled, and he kissed the back of my hand.

My heart fluttered as I took in his chiseled cheeks and full lips. Lips that tasted as good as they felt. My body warmed, and a cocky smirk crossed his face.

Right. He could feel that now. Refusing to be embarrassed by my desire for my mate, I quirked a brow at him.

"Great, another couple I get to see want to hump each other all the time," Sierra growled. "While all I have is a hand and a glass of wine."

"Whoa." Killian jerked back and glared at her. "What the *hell*? Never say that again."

Our moment was effectively broken, which I was sure was her intention. Wanting to change the topic, I noticed we were missing key people. "Where are Ronnie, Alex, Griffin, and Levi?"

Sterlyn answered quickly, afraid of giving Sierra time to derail the conversation again. "Griffin and Alex went to watch the second-shift guard change. Ronnie and Levi are taking Bune and Zagan—that's Levi's father and another demon friend—inside the building to experience the situation firsthand and see if they notice anything new."

"What do we know?" Cyrus walked across the clearing and stood next to Annie. He glanced awkwardly at Savannah, who was silently rocking on the bench.

Where are the twins? I linked with Killian. Surely they hadn't brought them here.

Killian replied, *They're with Midnight, Annie's biological mother, and the rest of the silver wolf pack.*

"Nothing more than what he had earlier." Rosemary fluffed her wings, making them appear larger. "Bune and Zagan didn't notice anything extra, so we should have a solid plan. Thirty guards are strategically posted outside to keep an eye on everything. The building consists of three rectangular buildings with the largest one in the center. The outer two buildings appear to hold equipment. The middle one is where the wolves are imprisoned and the tests are conducted. The main entrance is a lobby with five guards stationed there. A door in the center leads to the rest of the space. Beyond the door, there are four large rooms, two on each side, facing each other. The first on the left is where they're holding the children. The one directly across from it is where the women are, and the lab is on the same side as the children with the men directly across."

Rosemary paused, about to reveal something we hadn't heard before, and my chest clenched.

She inhaled. "At the other end of the building, they've set up a surgical center. As of now, they haven't used it."

My stomach soured. We *had* to get them out. "What about where they were forcing the men to shift?"

"They were forced to shift in their cages. Those take up most of the building. The wolf shifters are in various cages, positioned so each one has an IV in their arm at all times." Rosemary wrinkled her nose. "These humans are cowards."

"Okay, so there are thirty guards outside and five in the lobby. Are there any guards with the wolves?" Darrell placed his hands behind his back, a nervous tic of his.

"Ten in the hallway," Rosemary answered simply. "Had we gone in the other day, it would have been less than half that, and I worry there may be more tomorrow. We have to move tonight."

Eleanor huffed. "They're amping up for something, likely something to do with the surgery setup."

Oh, how I wished she hadn't said that. Fear seized my heart, and I could've sworn it stopped beating for a second. Killian squeezed my hand and moved closer to me, and I finally breathed.

"Do you know anything that might be helpful?" Eliza asked Savannah.

Squaring her feet underneath her, Savannah rubbed her hands together. "Not really. I know they want to see if they can find a way to use shifters to enhance the military. So the setup confirms what they told us."

They wanted to create humans with shifter strength and abilities.

"When Bune, Zagan, Ronnie, and Levi get back, we'll work through the plan. Until then, everyone, get some rest. We'll head out an hour after sunset, when they won't expect us to hit." Sterlyn gestured toward the house. "Relax, eat, decompress. We have to be ready for war."

I wanted to insist that we stay out here, but as Killian tugged me to the house, I linked, *Shouldn't we stay with Sterlyn and the others to plan?*

We have nothing to go on yet. Killian led me inside. *You didn't have lunch, so let's get some food and a bath, and rest.*

Not wanting to waste energy fighting him, I followed him inside and decided to enjoy the next two hours I had with him...alone.

WE LAY in the room I'd been staying in, my head on Killian's chest. I'd finally found a sound that relaxed me more than classical music—Killian's heartbeat.

We'd taken a long shower, devoured each other again, and eaten something afterward. This past hour, we'd been cuddling, enjoying the last quiet moments we'd have together until we had to leave.

A loud knock on the door was like the drum before a battle.

It was time for war.

CHAPTER TWENTY-SEVEN

OUR TIME of solitude was up, and it was time to save the others. Though I was eager to rescue them, a selfish part of me didn't want to get out of this bed. When I did, Killian would go to the facility with me, and he'd be at risk, just like the others.

What if I lost him?

My chest seized, and my eyes burned. This burgeoning sense of fear for his life was why I hadn't wanted to complete the bond. But even if I hadn't, I was certain I'd still feel this way.

Baby, what's wrong? Killian turned onto his side.

I scooted back until he could see my face. I hated feeling this way. I shouldn't have been hesitating to run into battle to save the people I loved, yet here I was. Any other time, I would've rejoiced over him using that term of endearment, but all my mind could focus on was the threat of him getting hurt.

Tell me, please, he linked as he cupped my face. *I can feel you're upset. Is it because of your family?*

No, but it should be. The guilt hung heavily, weighing me down. *But I'm more terrified that you'll be captured or killed.*

He mashed his lips together. *You do not need to feel guilty over that. I'm worried about the same thing, and so is everyone else, including the other mated couples who're going with us. It's part of being the other half of a person's soul. If you didn't feel that way, I'd be worried.*

Then how do mates do this? My fear that something might happen to him was crippling.

He kissed my forehead and leaned back again. *We do it like we'll do everything else for the rest of our lives—side by side and with a little trust that Fate is on our side.*

That was the problem. I wasn't sure Fate *was* on the silver wolves' side. Silver wolf history wasn't the kindest, especially with the annihilation of my uncle's pack. Add in my father's traumatic death, and I wasn't sure I trusted Fate to make sure no harm came to Killian. *Why don't you stay here in case we need to bring back the wounded?* If he wasn't at risk, then I'd have no hesitation.

He booped my nose as he smiled. "Jewel, I can't do that and ask my pack to go with Sterlyn. If *you're* open to staying here—"

I rolled my eyes and growled, "I'm not staying behind." *My* family had been taken when I hadn't been there to fight for them. Now that I was here and able, there was no way I was staying back safe...*again.*

Then it sounds as if we're doing this together, like I suggested, he linked, and kissed my lips sweetly.

My heart rate increased, and I licked his lips to taste him one last time before we left.

Uh... Sierra connected, ruining the moment. *Everyone is out here except you two.* Everyone. *All the singles and couples except for you. Are you getting the point yet, or do I need to repeat the same thing over and over again in slightly different ways?*

We got it, Killian growled as he kissed me slightly harder, then pulled away. *You can shut up now.*

I inhaled deeply to clear my head. One thing was certain: we were going to free my family, and neither Killian nor I was willing to stay behind. I'd try to stay as close to him as possible, but there was one other thing I knew, despite never having been in battle—we couldn't plan for everything. It was highly likely we would become separated.

I stood and pulled on my black long-sleeved shirt over my dark jeans. We'd agreed to wear dark clothing to blend in with the night. Unfortunately, the captive shifters didn't have that luxury, but it should help during our break-in.

Killian took my hand and opened the bedroom door, which led into the living room. Circe and Eliza were placing herbs by the windows and in front of the external doorways, chanting, "*Serva hominem intus.*" Savannah sat on the couch, picking at her fingernails. Though she'd become more friendly and was intrigued by our history, she was still uncomfortable around us. That was her survival instinct kicking in. Most humans didn't feel comfortable around supernaturals, despite our mysterious allure to them. They wanted to be next to us, yet...not.

What are they doing? I linked with Sierra and Killian.

Spelling the house so Savannah can't leave while we're gone, Sierra answered quickly. *Something you two would know if you hadn't holed yourself up in that room.*

Killian smirked as he led me to the back door and linked, *So you wanted to see us dry hump?*

I stopped walking and smacked him on the arm. "What

the *hell*?" Sometimes, saying things out loud had more impact, and I wanted him to hear my inflection.

He smirked without having the decency to look ashamed. Eyes sparkling, he shrugged. "Well, we did hump a little."

My cheeks flamed, but he was right. He'd forced me to lie down and rest because I wouldn't get off him. I'd never had sex before today, and I was pretty sure I was already a nymphomaniac.

I didn't see the problem.

Hey, I love it. He kissed my cheek and opened the door that led outside to the others. *That better never change.*

You have nothing to worry about. I slid out the door, brushing against his side, and my hand gently skimmed his crotch. If he was going to call me out, I might as well own it.

"Okay, ew." Sierra closed her eyes and shook her head. "I did *not* need to see you cop a cheap feel as soon as you came into view."

Ha! I'd finally gotten a reaction out of her instead of the other way around. "Then why were you looking there? That doesn't seem too sisterly."

Her mouth dropped, and her eyes widened.

"Well," Eliza said as she stepped out the door behind me. "I never thought I'd see the day when Sierra speechless."

Once Eliza and Circe had walked outside, Killian shut the door, and I looked around. We had twenty-six people on our side, including me. Twenty-six of us against forty-five guards and five lab techs, since fewer people worked the night shift. So two to one, which were decent odds.

Two men I'd never seen before had joined Eleanor, Levi, Rosemary, Ronnie, and Alex. They had to be Zagan and Bune. The taller one stood next to Levi. His coffee-brown hair and light golden skin matched Levi's looks, and his rich hickory eyes held wisdom, though I couldn't explain how I knew. He seemed timeless, and with Levi's resemblance to him, I assumed he was Bune. It helped that Eleanor had kept referring to Zagan, and now she was standing close to the man. His tan, clay-colored skin shone under the moon, making him seem otherworldly, and his shoulder-length raven hair hung in his icy black eyes.

Alex stood at the edge of two large oak trees that led into the woods toward the building, wearing a huge smile on his face. "I must say, this day will be remembered. Talking about Killian's—uh...*little* Killian will make Sierra speechless."

"*Little* Killian?" Sierra pivoted and moved to the side to see around the wolf shifters blocking Alex from view. "You're three hundred years old, and you can't say *penis*?"

Alex hissed, and Ronnie touched his arm.

"We should really focus on the matter at hand," Sterlyn interjected, and stepped past Alex toward Killian and me, holding two knives in ankle sheaths in her hand. "We've come up with the best plan possible, given the situation."

Here it was. Everything we'd been leading up to.

Bune began, "Levi, Zagan, and I just came back from taking one last look inside. As expected, the second shift has been on watch for a couple of hours, and now that darkness has fallen, they've let their guard down." The demon paced in front of us. "Most break-ins occur during daylight hours, and if there is a break-in later, it's usually around ten or eleven, close to when their shift ends. Attacking around seven should catch them off guard."

"And it helps that it's their break time," Luna added

from where she stood beside Sierra. "Guards are all about their breaks and consuming food. Believe me."

I linked to Killian, *How does she know that?*

In Shadow City, she was imprisoned and in near-isolation for over six months. For reasons I won't get into now, Rosemary was jailed next to her for a couple of days. Killian moved to my side. *Levi and Eliza broke them out before the demon war.*

Whoa. So much had happened while I'd been away.

Ronnie stepped closer to Alex. "That's what Rosemary said, too. We've determined that the safest option is for Levi, Bune, Zagan, and me to go inside the building in our shadow forms and take out the inner guards. Rosemary and Eleanor will fly overhead and keep an eye out to ensure no other guards are on the way while the rest of you incapacitate the outside guards. That way, when we free the shifters, the guards won't be a threat."

Frowning, Alex stiffened, resembling a statue, and I understood all too well what he was going through now that Killian and I were mated. He didn't want Ronnie to go inside and be apart from her. My heart ached for him.

"That's it?" Lowe chuckled. "That sounds easy. So what if they have ten on us? They're human. We can take them down easily."

"And people say angels are arrogant," Rosemary scoffed, and placed her hands on her hips, staring Lowe down. "You do realize those *humans* have firearms, bulletproof vests, and gods know what else, right? It's not like they'll fall to the ground in fear when you attack them."

Killian led me closer to Lowe and the rest of his—er —*our* pack. "When Chad was taken, our group learned that these humans cannot be underestimated. They have special military-style training and gave us a good fight." Killian spoke clearly, sounding as much the leader as the others. "If you walk in there overconfident, you'll likely be the first casualty."

My chest swelled. Seeing and hearing him lead made me believe we could survive this, especially if we all kept our heads on straight.

It also made my body warm, and now I wanted to do more than just brush his crotch.

"That's why we're here," Circe said, standing tall across from the shifters. Her hair was so dark, it almost blended in with her shirt, even to my sharp shifter eyes. "We will help with spells where we can, but remember, with the six of us splitting up to help as many groups as possible, our magic will drain faster since we won't be channeling spells together. We'll use magic only when needed."

Sterlyn handed the knives and sheaths to Killian and me. She commanded, "Strap this on your ankle in case."

Not needing to be told twice, the two of us obeyed, and the weight of the weapon provided some relief.

Griffin stepped forward. "There will be six groups, each with a witch. Because of the human and demon issues back home, we didn't want to bring any weapons that would make noise, especially since we don't want to actually harm the humans. We'll be fighting by hand and with our knives. That's why more witches came." A muscle in his jaw twitched. "That's not saying once we've disarmed some guards, we can't use their weapons against them."

Remembering the cold metal of the gun in my hand sent a chill down my spine. It hadn't felt natural, but it had helped us multiple times while we'd been under attack by the cabins. Still, I'd rather fight with my hands or in wolf form.

Levi planted his feet on the ground, shoulder-width

apart. "Keep in mind, Savannah said that once they call in backup, we'll be on borrowed time. We need to get in and out as quickly as possible. It's important to take out as many guards as we can, *quickly*. The shifters may be fully sedated, and we'll need time to move them to safety."

Circe rubbed her hands together. "I think we may have something that could work, but we won't know until we get there."

When no one else spoke, I realized this was our entire plan. Though we were clearly at a disadvantage, we had enough strength on our side to pull through. I only hoped that some of the captive wolves could move on their own.

"Any questions before we go?" Sterlyn's skin glowed under the moonlight as her silver hair shone. It was another reminder that she was the silver wolf alpha. She was stronger than any wolf, even the silver ones. With Darrell and Cyrus flanking Griffin and Sterlyn, it was noticeable how much more power ran through her than the rest of us. Dad had told me that when a true leader was in charge, they didn't have to throw their power in everyone's faces. He'd been like that, but Sterlyn was even more grounded.

I did have one burning question, one I probably shouldn't ask, but...I needed to know. "Has Mom or Chad woken up or been..." The word *tortured* refused to pass my lips. "Hurt?"

The corners of her eyes tightened. "No. But if we don't get to them soon, there's no telling when they might be."

At least nothing had happened since earlier when Chad had connected with me. Mom was with the women, and Chad was with the men. Unless these assholes were going after the children, with whom Sterlyn couldn't connect...

Bile inched up my throat. Instead of comforting myself, I was making it worse.

Killian squeezed my hand and waved his free one toward the trees. "Let's go."

No further words were spoken as Sterlyn spun on her heel. She and Griffin took the lead, with the angels, demons, Alex, and Ronnie following.

"It'd be great if you six didn't mind staying in the middle in case we need one of you to cast spells ahead of or behind us," Cyrus said as he looked at the witches. "Though I don't expect to run into any issues on the way there, it's better to be safe than sorry."

"Very well." Circe turned to the five others. "Conserve your magic until it's needed."

Nodding, the witches went next, Sierra and the other members of my new pack on their heels. The final group consisted of Cyrus, Darrell, Annie, Killian, and me.

Patting my arm, Annie smiled at me, her honey irises shining. "We'll get them out of there."

Pressure built in my chest, and I swallowed, trying to hold back my sadness. If I let my nerves get the best of me, I would become a liability. I had to keep my head on straight. But she was being kind, and Chad and Mom were part of her pack. She wanted them back as badly as I did. "I hope so."

"We've been in worse situations, and we take care of our own, which includes your grandparents and their pack." Darrell puffed out his chest the way he did when he got emotional. "And you will always be one of us, even though you're no longer a pack-linked member." He walked behind Killian and smacked his back in affirmation.

They love you almost as much as I do, Killian connected. Instead of jealousy swirling inside him, it was contentment, easing some of the anxiety pumping through my veins.

"We don't want to fall behind." Cyrus popped his neck on each side and moved forward.

We hurried to catch up with the others, which wasn't hard since the witches moved more slowly than the rest of us.

Cyrus was in the lead, with Annie just behind him, then Killian and me, and finally Darrell. The five of us walked easily through the woods, dodging trees but keeping pace with one another as if we were in animal form. The slightly less than half-moon was rising, and I could feel the magic within, though it wasn't as strong as on the night of a full silver moon. Raccoons scurried away, and a flying squirrel jumped from one red cedar to another close to me.

We moved slowly and deliberately, listening for anything out of the ordinary. When we reached the trail that led to the cliff overlooking the facility, we hung right instead of left to go around it. We needed to be able to run and reach the humans as soon as possible.

Are we going to shift? I'd meant to ask earlier. I had a feeling we wouldn't, but I wanted to make sure I was assuming correctly.

No. We're afraid that might scare the humans more, and we need to be able to open doors to get the wolves out, Killian replied. His anxiety bubbled from our connection, adding to mine. *We also need to communicate with the entire group and not only those we're linked to.*

I couldn't rest against his heartbeat out here, so I settled for my old, faithful calming technique—a classical song. In my mind, I replayed "Water Music" by Handel, opening my connection to Killian instinctively. If music helped me, maybe it would help him as well.

His anxiety smoothed through our bond, and a smile

spread across my face. The fact that this brought him some peace made me feel more in sync with him.

Through the leafless branches of the oak trees, the side of the building came into view, along with the first group of guards. They each had a rifle and pistol. We needed to spread out the best we could, though the cliff on our left would hinder us from attacking both sides discreetly.

We're going to split into our teams and move while Ronnie, Levi, Bune, and Zagan head inside the building to look around, Killian linked with me and the others of his pack. *Jewel, Sierra, and Herne are with me. Lowe and Scott, head with Griffin and Eliza. April, you're with Sterlyn and Cordelia. Luna, you're with Darrell and Circe, and Collin, you're with Annie and Aurora. That leaves Cyrus, Aspen, and Alex together. Get into your groups, and the alpha of each team will take you to your spot.*

Out of the corner of my eye, I watched as Sterlyn gestured to the witches, indicating which leader each should follow.

Being told what to do was normal for me, but hearing my *mate* be all alpha-y made my body warm and tingly, which was *very* unfortunate timing. It didn't help my situation that he'd made sure we were together. Some of my worry eased, knowing we'd be in the same group. But my desire for him...not so much.

We're staying here, taking the closest left corner, Killian instructed as the other five teams spread out and ran the perimeter.

Rosemary and Eleanor took to the sky. The guards didn't notice, I assumed because their human eyes couldn't see well in the dark. The five guards were talking and barely scanning the woods. Bune and the others had been right—they weren't paying attention.

Herne and Sierra stood close together, while Killian wrapped an arm around my waist, anchoring me in a way I hadn't known I needed.

A few minutes passed, and Killian tensed.

CHAPTER TWENTY-EIGHT

IF I HADN'T KNOWN any better, I would've thought weights were holding me in place. That was how damn heavy my body felt, weighted down with dread. What if I'd brought twenty-six people here to meet their deaths? But leaving the pack in these humans' hands wasn't an option.

Pushing away my concerns, I forced myself to focus.

You don't have to leave the tree line, Killian linked, and touched my arm, bringing me back to him. *I can feel the turmoil churning inside you.* More warmth exploded from his end of our bond.

Of course he wouldn't judge me. Almost any other wolf would, but not him...not my mate.

Just similar concerns from earlier, but I'm fine. I focused on his touch and let my wolf inch forward. I needed her to take charge and guide my actions.

He nodded, wisely choosing to drop the matter. He then linked with Sierra and me while gesturing to Herne, *It's time.*

Out of the corner of my eye, I watched as Sterlyn raced from her spot nearest the front door, Cordelia and April just steps behind her. Griffin went to the other corner of the front building, launching his own attack.

Everyone but our group was in motion.

Shit.

I'd delayed our group slightly.

Tapping into my wolf, I surged forward, wanting to make up for the brief delay I'd caused. Killian growled behind me, not liking that I was the first one the guards would focus on. Though that hadn't been my intent, I was fine with it. Anything to make the others in our group less of a target.

Gunshots fired near me, and I almost tore my gaze away to see if anyone had been injured, but years of training kicked in, and Dad's voice echoed in my head: *Focus on your own target; otherwise, you'll be injured, and you won't be able to help anyone else. Help others when you aren't under threat.*

Hearing his voice, even inside my mind, lent me strength. For once, I truly might believe he wasn't completely gone.

The five guards we were attacking were focused on Griffin and Sterlyn, which was why we were supposed to attack all at once. That way, each group would only have a few guards to contend with. All five had their weapons drawn and aimed away from us.

We have to do something before the guards fire, I linked to Sierra and Killian.

"Herne—" Killian started, but before he could say more, Herne mumbled, "*Ventus inimicos meos circumvolvam.*"

The breeze picked up, blowing past me toward the guards. Two gunshots came from our group of guards, and my stomach lurched.

But the wind was already swirling around them like a

tornado. The air pushed the bullets up, forcing them off track. I watched the bullets miss Sterlyn by mere inches.

I continued on my course, just a few feet from the swirling winds. I could reach them.

Jewel, wait! Alarm infused Killian's words. *You can't attack them until the wind dies down, or you'll be caught up in it, too.*

The wind knocked me back a few feet from the circle. Showed how little I knew about witchcraft. *So even though we're on their side, we aren't immune to their spells?* Some of the books I'd read growing up had the allies of the witches protected, but this was the real world, not some fairy tale.

That would be badass if we were, Sierra replied. *We need to talk to them about that! Uh...later.*

I wasn't surprised she was making quips in the heat of the moment. I was almost afraid of what I'd hear now that I had a link with her.

As if Sierra hadn't made a comment, Killian answered my question. *They can control the elements but have to target an area. Right now, she's targeting all five guards, so if you step into the area, the wind will affect you too.*

It's almost like a gun. You aim and shoot, and anyone who doesn't want to be shot better move out of the way, Sierra interjected. *Or sometimes it's like a missile with a huge-ass area of impact, so if you don't want to get caught up in the missile tornado, stay the hell away.*

Both explanations worked, but Sierra painted a better picture. I sighed. *So what do we do?*

We circle them and wait for Herne to stop the spell, Killian replied as he ran around me, avoiding the tornado, and took up a spot between the guards and the side of the building. I moved closer to the door so Sierra could take the spot against the tree line.

Killian linked with me, *I hate to ask, but are you good with taking out two guards?*

Somehow, his question made me feel stronger. Even though I was less experienced than Sierra, he was asking me to take on two guards. He wasn't underestimating my strength as a silver wolf. *Yes, and I'm assuming you plan on taking two as well.*

Yes. Sierra has gotten better, but now that I can actually feel your connection, you're stronger than every other person in this pack, including me. So despite being the last person I want fighting two people, you're the one who makes the most sense.

He'd proclaimed I was stronger than him without any malice or jealousy. Not many men would feel that way, which further proved how amazing he was. Few alphas could admit that someone else was stronger than they were, especially if they were part of their pack. Not only had he just admitted it to me, but he had also recognized that Sterlyn and Griffin were stronger than him. He was born to be the type of leader that most could never be.

The wind died down as more guns were fired and the guards tried to fight off the group overtaking them. Herne shouted, "I need a break, or I'll use everything I have."

"That's fine!" Killian said loudly enough for her to hear.

It was time for our fight. *I'll take on two.*

Our bond cooled slightly as his concern washed over me, but there was no going back. We were here and so damn close to saving the pack.

The wind slowed, and the breeze slipped past me again, heading back toward the woods as if it were heading back home, wherever that might be.

The five guards' eyes were wide, and I noted that one of them was a woman. I linked, *Sierra, take the one closest to you*.

You mean the one with boobs? she replied, but she was already crouching, ready to fight.

Yes, that one. I hadn't wanted to point out that I was giving her the female, but at least I was certain she knew which to attack.

My attention went to the two men closest to me. The five guards had formed a circle, and now that the wind had calmed, they were breaking apart. Not wanting to give them a chance to go for their guns, I followed my gut and ran toward them.

A guy with dark scruff laughed. "She thinks she can take us."

"She's probably one of *them*," the more burly guy gritted out, and went for his gun.

I'd need to pull out my knife soon because it would take more than strength to fight a gun.

As I reached them, I spun and kicked Burly Guy in the wrist. I'd used the leg my knife was strapped to and took the opportunity to pull it from the sheath.

Burly Guy grunted and reached for his gun again, but I thrust the knife at his wrist and sliced into it. He groaned, "See!"

"Holy shit," Scruff Guy exclaimed, and went for the rifle strapped to his shoulder. He wasn't going for the pistol, which boded well for me. It would take more time to remove the rifle from his shoulder than to pull a pistol from the hip.

Not worried about Burly Guy yet since he couldn't move as well with that sort of wound, I tapped into my moon magic and leaped toward Scruff Guy. As he grabbed the strap to remove the rifle from his arm, I punched him in the jaw.

His head snapped back, but there wasn't any sound of bones breaking, and he didn't pass out.

I hadn't hit him hard enough.

None of these guards had maliciousness wafting off them, meaning they were doing what they thought was right, like Savannah. Whether they were being manipulated, scared, or a combination of the two, they were just protecting their own kind. Inherently, I didn't want to hurt them any more than I had to.

I had to find a balance, preferably sooner rather than later.

Scruff Guy hadn't paused, and he now had the rifle in hand. Whatever training these guards had included hand-to-hand combat, and they were reasonably used to punches and kicks. I'd have to hurt him as badly as Burly Guy.

Lovely.

I pivoted as if to kick him, and he countered, ready for my leg. He was still underestimating me. That would've pissed me off in training, but in a real battle, it gave me an advantage. Just because I was a woman didn't mean I wasn't a worthy adversary. Human men were just as stereotypical as supernatural men, which was a damn shame. At some point, didn't *someone* have to evolve?

Since he was ready for a kick on the side opposite the rifle, I reached out and grabbed the firearm from his hand. There was a little resistance, and I yanked harder one second before he realized I'd faked him out.

The strap jerked the side of his body forward, throwing him off balance. Using his forward momentum, I redirected the rifle down so his head was closer to the ground. When his face was a foot away from me, I kneed him in the nose.

A sickening crunch followed. Then the metallic scent of blood wafted over me, and warmth spread over my knee. I'd broken his nose this time.

To the right, I sensed Burly Guy moving. Not good. He wasn't underestimating me.

I dropped my elbow on the back of Scruff Guy's neck, knocking him out.

One down, I linked to Killian and Sierra, and turned to Burly Guy.

Blood poured down his hand from the gaping wound where he'd removed the knife. He clutched his injured hand to his chest and lifted the pistol with his left hand, aiming right at my head.

Argh, I'd spent too much time on Scruff.

A sick smirk spread across Burly's face as he pulled the trigger.

I jerked to the side, tumbling to the ground and praying I'd moved quickly enough to dodge the bullet.

"*Opprimere minas*," Herne chanted loudly behind me.

Something hit the ground beside me, and I flicked my gaze to the bullet hole mere inches from my nose.

I glanced back at Burly Guy as he fired another shot, his aim centered on my heart.

I lunged left, wanting to switch up my actions. If I favored one side, he'd take note and plan accordingly.

Sharp pain seared into my shoulder as the bullet hit me. I gritted my teeth, thankful it wasn't a kill shot.

Jewel! Killian linked, his fear taking hold as horror pulsed through the bond.

Well, that was one bad thing about the mate and alpha bonds. He could feel my pain, and I wondered if it was worse since I was now both his mate and part of his pack. *Focus on your own fight.*

"*Habeat eum arma sua stillabunt!*" Herne shouted.

Burly Guy's gun hand shook. He leaned forward, trying to use his weight to counter the strain. He was struggling against whatever Herne was doing.

I couldn't let her drain her magic. I had to move.

Climbing to my feet, I spared Killian a glance. He was fighting the other two, who were smaller. Somehow, I'd picked the largest two, but I'd take it. Killian had one of the rifles turned on the two men. He had a black eye, which I hadn't felt, but overall, he was okay.

His frantic gaze landed on me, and I connected, *Herne has him occupied. I'm fine.*

Now that I was on my feet, I channeled my adrenaline and ran toward Burly Guy. His hand shook so hard that his teeth clacked, and the gun dropped.

I threw my left hand, aiming for his face, but he blocked it with his good arm. He was going to be a pain in the ass to take down, so I had to strike him fast and hard. I pivoted, kicking the injured wrist he had clutched to his chest.

He groaned and hunched over.

Gunfire hadn't sounded around us since Burly Guy had lost his weapon, so I hoped we were winning the battle. Thank gods. I just needed to bring him to his knees.

Grappling for the rifle strapped around him, Burly Guy wasn't going down without a fight.

Tapping into the moon, I vowed not to show this prick any mercy. He was beginning to become a thorn in my side. He'd fucking shot my shoulder.

I grabbed the knife off the ground just as he swung the rifle at me. I wouldn't let him shoot me again. I threw the knife at his shoulder as he struggled to pull the trigger with his non-dominant hand. My knife hit its mark, and the rifle dropped.

"Don't—" Killian started, but I ran and kicked Burly Guy in the side of the head, knocking him out. Finally.

"—move," Killian finished, but I'd already ensured that Burly Guy wouldn't.

I turned my attention to Killian and saw he had three of the five guards held at gunpoint. Sterlyn's group had knocked out their five, and Griffin was holding his group captive. I tapped into my wolf's hearing and didn't hear any fighting. I almost lifted my non-injured arm in triumph.

Now we just had to get the wolf shifters out of the building.

Has anyone heard from the demons? I linked with all our pack members.

But they didn't answer. Instead, an alarm pierced the air.

CHAPTER TWENTY-NINE

THE NOISE WAS SO loud that my eardrums screamed in protest. If the humans hadn't warned anyone before, they sure as hell had now.

Someone blurred around the side of the building near Griffin toward the front door.

Only one person out here could run that fast.

What's wrong with Alex? I linked with all my new pack members. This was the first time not being able to link with the silver wolf pack had been problematic. If I could have, I'd have asked Cyrus, since he'd been with Alex during the fight.

Killian replied, *Sterlyn just connected with me. Ronnie and the demons inside are in trouble. They took out all the guards, but when they went into the rooms and began opening the cages, gas filled the room. It's making them groggy.*

My blood ran ice cold. This was *horrible* and something we hadn't accounted for.

I should've known things had seemed too easy.

It was so hard to think while the siren blared, but I

focused on the words inside my head. *At least one of these guards must know the codes.* There had to be a backup procedure in case of an attack. *Tell everyone to ask the conscious guards how to turn the gas off.*

A loud barreling sound caught my attention, and I jerked up my head to see a black streak shooting across the sky toward us.

Rosemary.

With her connection to Levi, she either felt or knew he was in danger. Neither she nor Alex was thinking clearly, and they wanted to save their mates. Someone had to help.

I took off toward the front door at the same time as Sterlyn. That was good since I couldn't link with the other silver wolves.

Where are you going? Killian asked, and my blood ran colder from his fear.

I despised causing him more discomfort, but if the humans got hold of an angel, a vampire, and a demon, I didn't want to think about what more they would do. *I'm getting them out of that room. You're the one with the gun keeping three guards hostage. Focus!*

He didn't respond, but he didn't need to. His displeasure floated through the bond, and I struggled to breathe.

Rosemary landed and yanked open the door just as Sterlyn and I reached her. She went inside, and Sterlyn and I followed right behind.

The door shut behind us, reducing the blare of the alarm to a more bearable volume. The sound was outside, likely to scare invaders away.

The front lobby looked like a standard reception room. The walls were off-white, and the floor was a smooth gray cement. The room didn't contain a desk or chairs, only an intercom by an oversized steel door. To the right of the door, a small box was set in the wall at shoulder height. Five unconscious guards lay on the floor.

Alex leaned over a guard, fangs extended and irises crimson. There was no blue in them whatsoever. For a second, I thought he was draining them of their blood, but my heart squeezed when I realized he wasn't. He was merely searching their pockets, likely for the keys to the door.

"Which ones haven't you searched?" Sterlyn asked, hurrying toward them.

Now that I'd noticed, they were lying face-down with their feet pointed inward, as if they'd been standing in a circle when taken out. If I'd been with a group of fighters while being attacked by an invisible foe, I'd have positioned myself with my back to my allies so we'd have to fight only what was directly in front of us. That must have been what they'd done.

"*Thooose twoooo,*" Alex hissed, and nodded at the two by the farthest wall.

"What are you looking for?" There wasn't a lock on the door, so I was at a loss.

Sterlyn gestured at the door. "There has to be a way to get in. A card or something."

However, the box didn't look like a card swiper. I hurried to it as Alex, Rosemary, and Sterlyn continued their search. If this was a government facility that wanted to keep people out, they would make it more complicated to get in—something the demons hadn't needed to worry about since they could slip through the cracks.

We hadn't been as thorough as we'd thought.

"There's nothing here," Sterlyn murmured. "I don't understand. There has to be a way *in*."

"I'll make one," Rosemary said determinedly.

"Wait," I said as I touched the box. There was a seam at the bottom as if there was a lid that could be flipped open. "If you crash through the door, we could set off something else, putting everyone in more danger."

Rosemary frowned. "I hadn't thought of that. This is when emotions are bad."

I stuck my thumbnail under the seam and pushed it up. The lid resisted for a second; then it flipped up, revealing a scanner. Within a second, the red light came on, and the screen lit up.

My heart pounded in my ears. "It's a fingerprint scanner. Bring one of the guards here." Hopefully, any fingerprint from the five would allow us in.

"You're a genius!" Sterlyn exclaimed.

I wouldn't go *that* far. I just liked to think a situation through and figure out what I would do if I were in the other person's shoes.

Throwing a guard over his shoulder, Alex raced the few steps to me. He turned his back so the guard was facing the scanner. Without missing a beat, Rosemary lifted the guard's right hand and grabbed his thumb.

I helped lay the thumb flat on the screen, and the scanner scanned.

The door clicked, and I almost cried with relief, but this was just the beginning.

Due to everyone's supernatural hearing, I didn't have to tell the others that the door was unlocked. They'd all heard, so Alex dropped the guard, not bothering to cushion the poor guy's landing, and dragged him over so his foot propped open the door. At this point, the guard couldn't be bruised *that* much more.

I opened the door, and Rosemary and Alex piled in, desperate to get to their mates. I couldn't blame them.

We followed Alex to the first door on the left, where the children were, while Rosemary placed herself at the second door down on the right where the men were. They knew where to find their other halves.

The same long hallway led to yet another steel door. In here, the walls were cement, and there wasn't any natural light, just the bright glow of the fluorescents on the ceiling. The place smelled of disinfectant, adding to the eerie vibe. As Ronnie and the demons had stated, there were two doors on each side of the hallway across from each other. A small window sat at the very top of each door, with bars on the inside of the room.

I was almost afraid to look.

Alex pounded on the door. "Ronnie! Wake up!"

The gas had knocked the demons out before they could leave. The ten guards lay every few feet on the cement hallway floor, and someone in a lab coat lay outside the last room on the left. It had to be the laboratory, and it was the only open door.

"Each room has a panel like a thumbprint one outside," Rosemary said, remaining more objective. "Maybe that's how we turn the gas off."

Wanting to check on Mom and my grandmother, I hurried to the first door on the right.

I looked through the window and wished I hadn't. It held seven rows of ten cages and an additional five against the wall that joined the room and hallway. The cages were big enough for a person to lie in and for the lab techs to walk inside. An IV bag full of liquid hung on a rod next to each cage, and it looked like the IVs had been inserted into the occupants' legs or feet.

The only blessing I could find was that they were all clothed, leaving them some dignity.

Either Bune or Zagan lay passed out on the floor. I wasn't sure who, since the demons were in shadow form and I couldn't see the figure's eyes, but I knew it wasn't Levi or Ronnie. The room was foggy, filled with whatever gas had knocked the demons out, but the demons had gotten inside the rooms somehow, so they couldn't be airtight.

What were we missing?

I examined the corners. There had to be a crack. Then I saw a very small trickle at the top edge of the steel door. Whatever this gas was, it was lighter than natural air and hovered toward the top of the room, but as the trickle continued, it would filter through the hallway.

We were *all* in danger.

"Guys, look." I hated to be the bearer of bad news, but we had to realize what we were up against. "The demons got in, so the rooms must have a crack. Gas is leaking out."

Sterlyn appeared beside me, her face lined with worry. "Okay, so the scanners should be the same as the one beside the main door." She lifted the panel, and a scanner appeared, but this one held a circle, like for an eye.

A retinal scanner.

Something flashed in the right corner of the screen of the scanner, and sixty seconds popped up and began counting down. We did *not* want that to reach zero.

"Guys, grab a guard and move!" I tried to keep the panic out of my voice, but it was futile. "We have less than sixty seconds to get in there before something else happens."

I expected them to freeze, but both Alex and Rosemary blurred. Within a second, Alex had the first guard. Sterlyn helped lift him up as I peeled the guy's eye open. The scanner read him, but a red X flashed across the screen.

"They have this locked down more securely." My voice cracked as my panic flared.

Alex tossed the guard to the side, and Rosemary took his place while he ran to get another. Once again, an X marked the screen. Fifty seconds.

Jewel, what's wrong? Killian linked, his concern compounding mine.

I hated to answer him, but this could be the last time we ever talked. *We initiated a countdown while trying to break into the pack rooms.*

What? he replied. *Get the* hell *out of there.*

My heart palpitated. *You know I won't do that.* What kind of person would leave her family behind? Not me.

Quickly, we worked through the guards. Every time the X flashed across the screen, the world tilted more. Sweat beaded my forehead.

The countdown read ten seconds, and we'd gone through every guard.

"What do we do?" Alex sounded broken.

"We must be missing something." Sterlyn glanced at the pile of guards around us. "We need to try the first ones again. Maybe we didn't do it correctly."

We all knew the truth, but we couldn't give up.

"Wait! We assumed a guard. Grab a lab person!"

The timer read five seconds now.

Alex disappeared, using his vampire speed. With three seconds left, he blurred back beside me with the person who'd been lying outside the lab, a woman with long gray hair, dangling over his shoulder.

Sterlyn yanked the woman's front upward, not bothering to be as careful as she had been with the others, and I opened her bloodshot brown eyes.

We had one second.

The scanner read her eye, but the timer went to zero.

We'd failed.

Jewel! Killian's fear strangled me, but hell, it could have been my own. At least we'd had a few moments together before I died.

Then instead of a red X, a green check marked the screen. A voice said over the intercom, "Backup measures disabled. Please wait one minute before entering the room." Then a loud vacuuming noise came on inside, and the fog dissipated.

We're fine, I linked to Killian. *We figured out how to get into the rooms.*

The sirens just turned off out here, Killian replied as our bond relaxed. Both of us were okay...for now.

"Is it working for all the rooms?" Sterlyn asked, bringing me back to the present.

Rosemary flew the small distance to the men's room, while Alex rushed to the children's room with the lab tech on his back.

"Yes," Rosemary exhaled. "It's dispersing here, too."

"Same here," Alex confirmed. "Thank gods you were here with us, Jewel."

My cheeks warmed. I wasn't used to that sort of attention.

The door in front of me clicked, and the voice came back on over the intercom. "You can now enter the room."

"The other doors didn't unlock." Sterlyn looked down the hallway. "Go inside and get the wolves out of the cages while I help Alex and Rosemary open the other doors."

I took a deep breath and ran inside the women's room, careful to step around the demon. I was going to hold off breathing just in case some gas still lingered, though I doubted there was any left. I'd seen and heard the vacuum noise.

I wasn't sure where Mom and Nana were, so I started

on the section against the left wall. Each person had their feet facing the wall opposite the hallway, and each cage had an opening with a chain over it. "I can't open these without a key," I said loudly.

"Just pull out the IVs. I can break the locks with my wings," Rosemary replied as the door across from my room clicked. She sounded better now that she knew she could get to Levi.

That was enough for me. I'd seen the damage Rosemary's wings could do.

I went one by one, removing the IV from every person's ankle. By the time I reached the middle row, my lungs were bursting. I had to breathe.

Taking in a deep breath, I waited for fatigue to hit, but nothing came.

The vacuum *had* removed all the gas.

Continuing on with no time to waste, I almost cried when I stumbled upon Nana. Her long chestnut hair with silver streaks lay greasy against her face, and her olive skin was sickly pale like all the others. But she was breathing.

Since most of these humans weren't evil, the measures they'd taken to secure the pack showed how scared they were of us. *This* was why we'd kept our existence secret for so long. But none of that mattered now. We had to figure a way out of this.

Rosemary appeared in the room. The area around her eyes was still tight, but her face wasn't quite as lined. She moved from cage to cage, breaking the chains and going much more quickly because I was being careful not to injure the shifters as I removed the IVs. They'd already gone through so much.

"Did you find Chad?" I wanted to know about PawPaw, too, but she had no clue what he looked like.

She nodded without pausing.

Thank gods. At least there was that. However, the farther down the rows I went, the more my stomach churned. I still hadn't found Mom. What if something had happened to her?

Needing to remain calm, I recalled Satie's "Gymnopédie No. 1" and concentrated on the calming tune to ease my racing mind. Rosemary had almost caught up to me when I reached the very last shifter.

Mom.

"Thank gods," I whimpered, unable to hold in my relief. I linked with Killian, *I found Nana and Mom.*

Good, Killian replied. *Eliza, Circe, and Aspen are heading inside to see if they can do a spell to wake everyone.*

I hadn't even thought about how to wake them, I'd been so focused on finding Mom and Nana. But that was the point of having a team, Dad had said. Every person thought of something the others didn't.

Again, Dad proved how wise he had truly been.

I removed the IV from Mom's ankle, and the strong woman I knew was missing. Her hair was more brown with a touch of cinnamon, and like all the others, her usually dark olive complexion was pale. I wanted her to open her eyes so I could see the familiar warm cognac I'd admired all my life.

"Move. I still have to get to the children," Rosemary commanded as she slipped past me and unlocked Mom's cage. She yanked the chain from its place and opened the door. Glancing at the demon stirring on the floor next to the door, she said, "Keep an eye on Bune, too, please."

"I will," I replied.

I walked to the door, wondering how everything was

going outside, and saw the three witches breeze in through the main door propped open by the guard's foot.

Circe gestured to the children's room, which held about twenty kids from two to sixteen years old. "Aspen, take this room, and Mom, take the women. I'll head down and spell the men."

Following their priestess's instructions, each witch went to the room they'd been assigned.

When Eliza slid past me, her light green irises darkened. "It's almost over, child."

"You can wake them up without also waking the guards?" I asked. Killian had made it sound as if that were uncertain.

Eliza pursed her lips and turned toward the cages. "The spell was created to wake them from a chemically induced sleep, not one caused by injury, *if* it works."

My heart thudded as she lifted her hands and chanted loudly, "*Evigila a somno!*"

Then I waited, praying to the Heavens for the spell to work.

CHAPTER THIRTY

A FEW HEART-POUNDING SECONDS LATER, nothing happened.

Zilch.

My heart dropped into my stomach. We would have to carry out all one hundred ninety-nine members of my grandfather's pack, which didn't include Mom and Chad. This would take forever.

The only blessing was that Bune had sat up and transitioned back into human form. He rubbed his eyes and yawned. "What happened?"

Since Eliza had to keep repeating the chant, I figured that I should answer. "You were gassed when you tried to break one of them out."

"That's *right*," he said as he stood on shaky legs. "I...I yanked on that first cage." He gestured to the one I'd started with. "And I set off the alarm, and...then I don't remember much past that."

Whoever was in charge was smart. They didn't want a wolf shifter to escape a cage, so they'd set up a fail-safe to prevent escape. They hadn't accounted for our style of rescue, however, which lifted some weight off my shoulders. They were relatively clueless about supernatural abilities, but with us getting into the facility without any fatalities, they'd eventually figure out that we were stronger than they suspected.

Mom groaned, snapping my attention back to her cage. Hers was against the wall that backed to the hallway and furthest from the door.

"Mom!" I shouted, unable to control my volume. I hurried to her side and took her hand.

Her cognac eyes flew open. "Jewel!"

For a moment, the world didn't feel quite as dire. I had Killian, and the people I loved were close to being rescued. The spell was working. "Hey."

"You need to get out of here before..." She trailed off as her gaze landed on Eliza, then Bune. Blinking, she glanced around at the cages. "You broke us out?" The last word rose an octave higher, making it sound like a question.

"Mortals ask very odd questions sometimes." Bune plucked at his black shirt, readjusting himself. There was a faint bruise on the right side of his cheek where he must have hit his face when he'd fallen.

Eliza continued to chant, and another woman groaned from across the room. They were all stirring.

"I'm going to help Levi in the men's room," Bune said. "Let me know if you need me," he added as he left.

"I'll help you up." I leaned farther into the cage and slid my arm around Mom.

They'd been pretty much comatose for over a week, so they'd be stiff and off balance. Add in the fact they probably hadn't gotten enough calories because humans were unaware of how fast shifter metabolisms worked, and no doubt, weakness would exacerbate the problem.

Mom's hands shook as she braced herself on me.

Two Suburbans just pulled up, Killian linked with me. *That means more are on their way. You need to get them out of there quickly.*

That was easier said than done. *They're waking. I'll ask the witches if they can speed up their recovery.* I helped Mom into a sitting position and turned to find Eliza's face strained, sweat beading on her upper lip.

She was already running low on magic. I couldn't ask more of her.

Footsteps padded into the hallway, and Sterlyn called out, "Eliza, Circe, and Aspen, I *hate* to ask, but backup is arriving. Is there a way to speed things along?"

Their chanting grew louder, their voices merging despite being in different rooms. Eliza cupped her raised hands as if more of her power were flowing out. Within seconds, her arms were shaking.

If she was like this, I worried about Circe. She had twenty-six additional shifters to wake, so the draw on her power had to be higher.

I couldn't hear what was happening outside, but I could feel panic swirling into me from Killian. We'd known this would be hard, but knowing it and experiencing it were completely different.

More and more women woke, and I helped Mom slide out of the cage. "I'm going to help the others. Head outside as fast as you can, and hide in the woods before more humans arrive."

Mom squared her shoulders and inhaled deeply...and her body went slack. "You're *mated*—to *Killian*?" She rubbed her chest where the pack links were located. "I can't feel you anymore. You joined *his* pack?"

She had a habit of zeroing in on things that upset her,

even while in danger. "Mom, yes. It's Killian. But now is not the time to talk about this!" I cupped her face with my hands and rasped, "I'll tell you about it when everyone is safe. Not in a room full of *cages*. Now, I'm going to go help the other women." I spun on my heel and raced toward Nana. Though I would help everyone, my family took priority, and I needed her to talk to PawPaw and the others through their links. It would move things along faster.

When I reached her cage, she was already inching forward to get out on her own. She was a fiercely independent woman, a perfect match for the alpha, and felt the need to model the behavior she expected from others. Her golden-green eyes locked on me, and she clutched her neck. "They captured you, too?"

"My friends and I are here to break you out, but we need to move. Two vehicles filled with humans have arrived, and more will surely be coming. Can you link with everyone and light a fire under them? Because we *have* to move."

I reached for her hand, but she pushed mine gently away. "If we're going to expect the others to make it out on their own, then the same should be expected of me. I'm linking with them. Everyone is awake."

Nana had always been a strong woman, and sometimes I wondered if I was even half the person she was. At least I had a good person to emulate as an alpha's mate.

Everyone's movements soon became frantic, confirming she had informed the pack about the situation. A few women were out of their cages and heading for the door, likely looking for their mates and children.

As I moved down the aisle to see if anyone needed assistance, I glanced at Eliza. She was pale, but her hands were now lowered, and her lips weren't moving. Hopefully, she could recharge a bit before we headed out.

I refocused on my purpose and helped an older woman from her cage. *Killian, they're heading out soon. Is it safe?*

Alex, Annie, Cyrus, and Griffin are shooting at the Suburbans to hold them off, and Eleanor has been fighting and distracting the new guards who showed up. It should be enough chaos for the pack to slip through. We'll lead them to the edge of the cliff—the rest of us are ready for the pack outside, he replied.

What about the guards you were holding hostage? As soon as I asked, I wished I could take the question back. It might be better if I didn't know.

We knocked them all out, Killian replied. *They'll be unconscious for a while.*

The ringing in my ears calmed. Though I hadn't thought they'd kill them, this was war.

The shifters milled into the lobby, and the door opened to let them outside. I glanced at the door to find Nana heading toward the men's section to look for PawPaw.

"I'll check the last aisle," Mom called as she breezed past me.

That would save some time.

When I reached the end of the aisle, Chad's familiar scent drifted to me, and I heard the familiar cadence of his walk. He called out desperately, "Mila, I can't feel Jewel. Something must have—"

Not wanting him to cause more panic, I sped back toward the door, wanting him to see me. "I'm *fine!*"

"Wait!" Chad's brows furrowed as he focused on me. "How come I can't link with you?"

Dear gods, this question was going to drive me up the

wall. "Because I mated with Killian, and I'm part of his pack now."

"*Ohhh*, that makes—" He stopped, his face blanching. "Wait. WHAT?"

I wanted to punch them all. "We can talk about this *later*."

PawPaw's black hair, with its gray streaks at the sides, caught my eye, and I smiled as he stepped through the doorway with Nana, Levi, Circe, and Bune behind him. His warm brown eyes found me as he rubbed the gray beard that had grown quite long while he'd been out. "I'd like to be part of that discussion."

Of course he would. The only person as protective of me as Dad had been was PawPaw. "Fine." I turned to Mom. "Is there anyone else still down there?"

"It's clear," Mom said as she stepped back into the area in front of the door.

"We're the last ones." PawPaw nodded, gesturing toward the men's door.

Mom, Chad, Eliza, and I converged into the hallway. I avoided looking at the guards, who were still in a pile, paying just enough attention to step around them.

Sterlyn, Ronnie, Alex, and Aspen waited by the outer door.

My heart froze. "Did anyone take care of the samples? I'm sure they uploaded most data onto their computers, but anything recent they ran or had tested could be destroyed."

Alex nodded. "I already did that before coming out here."

Sterlyn's face gave me pause. Her eyes were narrowed as if she were in deep thought, and she held the door closed. "Something isn't adding up."

"What do you mean?" Ronnie asked.

Another four Suburbans just pulled up, Killian linked. *We need to get out of here. We're running out of time.*

A low growl emanated from Sterlyn, and she yanked open the door and rushed out. Griffin must have informed her of the same thing, and if both Killian and Griffin were concerned, things were becoming dire.

I pushed past Ronnie, following Sterlyn. If Killian was in danger, I wanted to be beside him.

I was only a few steps behind Sterlyn, and I could hear Rosemary's wings flapping behind us. She would fight alongside us as well. The last of the freed shifters were running into the trees, but we had a parking lot and a huge clearing to get past before we hit it ourselves.

The four vehicles were already in the lot.

Cyrus and Annie had their backs against the building, and Griffin and Killian were a few feet away, glaring at the guards that had arrived. Griffin and Killian were close enough to the edge of the building that if the guards opened fire, they could find cover easily.

Eleanor flew erratically, attempting to draw the guards' focus to her, but there were too many of them.

From the closest Suburban, a guard pulled out the largest gun I'd ever seen. My stomach churned. I didn't have to be knowledgeable about guns to know that one was bad news.

Jewel, move. That's a fucking machine gun, Killian linked desperately. *We've got to get out of here before they open fire.*

I glanced behind me, relieved and terrified that Sterlyn and the others had caught up.

"I'll take care of this," Rosemary said as she soared toward the man with the gun. Her wings pumped quickly as the guy pointed his weapon at her. "Get to the woods. I'll meet you there."

"You aren't going without me," Levi said as he flickered out of view. All four dark demon figures flew past me. They were going to distract these new enemies to give us time.

Eleanor swooped down beside Rosemary, forcing the man to choose between targets. Though the gun might be large, it could only be aimed in one direction at a time.

"Run," Sterlyn commanded.

Our group broke into a sprint, and I ran directly to Killian. He and Griffin were the only ones still out here. He must have had Chad, April, Lowe, Sierra, Luna, and the others lead the shifters back to the farmhouse.

My heart sank as I realized how little manpower we had left. That would be yet another conversation for another day.

The machine gun began to fire, and I understood why Killian had sounded so concerned. Each bullet was shot only a millisecond behind the previous one. I paused, turning toward the demons, angels, and Ronnie.

"Don't stop *moving*," Killian said, and he grabbed my hand and dragged me toward the woods.

Griffin turned around, staying next to Sterlyn, who was in the middle of PawPaw, Nana, Mom, Eliza, Circe, and Aspen, watching everyone in the front or back. Her gaze was glued on the threat as she, no doubt, tried to anticipate their next move.

"For the love of any and all gods, *listen to him*," Alex murmured as he blurred beside us. "Otherwise, I'll march over there and help my *mate*, but unfortunately, I'm not invisible to them." His cheeks were red, his irises had turned crimson again, and his fangs had descended. He was struggling not to rush to Ronnie, proving how much he trusted her abilities against his natural instinct to protect her.

Halfway to the tree line, I slowed so I could turn around and check on Mom, Nana, PawPaw, and the others. They were all a few steps behind me. "Run as fast as you can."

The witches straggled, their weakened states impacting them more than I'd expected. All three looked deathly sick.

Something hot stung my leg, and I glanced down to see that a bullet had hit me.

Holy *crap*. Not again!

I'd gotten more injuries this past week than I ever had in all my years of training.

Jewel! Killian growled, and leaned down to examine it.

"What are you doing?" I hissed. He didn't need to be kneeling in the exact spot where I'd been shot.

Another bullet hit the ground a few inches from Killian, causing grass and dirt to fly up from the impact.

We had to get out of here.

"Damn it, you aren't supposed to *hit* them," a guard rasped in a whisper, but we could still hear him perfectly.

If they weren't supposed to hurt us, then why the hell were they firing at us?

The rest of the group passed us with Annie and Cyrus flanking PawPaw and Nana. Behind them were Sterlyn, Griffin, and Mom, with Eliza, Circe, and Aspen at the back. Killian and I fell in at the tail, and no one realized I was injured.

I'm fine. We stumbled together toward the tree line, keeping watch at the back of the group.

I gritted my teeth, trying not to limp. The pain wasn't completely unbearable, but it was worse than I would have preferred.

I can carry you, Killian offered. His concern slammed into me, seizing my lungs. His fear was nearly paralyzing.

If we don't keep going, we'll both get hurt worse than I am now. I wasn't trying to be mean. I understood where he was coming from. I'd be in a similar frame of mind in his position, but that didn't mean it was our best course of action. I tamped our bond down enough that he wouldn't feel my pain as intensely.

When we finally reached the tree line, some of his tension eased. I almost dreaded calming down because my adrenaline was numbing the pain. I didn't want to know how much worse it would hurt when we had time to rest.

The scent of a strange wolf—no, *wolves* infiltrated my nose.

We've got a problem, Sterlyn said through gritted teeth. *A really big one. We're surrounded.*

I sucked in a breath as realization struck me. The new humans hadn't been trying to kill us. They'd been herding us toward something.

A tall man close to Mom's age stepped through the bare trees into sight. He had short, spiky, light blond hair and ice-gray eyes. His attention was entirely on Mom as he smirked cruelly.

"Tom!" Mom gasped as she stepped forward between PawPaw and Nana. "Is it really you?"

"It is." He took a step toward her and ran a finger across her face.

My heart sank. What was going on?

She flinched but didn't step back, knowing not to show fear or weakness. "I'm assuming you're not here to help us."

"Gods, no." He chuckled darkly. "I told you once that you'd regret leaving me. Now I'm going to need you and your friends here to head back inside that building. There's *so* much more testing to be done."

I'd always wondered how the humans had located a wolf pack so quickly, especially one hidden in the mountains.

As if he'd read my thoughts, PawPaw spat, "*You* told them about us."

My stomach dropped. I knew who this man was. This was the man my mother had almost mated with. There was no other explanation. I connected to Killian and the others, knowing my mate would want to know the answer. *Please tell me you're safe.*

We are. We just got everyone in the house, and we're waiting on you, Sierra answered. *Where are you?*

"I did. I've been waiting for the perfect opportunity to make things even between Mila and me." He tilted his head. "It's a damn shame you're just as beautiful now as you were in high school. Such a waste."

"I can't *believe* I ever dated you," my mother sneered. "You're a traitor to your own kind. You disgust me."

He shrugged. "You can't hurt me now. And it's fine. You took everything away from me...my heart and my future. It's time I return the favor. Now, turn around and get back inside."

On his last word, fifty wolves inched from the tree line, ready to drive us back into the facility.

Killian linked to his entire pack, *We need backup. Now! Bring any weapons you can find.*

As my hand found my mate's and I sent all the strength and love in my heart to him, I knew he had one thing right.

We weren't going down without a fight.

We'd stay free...or die trying.

LEAVE A REVIEW

Did you enjoy this book?
Please leave a review for it on Amazon.

Join Jen's newsletter to get exclusive content, enter giveaways, and receive free books and excerpts.

Join Jen's Newsletter here.

Follow Jen L. Grey on Facebook here.

Join Jen L. Grey's Facebook group here.

ABOUT THE AUTHOR

Jen L. Grey is a *USA Today* Bestselling Author who writes Paranormal Romance, Urban Fantasy, and Fantasy genres.

Jen lives in Tennessee with her husband, two daughters, and two miniature Australian Shepherds. Before she began writing, she was an avid reader and enjoyed being involved in the indie community. Her love for books eventually led her to writing. For more information, please visit her website and sign up for her newsletter.

Check out her future projects and book signing events at her website.

www.jenlgrey.com

ALSO BY JEN L. GREY

Shadow City: Silver Wolf Trilogy

Broken Mate

Rising Darkness

Silver Moon

Shadow City: Royal Vampire Trilogy

Cursed Mate

Shadow Bitten

Demon Blood

Shadow City: Demon Wolf Trilogy

Ruined Mate

Shattered Curse

Fated Souls

Shadow City: Dark Angel Trilogy

Fallen Mate

Demon Marked

Dark Prince

Fatal Secrets

Shadow City: Silver Mate

Shattered Wolf

Fated Hearts

Ruthless Moon

The Wolf Born Trilogy

Hidden Mate

Blood Secrets

Awakened Magic

The Hidden King Trilogy

Dragon Mate

Dragon Heir

Dragon Queen

The Marked Wolf Trilogy

Moon Kissed

Chosen Wolf

Broken Curse

Wolf Moon Academy Trilogy

Shadow Mate

Blood Legacy

Rising Fate

The Royal Heir Trilogy

Wolves' Queen

Wolf Unleashed

Wolf's Claim

Bloodshed Academy Trilogy

Year One

Year Two

Year Three

The Half-Breed Prison Duology (Same World As Bloodshed Academy)

Hunted

Cursed

The Artifact Reaper Series

Reaper: The Beginning

Reaper of Earth

Reaper of Wings

Reaper of Flames

Reaper of Water

Stones of Amaria (Shared World)

Kingdom of Storms

Kingdom of Shadows

Kingdom of Ruins

Kingdom of Fire

The Pearson Prophecy

Dawning Ascent

Enlightened Ascent

Reigning Ascent

Stand Alones

Death's Angel

Rising Alpha

CPSIA information can be obtained
at www.ICGtesting.com
Printed in the USA
BVHW040306090623
665683BV00014B/52